Rude

D0355511

He heard movements from the corridor outside—a soft, regular thumping sound. They didn't want to shock him, possibly risk driving him insane by confronting him too suddenly with what the human race had become.

That had to be the answer. They were breaking it to him gently, giving information by indirect means, even to the extent of supervising his revivification at a distance.

Ross thought that he was prepared for the shocks now.

"Come out, come out!" he yelled at the top of his voice, "wherever you are!"

AND THEN THEY CAME OUT....

Monsters
and
Medics

James White

A Del Rey Book

BALLANTINE BOOKS • NEW YORK

To Dr. Ian Ross McAulay
who provided the encouragement,
the home-brewed beer and the
trouser turn-ups

In Appreciation

A Del Rey Book
Published by Ballantine Books

Library of Congress Catalog Card Number: 76-30333

ISBN 0-345-25623-9-150

Manufactured in the United States of America

First Edition: March 1977

Cover art by H. R. Van Dongen

Contents

Introduction

Reality in Science Fiction

THE QUESTION MOST often asked of science-fiction writers is, as we all know, "Where on Earth do you get those crazy ideas from?" This is a deceptively simple question, whose answer, dealing as it must with that peculiar synthesis of the input of firsthand experience of the real world and the exercise of a disciplined and science-oriented imagination, can often take the form of a long, detailed, and complex discussion covering the whole creative literary process. To achieve success in his or her profession a writer should, in addition to possessing the skills associated with the craft, have wide-ranging and personal experience of a great many aspects of the world around him or her.

Judging by their book-jacket biographies, a large number of these writers have served a long and grueling apprenticeship to their profession before setting typewriter to paper. They have performed such varied tasks as shoveling coal on a tramp steamer, driving New York taxis, prospecting for uranium, Hot Gospeling, sexing day-old chicks, kicking various drug or alcohol addictions, and, of course, building up the stamina for

1

the kind of firsthand experience which has to be read between the biographical lines and which surfaces in the book as the sexy bits.

No doubt it is the latter kind of firsthand experience which makes the writer's photograph appear to be that of a much older person, and, regrettably, not all of us are lucky enough to have it.

Science-fiction writers have another reason for appearing prematurely mature. They have to bear the extra burden of worry and guilt caused by their complete lack of firsthand experience of the subjects about which they write.

For example, how many s-f authors have flown an Earth-orbital mission, much less traveled to the farthest stars? And who among our talented female writers has experienced the stock situation of being chased, while clad in a gold-plated bikini, by a psychiatrically suspect extraterrestrial whose amorous advances should properly be directed toward a member of its own species? Who of us has traveled into the past or future, except by studying history or reading s-f? Because the s-f writer is dealing with events that have not happened and may never happen, disciplined imagination must of necessity take the place of firsthand experience—but not entirely. Even the wildest flights of imagination require a launching pad of solid, factual experience; otherwise, the reader would have no hook on which to suspend his disbelief.

But there is a solution to the apparently insoluble problem of writing realistic s-f. By dint of a little judicious poaching from real life, it is possible to modify firsthand experiences and characters so that they can be transplanted, without danger of rejection, into alien but believable surroundings. Real-life events rarely proceed in a tidy and dramatic fashion, and have to be heavily edited if they are to make acceptable fiction, but real-life characters and character conflicts are a different matter. They can be used with little or no modification, which enables the reader to suspend willingly his disbelief by identifying with one of these credible characters in what can very often be a wholly incredible situation.

Any good writer—or, for that matter, any mean, nasty, drunken or depraved writer of good stories—knows that the best stories are those in which ordinary people are faced with extraordinary situations. It is in this area that the s-f author has a big advantage over the mainstreamer, who has to be content with the more mundane kinds of emotional and environmental catastrophes associated with unfaithful wives, girl friends, husbands, and whatever, or physical threats from tidal waves, mining disasters, urban-guerrilla activity, or outsize sharks nibbling away at one's circle of friends. If the s-f writer can provide the reader with characters he can believe in, that same reader will have no difficulty in accepting alien situations and surroundings which otherwise would have been completely incredible.

It is also possible to achieve this effect by introducing an alien character into completely mundane surroundings. Even my six years spent in the tailoring section of a big department store were not wasted, science-fictionally speaking.

As the salesman responsible for measuring ladies and gentlemen for the bespoke-tailored or custom-fitted suits (depending on which side of the Atlantic you are reading this), I was becoming strangely dissatisfied with my job. The chief problem was that all the young and nicely shaped ladies and normally sized gentlemen bought their gear off the peg, while my department got only the people who *needed* their clothing made specially for them. I began to cast covetous eyes on the job of the night security man, a simple, philosophical soul who could get through a book of crossword puzzles in three nights, and who would never even dream of borrowing a typewriter from Office Supplies and spending the time, as I would have liked to do, writing s-f stories.

Then one night I had to work very late on a new display, and I discovered what an eerie place a dark and deserted department store could be at night, and in the process I also found the plot for "Counter Security."

Another plot I found lying in the gutter one pouring-

wet morning when I was hurrying for my bus to work.
There was a large, fat and very old dog of very mixed
ancestry crouched in the street alongside the curb. I had
known the dog for some time, although not by name,
having seen it playing with some of the very young children of the district—it preferred them small and gentle,
because it, and they, could not run fast.

It was lying with the rainwater gurgling around it,
eyes closed, head on paws, whining and barking quietly
to itself, the way some old dogs do when they are chasing rabbits in their sleep. The odd thing about this dog
was that as it lay there, ignoring the odd passers-by who
called to it or patted it, it showed not the slightest sign
of being miserable or even uncomfortable.

I was a few minutes late that morning, and the departmental buyer looked pointedly at his watch. But
while I was doing my thing with the tailor's chalk, pins
and measuring tape I kept thinking about that dog,
about the almost human nature of dogs and the often
animal nature of men. The result was "Dogfight," one
of my very few war stories.

Regrettably, not all stories proceed from real-life experience to complete plot outline in such a tidy and
rapid fashion. The elements of "Nuisance Value" were
festering away in my subconscious for many years before the story came to be written—and "festering" is
used advisedly, because that is what happens when a
sore is left untreated for a long time.

The sore spot in question was caused by the growing
practice in recent years by people in positions of power
of avoiding the consequences of their mistakes by com-
pounding physical killing with character assassination.
Take the example of an ordinary citizen—hard-
working, politically inactive, and much more interested
in seduction than sedition—who is shot or blown to
bloody tatters or otherwise killed by mistake. The death
of this obviously innocent bystander will cause a loss of
public support for The Movement or some similar em-
barrassment, and, rather than admit to a mistake by
apologizing to the next of kin, the slower and more in-

sidious killing of the victim's character is begun. He was a police spy, people say—although the people who said it first are impossible to find. But the rumors grow, and, as everyone knows, there is no smoke without fire.

The victim cannot possibly defend himself against this sickening and wholly reprehensible process, and only his closest friends and relatives know that the target of the character assassin was innocent. But if the assassins are good at their job, even the most loyal of friends will be unable to prove, even to themselves, the victim's innocence.

In "Nuisance Value" a quiet, dutiful and very persistent son spends virtually the whole of his adult life trying to find out the truth about what happened to his long-gone father, and to resuscitate his parent's good name. He persists when civilization is falling apart all around him and nobody cares anymore.

There are occasions in a writer's life when a story has to be written to meet a deadline and he hasn't a single useful idea in his head. When it happened to me there were plenty of ideas in my head, as I remember, but they were useless so far as an s-f plot was concerned, because the New Wave permissiveness was then only a tiny cloud on the literary horizon.

My problem was that I had met this tall, slim, dark-haired, terrific girl (I have to describe her this way because, twenty-three years later, having provided me with three children and many other fringe benefits, she also corrects my typescripts), and contacts of an extraterrestrial nature were very far from my mind. After discussing the problem with a writer friend who was also "between stories," we arrived at a solution—or possibly it was another problem. It was, in any case, a challenge.

We decided that we would each make a start on a story, the same start, which would begin with a man sitting on a rock, and see what developed.

What developed in my case was "In Loving Memory"—probably because I was feeling a bit romantic and sentimental at the time. My friend, using a different man and a smaller rock, sold his story, too.

To hold the attention of the reader a story must have conflict, which means that it must incorporate physical or emotional violence of some kind. But if a writer dislikes violence, senseless killing and all forms of war, and is convinced that killers, no matter what their excuse, are something less than heroic and most certainly unworthy of being given sympathetic treatment in a story, he faces immediate difficulties. Avoiding these difficulties is the chief reason why so many of the leading characters in my stories are medics.

In a medical s-f story the violence and bloodshed usually come about as the result of a natural or technological catastrophe—Lester del Rey's *Nerves* of the early forties made a deep impression on me when I was still in school, and there have been many other fine examples since. But if there *is* a war situation in such a story, then the leading characters are fighting to save lives, and doctors and nurses do not as a rule admire the "heroes" on either side who are making so much medical repair work for them.

Another reason why I prefer medical characters is that I wanted to be a doctor myself, but had to go out to work instead. By that I mean I had to go to work instead of completing my education, not instead of doctoring. This was probably for the best, since writing enables me to enjoy all the drama and excitement that go with the practice of medicine without actually risking anyone's life in the process. With the five not very dexterous thumbs I have on each hand, there are probably a lot of ex-patients walking around today who would not have made it if I'd been a doctor.

Unlike the self-taught psychologist of "Nuisance Value," who specializes in the treatment of one patient, the medical student of "Second Ending" cannot find even one patient on whom to practice, because he is the last surviving member of the human race.

One problem in writing Last Man stories is that there is a severe shortage of characters, and if the material is not to consist entirely of flashbacks, monologues and the hero thinking to himself, an animal, alien or mechanical Man Friday is usually introduced to carry along the necessary explanatory conversation—even if it has to be a strictly one-way conversation. In "Second Ending" the Man Friday role is played by a medically programmed robot who, as the sole companion of the protagonist, is a very important character indeed. To make such a character believable it must be shown acting as we think a machine would act in this particular situation, as the fussy, literal-minded and not too bright—at first—servant and protector of the last human being.

There is a stage in every writer's career when he feels an urge to develop his own particular idea of a First Contact story, a Last Man on Earth story or a World Disaster story—in my case, it was a combination of the last two. This must be something a writer has to get out of his system, and it resembles literary measles or chicken pox. Fortunately for the reader, authors tend to display highly individual symptoms while the malady is running its course.

The peculiar course taken by my own attack of Last Manitis was due chiefly to two friends. One of them insisted that I could not do a Last Man story because all my stuff was upbeat, but he added that if I did try then he wanted the story to go beyond the far-future episode in Wells's *The Time Machine,* in which the time traveler finds himself on a beach lit by an aged, dull-red sun, with the only life visible a small, slow-moving creature resembling a tentacled football. Meanwhile, the other friend was listening and drinking beer and complaining about the lint and sundry unidentifiable material which had collected in the turn-ups of his trousers (or, if you prefer, the cuffs of his pants). When I began researching the idea, however, it soon became plain that aging suns got brighter and hotter, not cold and dull, and the last days of the dying Earth would be somewhat different from the scenario visualized by H. G. Wells and my friend. As for the other friend's trousers . . .

"Second Ending" is one of my own favorite stories, and not just because it was voted onto the short list of five novels for the 1963 Hugo award (Heinlein's *Stranger in a Strange Land,* a much longer, and better, story, won it that year). So strongly did I feel about the story that when it was submitted to my favorite editor and he requested a few changes—including a reduction in length to twenty thousand words and the introduction of a surviving island of humanity!—I demurred. It was the only time in my writing career that I said "No" to an editor in such forthright language. After close on a quarter of a century in the game, I have now learned how to make all my "No's" sound like "Well, maybe's."

Returning to the original question, "Where on Earth do you get those crazy ideas from?", it seems that in my case they come from unfulfilled ambitions, feelings of injustice, meeting a bedraggled dog or a beautiful girl, or from a friend with polluted pants. But the simple answer is that all of the ideas have a solidly terrestrial origin, and so the question answers itself.

Second Ending

1

FOR ROSS THE process of awakening was a slow thaw. Gradually there was growing within his mind a spot of warmth, melting and clearing the long-unused channels of memory and perception. For a time he knew only that he was somebody and that it was very cold, and then he began to remember other cold awakenings and the nightmares which followed them. He tried to tell himself that this was all wrong, that nightmares preceded awakening and not the other way around, but his memory insisted otherwise. It insisted so strongly that, had such a reaction been physically possible, Ross would have broken into a sweat of fear. Eventually sound and vision came to him, the icy fog of Deep Sleep cleared and he saw Beethoven.

Someone had given Beethoven's hair a coat of black enamel, painted the face with a realistic flesh tint and touched in the eyes with blue, but it was still the same bust which had occupied a place of honor in Pellew's consulting room. That someone, Ross knew, was in for trouble, because Dr. Pellew was not a man who took kindly to practical jokes. All at once that line of thought became a very comforting one for Ross, because it opened up the possibility that the nightmares had been practical jokes also. He seemed to remember that there had been quite a few jokers in this place, especially on the thirty-first level. But why such a needlessly cruel trick, and why had they picked him? Who, exactly, were *they*? What was this place, what was he doing here, who was Pellew . . . ?

Ross didn't know, exactly. His mental processes were quickening, but he was demanding answers from a memory which was still woefully incomplete. He sighed audibly, and suddenly Beethoven was talking to him.

"When the patient has recovered consciousness," Beethoven said in a dry, lecturing voice which was remarkably like that of Dr. Pellew, "it is important that he make no sudden movements, which at this stage could result in severe muscular damage. He, or she, must be urged to move *gently*. The patient should also be assured, as often as seems necessary considering his emotional state, that he has been cured he has been cured he has been cured he has been cured . . ."

Like a record with a faulty groove, the same words droned out over and over and over. Ross stuck it out for as long as he could, which was about six minutes; then he croaked, "Shut up, I believe you!"

The voice ceased. Ross became aware of a steadily mounting pressure at the back of his head and shoulders. Chest, neck and leg muscles cracked painfully, and he realized that his posture was altering. The padded surface on which he lay had broken in two places. It was swinging upward from a point below his waist and falling away at the level of his knees. He was being forced from a supine into a sitting position. The process was slow and was probably meant to be gentle. Ross would have yelled in sheer agony, if he had not known that filling his lungs for the yell would have expanded his chest muscles suddenly and added to the pain. Finally he was sitting upright, held by a strap around his middle. He *felt* the strap, because his eyes showed little more than drifting patches of blackness. Strain as he might to see more, for the moment the blackness continued to prevail. The voice began again:

"With long-term patients there will be psychological difficulties as well," the bust said through its motionless, painted lips. "He is awakening into an environment which is completely strange, and perhaps frightening, to him. Someone with an understanding of his background should be present, and the shock can be lessened by surrounding him with his more valuable personal possessions . . ."

Ross blinked until the black patches faded from sight. He was in a small room which contained, in addition to the contraption he was sitting in, a bed, some recessed cupboards and a floor which was neatly paved with what looked like foam-rubber mattresses. Close by was an instrument trolley containing the talking bust of Beethoven, three shiny cans and his wallet, opened to show the picture of Alice.

". . . At the same time the patient must take nourishment and exercise his muscles as soon as possible after revivication. The method recommended is to raise him into a sitting position, massage, administer a light, liquid meal liquid meal liquid meal liquid meal . . ."

"Oh, for Heaven's sake!" Ross groaned, and reached out carefully for one of the food containers. This, he thought, was the most intricate and senseless joke he had ever heard of. He did not feel hungry, but doing what he was told seemed to be the only way of shutting off that maddening, repetitious voice.

The can warmed up as soon as he lifted it and the top flipped back, spilling some of the stuff onto his bare legs. He swore, sniffed, then began to wonder if perhaps he wasn't hungry after all. The stuff tasted every bit as good as it smelled, and it warmed him right down to his toes. But when he had emptied the can Beethoven continued to drone "Liquid meal liquid meal" at him. Presumably he was expected to empty all three.

The second can exploded in his face.

Several things happened at once. He jerked backward instinctively as the hot, foul-smelling liquid sprayed his face and chest. The sudden movement triggered off a cramp which nearly tied him in knots, and he began slipping toward the floor. The retaining strap took his weight for a moment; then it parted with a soft tearing sound and he collapsed onto the floor.

That drop of perhaps three feet onto a thickly padded surface brought a shock of pain worse than anything he had ever experienced. It also brought him finally and fully awake.

Up to now Ross had been treating everything which was happening as some sort of involved practical joke which was being played on him; he was both angered at the cruelty of it and relieved that he had not awakened to the nightmare of being crushed to death in a tubular metal cage which ticked. From his new position he could see a small extension speaker unit attached to the back of Beethoven's head, and a cable which ran from it across the floor and out through a hole in the wall. This *could* have been the sort of joke that his fellow students might have played on him—involving stink bombs, a talking bust and an edited playback of one of Pellew's lectures—but for one thing. The tape had led him to believe that he was cured. No one in the hospital would joke about that.

And if it wasn't a joke . . .

2

THE FIRST ATOMIC War had occurred fifty years before Ross had been born. It had started because of malfunctioning of some early-warning equipment and raged
for three weeks before the mistake was realized and all
parties agreed to the cease-fire. Had it continued for
another three weeks the world would have undoubtedly
been depopulated completely, but as it was, one out of
every ten people survived. Far from causing the collapse of civilization, the war seemed to give it an explosive boot in the pants. Scientific advances came thick
and fast; because there were no longer multitudes to be
thrown out of work, industry became fully automated,
and the world seemed well on the way to becoming a
Utopia—except for the nervous tendency of people to
build deep instead of high. Possibly because there was
still a lot of distrust about, and possibly through sheer
force of habit, improvements in nuclear weapons were
keeping pace with everything else.

Like everyone else, Ross had been cynical and uncaring about the war. He had never known an over-
crowded Earth, and was rather glad he had not been
born into such a period. He enjoyed having twenty-one
hours of leisure in the twenty-four. But then had come
the realization, when he was still in his early teens, that
the long-term effects of the war were still horribly evi-
dent. The incidence of male and female sterility had
passed the 40-percent mark and was still climbing, too
few children were being born, and if the trend could not
be checked the effect would be exactly the same as if
the war had not been stopped.

All at once human life became a rare and precious

thing, and promised to become rarer and more precious as time went on. No effort or expense was too great to save, extend or propagate a human life. No case was ever considered hopeless. If a patient could not be cured there and then, well, in the next decade the researchers were bound to come up with the answer, or perhaps in the decade after that. In the meantime the patient was put into suspended animation. They would develop a cure eventually, and while there was life there was hope.

So Ross had applied to train as a doctor in one of the "incurables" hospitals. As well as his basic studies, he had specialized in the techniques of what the purists called hibernation anesthesia and the patients called Deep Sleep, when they both weren't calling it suspended animation. Then, in his fifth year, at the age of twenty-two, it was discovered that he had a rare lukemic condition—one on which very little research had been done. He had been told that, owing to the fact that he was not likely to be awakened for some time, they would be putting him at the bottom of the heap.

As was customary with long-term patients, Dr. Pellew supervised the freezing personally. And now it seemed to be only hours ago since the old boy had murmured, "Good night, young man, and good luck," in a tone of voice which Ross had never before heard him use to a student, and had administered the shot which kept the patient from feeling the gradually increasing cold.

But it had been more than a matter of hours, obviously.

Ross was thinking of the food container which must have been improperly sealed and whose contents had gone off in both senses of the word. And of the thick retaining strap which had come apart like so much dry putty. An awful lot of time must have passed. Now that he thought back on it, even the recorded voice of Dr. Pellew had sounded older and more tired. But none of those things was important. Neither was the fact that his body was only a little fatter than a demonstration skeleton, or that every square inch of it ached.

He was *cured!*

Carefully, Ross pushed himself onto his hands and knees and began crawling slowly around the room. His cheek muscles ached because he could not keep himself from grinning, and if he had had the breath for it he would probably have been singing at the top of his voice. A period of sustained, gentle exercise was the next step, and although it was odd that the physiotherapist hadn't arrived, Ross did not mind taking it the hard way. He continued to crawl across soft sponge rubber, feeling the stiffness leave his muscles, smiling and occasionally laughing out loud. He tried not to think about Alice, or the fact that she was probably in her fifties by now and that a very awkward and painful situation would arise between them in the near future. He did not want any hint of sadness to spoil the moment in which he knew that he was no longer under sentence of death.

Eventually he was able to stand upright, with one hand steadying himself against the wall. He opened the locker which contained his clothing, and was met by a blast of cold air which made his eyes water. Moisture began condensing on everything inside the locker, and Ross decided wryly that there was no point in catching pneumonia through wearing damp clothing after all that had been done to keep him alive. He left the locker door wide open so that the room heaters would dry them. It wasn't that he was a prude, Ross told himself, but his blotchy, emaciated body looked horrible even to him. The sooner it was covered the better. Alice might come in.

Ross walked unsteadily to the bed and sat down. He was beginning to feel hurt by the lack of attention being shown him. Someone should have been around to welcome him back to the land of the living or to say a few words of congratulation—or to check on his condition, at least. There should have been a physician supervising the revivication, a couple of nurses or physiotherapists to walk him about before putting him to bed, and a psychiatrist to cushion him against the mental shocks of awakening. That was how things had been done in his time.

Instead there was a painted, bronze bust, a disjointed lecture tape played through a loudspeaker and rubber mattresses scattered about the floor to keep him from hurting himself. Ross was suddenly afraid. There must be a shortage of staff, he thought.

An acute shortage of staff.

Ross found himself standing with his hand on the doorknob, not remembering how he had got there but knowing by the way that his legs ached that he had moved too fast. The door slid open easily and he stumbled outside. Immediately he knew that he was in a section of the hospital which he had not seen before, perhaps an extension built after he had gone into Deep Sleep. It was a short, brightly lit and spotlessly clean corridor with three doors opening off each side. A few yards to his right the corridor came to a dead end and in the opposite direction it terminated in a semitransparent door which gave the suggestion of a sloping ramp on the other side of it. Just inside the door stood a small desk and chair. There was a pale green folder lying on the desk; there was nobody in the chair.

Propping himself against the wall, Ross moved around to the door facing his own and slid it open. It was dark inside, but light from the corridor showed a stripped bed, locker doors standing open and an empty Deep Sleep casket. He closed it and began a stumbling zigzag along the corridor, trying all the doors. The rooms were dark and empty, but looked as if they had been regularly cleaned—he tested some of the furniture with his fingers. There was a cleaning staff, then, as well as the people responsible for rigging the crazy equipment in his room. It was high time somebody put in an appearance, Ross thought as he moved toward the desk to sit down.

And began to laugh gently to himself, because the green folder lying on the desk had his name on it.

Since his revivication Ross had both fed and exercised himself without assistance, and now it looked as though he was expected to handle his own reorientation problems as well. Abruptly he stopped laughing, when he realized that there was nothing at all to laugh at in the situation. Ross split the folder's all-around seal with a fingernail—his nails had grown very long despite the fact that *all* body processes were supposed to be halted by suspended animation—and went through the contents quickly. There were seven of the green 508 forms—the type used for hibernation-anesthesia patients—and about ten sheets of various sizes which looked like interdepartmental memos. Ross went back to the beginning and began to read.

The first green form was familiar to him—Ross had been present when it had been filled in. It was dated 29th September, 2017, and gave his name and the details of the condition which required his going into Deep Sleep. It was signed by Dr. Pellew and his assistant. The next one was similarly signed, was dated 4th June, 2036, and stated that the patient had been revived but kept under complete sedation for three weeks while a new treatment was tested. It was unsuccessful. The third form was dated 1st May, 2093, and was signed by a Dr. Hanson. On this occasion he was revived but unconscious for six weeks while a complex treatment involving micro-injections of his bone marrow was tried, again unsuccessfully. His eyes went back to the date: *1st May, 2093!*

The problem of Alice was solved, he thought numbly, by simple mathematics: 2017 from 2093 was seventy-six years, and Alice had been twenty-two. His eyes began to sting and Ross hurriedly changed to a less emotionally loaded train of thought. The notes on his chart showed that medical science had left him far behind; relatively, his training was as outdated as bread poultices and bloodletting. And the growth of his fingernails was explained by the periods during which he had been revived but unconscious. He blinked a couple of times, then turned to the next form.

It was dated 17th May, 2233.

Ross could not believe it at first. He suspected a misprint or a new system of dating, until he began to read the notes of the physician in charge. They ran to around three hundred neat, closely written words which detailed a treatment so complex that Ross could only guess at what it had entailed. As before, he had been revived but kept under sedation. *Something* had been done to him—whether it was something injected or attached or surgically implanted he couldn't tell—which had brought about a long-term cure, because the notes ended with a terse "Treatment successful, to be revived permanently in 75 years from this day."

And it was signed by Dr. Pellew and a Sister. At least, the assistant's space had been rubber-stamped WARD SISTER 5B, but she had forgotten to add her initials.

Ross shook his head in weary confusion. It *couldn't* be Pellew's signature, not after two hundred and sixteen years. It must be a coincidence, he thought, or maybe a great-grandson. Yet he had heard Pellew's voice—his taped voice, rather—during his awakening. Would a tape recording keep for two hundred years? Ross wasn't sure, but it might. But then there was that signature . . .

The next green form, dated 17th May, 2308, was stamped REVIVICATION HALTED: REPROCESSED at the bottom by the Ward Sister of 5B, who was apparently either too busy or too well known to have to add her initials. There was no doctor's signature. The next sheet was practically a carbon copy, except for the date, which was four months later, and the last one bore the date 7th October, 2308, and was stamped PATIENT AWAKENED.

Now I know the date, Ross thought, a little wildly; *if I had the right time I could set my watch!*

3

ALL AT ONCE Ross felt so unutterably weary that he wanted to lie on the floor and sleep. For a patient just out of Deep Sleep he had been behaving stupidly indeed. Instead of a few minutes' gentle exercise, he had been stumbling about the corridor and sitting on an uncomfortable chair, of the kind designed to keep Night Sisters awake, for the best part of an hour. It was high time he got into bed. Perhaps his brain would be able to make something out of the confused mass of data, after he got some sleep.

Five minutes later Ross was between the sheets, which turned out to be of fine, woven plastic. Their only sign of age was a tendency toward yellow in places. He tried to sleep but his curiosity kept him awake. The green folder, which he had brought along and hidden under his pillow, lay a few inches from his hand. In those unread pages he might find the answer to everything or he might be thrown into worse confusion. He was *sure* that the contents of the folder would do nothing to increase his peace of mind. But Ross was beginning to be afraid again and he wanted to do everything possible to find out exactly what he feared.

Groaning, he levered himself to one elbow, drew out the folder and began to read.

Immediately following the 508s which he had already studied there was a two-page instructional circular dealing with the transfer of staff to the extension of the five-mile level. This would be devoted to the study of non-sterile mutations. Two Doctors and four Sisters were listed by name and there was a note stating that owing to the shortage of staff the cleaners would also serve as nursing orderlies and be allowed to administer simple courses of treatment without supervision. Dated March, 2062, the circular was signed by Dr. Pellew.

The next five sheets dealt primarily with the reorganization due to the shortage of staff and covered a period of about twenty years. Apparently some of the wards were then operating with just a Sister and two Cleaners. In addition to the cleaning and maintenance work, these people, who had once been considered the lowliest members of the staff, were being given increasingly responsible duties with regard to the patients. They had become Cleaners with a capital C, like Doctors and Sisters.

Ross's mind was bursting with questions. He turned quickly to the next page, hoping that the answers to some of them might be there.

Two short paragraphs, in bold type and underlined, practically shouted up at him.

During the Emergency all sections shall be rendered self-contained and self-sufficient. Transfer of staff, food, medical supplies and servomechanisms is forbidden. Penalty for contravening this regulation, regardless of circumstances, is exclusion from the home section. Contact between sections shall be by intercommunication phone only.

All Deep Sleep patients with a favorable prognosis shall be transferred immediately to the Non-sterile Mutations section. Patients to be transferred are . . .

A list of case numbers followed, Ross's being one of them.

So there had been an Emergency. Ross didn't like the sound of that at all. His hand was shaking with more than fatigue when he turned that page over.

There followed four closely typed pages which were the minutes of a meeting held by all the medical staff of the section, dated 6th July, 2071, Dr. Hanson presiding.

Under discussion were the new techniques for treating patients while actually in the Deep Sleep state. The only drawback was that the new treatment required many decades to effect a cure, and, with the exception of Dr. Hanson, who had been born in the section, all the Doctors were men in their sixties. They were therefore faced with the problem of reviving nearly thirty Deep Sleep patients in fifty-odd years later, at which time they themselves would have long since been dead.

The only possible answer was for the Doctors to go into suspended animation also until the time when their patients were due to be revived. However, at least one Doctor would have to remain awake to supervise and to continue with some of the more promising lines of research, which, if they were lucky, might result in cures for all of their suspended patients. A timetable of twenty years asleep and two awake was suggested, with a three-month overlap to allow the newly awakened Doctor to take over the reins. Being the youngest of the group, Dr. Hanson asked that his waking term be extended to five years, as he was working on a line which might produce a cure for the heart condition which had forced their previous director to undergo suspended animation. They must agree that if Dr. Pellew could be cured and revived, his help would be invaluable.

Mention was made of the psychological dangers present in the scheme, and methods suggested for guarding against them, and the report ended with discussion of the staff problem. It was decided to give Cleaners more responsibility and allow the Ward Sisters the right to diagnose, treat and perform limited surgery.

Staring unseeingly at the page, which was the last one, Ross thought, *And so endeth the first lesson.* For that was what it had been. Unbalanced, over-short, composed of medical charts and instructional circulars, but withal a history lesson designed to help him fit into a strange present.

Something caught in his throat as he thought of those wonderful old men, forced by their short life expectancy to spread out their remaining years to carry the torch of their knowledge across two centuries, in a relay race against time. And young Hanson *had* been successful, because the circular was dated 2071 and Dr. Pellew had signed one of his 508 forms in 2233.

Suddenly he began to feel the stirrings of hope. A wild, exciting and purely selfish hope. The record had made no reference to nursing staff, but presumably they would have had to go into Deep Sleep also. Suppose one of them was Alice . . .

The lights went out.

His brain froze in mid-thought and the cold sweat broke on his forehead, hands and at the small of his back. Without knowing why exactly, Ross was terrified. In vain he tried to tell himself that the lights had gone out to let him sleep, that there was nothing frightening about that. But this darkness was absolute, a negation of light which was possible only when all power has gone five miles underground. Ross had left his room door open in the hope that anyone passing would notice and maybe call in; it was just as dark in the corridor. The folder slid to the floor and he lay motionless, his heart banging deafeningly in his ears and teeth jammed together to keep them from chattering.

Then, above the relative din of his racing pulse, he heard movements from the corridor outside.

It was a soft, regular, thumping sound accompanied by a gentle sighing. Outside his door it stopped briefly, then grew louder as it entered his room. Ross strained his eyes desperately into the blackness, trying to give shape and substance to the blotchy retinal images which slid about in the darkness. The faint sighing and thumping seemed to be moving about the center of the room, and he could hear some small objects being lifted or laid down, quietly. The sounds were quiet but, somehow, not stealthy. Whoever was making them knew what he was doing, and could see very well in the dark. Undoubtedly they could see *him*. Any second now they would come over to his bed . . .

"Who . . . who's there?" said Ross.

"Ward Sister," replied a voice out of the blackness, a pleasant, impersonal and unmistakably feminine voice. "You are doing fine, Mr. Ross. Now go to sleep."

The sounds moved toward the door without approaching his bed and began to fade along the corridor. The door leading onto the ramp slid open and closed, and a few seconds later the lights blinded him.

Ross lay back and shielded his eyes until they became used to the lights again. Four self-heating food containers had been placed beside Beethoven, but otherwise nothing had changed in the room. He pulled the sheets up to his chin and relaxed for the first time since his revivication. Weariness made his mind work slowly, but the mental processes were clear and logical. At last he was beginning to make sense out of the mad puzzle facing him, and the Sister who had visited him in complete darkness was the key incident, he thought.

Beethoven, his case history, a Sister who could see extremely well in pitch-blackness . . .

The most urgent problem when Ross had gone into Deep Sleep had been the sharply declining birthrate, and according to the contents of the folder the problem had worsened steadily. Staff shortage was mentioned on every page. Human life had become a rare and precious thing—so rare, perhaps, and so very precious, that the meaning of the word had widened somewhat. *Devoted to the study of non-sterile mutations* . . . Ross thought. That might explain Sister's extraordinary eyesight, and her visit under a cloak of darkness. They didn't want to shock him, possibly risk driving him insane, by confronting him too suddenly with what the human race had become. That had to be the answer. They were breaking it to him gently, giving information by indirect means, even to the extent of supervising his revivication at a distance.

Ross thought that he was prepared for the shocks now. He probably wouldn't like them, but he wouldn't be terrified or disgusted by them. And if things got tough he could always console himself with the reminder that there were a few real, old-time human beings still in suspended animation. One of them might even be Alice.

The one piece of the puzzle which did not fit his theory was the nightmares. There had been two of them, almost identical, and he still had the conviction that they had occurred *after,* or at least during, the process of awakening. Thick metal bars pressing down on his head, chest, abdomen and legs. Others crushing his arms into his sides, jamming his legs together, threatening to squeeze in the sides of his skull. Fighting to escape that vicious, inexorable pressure, struggling desperately to see, to move, to breathe. But he could not see, he could only feel and hear: the savage construction of uncaring metal, and an irregular ticking sound . . .

Until that gap in the picture was filled, Ross thought, he would feel very uncomfortable about going to sleep. He was uneasily wondering who had introduced an Iron Maiden into the hospital when sleep sneaked up on him.

4

Ross awoke hungry. His first act was to remedy that condition, and he was lucky in that only one of the four food containers had spoiled. While the air conditioner was dispersing the stench of two-hundred-year-old soup, he moved across to his clothes locker and began to dress. His next action must be to go out and find somebody, the Doctor in charge, Sister, anybody, and while the sight of his unclothed body was unlikely to shock any member of the hospital staff, having a few clothes around him would boost his morale considerably.

He hadn't realized just how few clothes that would be.

His socks and underwear fell apart when he tried to get into them, his shirt had gone brittle and cracked when he forced his head into it, and the elastic in his shoes had ceased to be. The slacks were in good condition—they were all wool and had been rather an extravagance in a day of largely synthetic clothing—but his belt came to pieces in his hands. And his hips had shrunk so much that they refused to hold them up. Ross swore, feeling ridiculous.

One of the other lockers contained the woven plastic sheets, he discovered after a brief search. He opened out one of them and began to work at the middle of it with his teeth until he had a hole that he could get his fingers into. The stuff wasn't easy to tear. When the hole was big enough he put his head through it and let the sheet fall down around his shoulders. It came almost to his knees. Working his arms free, he tore one of the pillow coverings into strips, tied one around his waist and made two others into figure-eight bandages which held the shoes on his feet. In the locker mirror the effect wasn't too bad, he thought, but it needed something. A turban, maybe, or a chaplet of laurel leaves?

Ross made a face at himself, snarled, "You look horrible in white," and headed for the corridor.

This time he was able to walk without holding on to the wall. But when he began to ascend the ramp at the end of the corridor, dizziness overtook him and he began to gray out. He realized that he must still be terribly weak and that if he was going to get anywhere at all he would have to take it in easy stages. Climbing slowly, sometimes on hands and knees, Ross ascended to the next level.

He found himself in a long, brightly lit corridor with a T-junction at the other end. Everything in sight was shining, aseptically clean. *Matron must be the strict type,* he thought, and hoped that he did not encounter her first. But there were no signs of life or movement about and the only sound was that of his own breathing. Ross moved forward and began trying doors.

By the time he reached the intersection he was both bewildered and uneasy. Many of the doors had opened into small wards and rooms like his own. There could have been a good reason for their being dark and unoccupied, but some of them *should* have contained members of the staff, or at least shown signs of recent use. The diet kitchens, for instance, the power rooms, or the Sisters' and Cleaners' quarters. Those living quarters bothered Ross. He could not say for sure, because he had been seeing only by reflected light from the corridor, but those rooms had seemed to be large, featureless boxes which were completely devoid of furniture, fittings and personal decoration. Yet everything he saw was so *clean.* Somebody was responsible for the spotless condition of the place, but who and where? The whole thing was ridiculous!

Maybe they were playing hide and seek, Ross thought wildly; if so, he was getting tired of the game, tired of being "it" . . .

"Come out, come out!" Ross yelled at the top of his voice, "Wherever you are!"

They came out.

They were long cylindrical objects mounted on four padded wheels, possessing at least ten thick, multi-jointed metal arms and various other projections of unknown function. As they rolled steadily toward him, Ross knew with a terrible certainty that what he was seeing was his nightmare—multiplied by twenty. There was almost a score of the things coming at him from the left-hand fork of the corridor. The lights gleamed off their shiny metal sides and folded arms. He could see that each had a double lens arrangement mounted vertically atop a short, headless neck. The upper lens rotated slowly; the lower was directed forward. They advanced without a sound. Ross wanted to run, but his brain seemed to have gotten its signals crossed. All he could do was tremble and sweat, until . . .

"Our previous instructions were to conceal ourselves until after you had spent some time in Dr. Pellew's room," said a quiet, female voice behind him, "and we were warned that to do otherwise might result in severe psychological disturbance to yourself. The wording of your last order, however, is such that it overrides our previous instructions."

Ross turned around, slowly. The thing behind him was a large, erect ovoid mounted on three wheels and surmounted by one fixed and one swiveling eyepiece. There were no arms but the smooth, egglike body showed the outlines of several panels which might open to reveal anything. Clamped to one of the wheel struts was a large square box with a cable running from it to the main body. It gave the impression of having been stuck on as an afterthought. One of its wheels had a worn tread which emitted a faint sighing sound as it moved toward him. Ross thought of dodging around it and running—or trying to run; he felt almost too weak to stand now—for the ramp, but behind the egg there were more cylinders coming fast.

With his head jerking from side to side Ross watched them roll up to within a yard of him and stop. The rotating lenses turned slowly; the stationary ones were fixed on him.

After several unsuccessful tries Ross made his tongue work. He said, "What . . . what *is* all this?"

The cylinders began to tick like runaway clocks and then the egg spoke again. It said, "The question, requiring as it does complete and detailed knowledge of astronomy, anthropology, cybernetics, evolution, mass psychology, metallurgy, medicine, nuclear physics as well as other sciences about which I have no data, is beyond the scope of an electronic brain. For your information, sir, when asking questions or giving orders to a robot the wording must be detailed and non-ambiguous."

So they were only robots who could answer questions—simple questions—and obey orders. Ross began to relax. His first thought was to tell them all to get to blazes out of his sight, but then he decided that that, also, might be too confusing for them. He considered for a moment, then said timidly, "Go back to whatever you were doing before I called you."

They all began to move away, including the egg-shaped one. Ross called, "Not you. Wait. Your voice is familiar—are you the one who came into my room last night?"

"Yes, sir."

"But I'd thought . . . the mutations . . ." Ross stammered. "What happened to the mutants?"

"They are dead, sir. The research was discontinued before I was programmed."

Ross shook his head. He had been expecting mutants and had found robots instead. In a way he ought to have expected something like this, because the trend had been well developed even in his time. Full-scale automation spreading from the factories into the homes, guardian robots for small children—there had even been talk of a robot barber. But in his wildest moments Ross would never have thought of them turning one loose in a hospital. Ross had to check an urge to revise his picture of what had happened while he was in Deep

Sleep, because the revision would be based on incomplete data and would probably be as wide of the truth as the last one. Horrible mutations working under a cloak of darkness, indeed! He decided not to jump to any conclusions at all until he had been to Dr. Pellew's quarters.

Matching pace with Ross's weary shuffle, the robot led him through a series of short corridors, up another ramp for two levels, then into what appeared to be the administration and maintenance section. Ross was feeling quite pleased with himself. He had had a horde of robots sprung on him without warning only minutes ago, and now he was talking to one of them, almost naturally. Such powers of adaptability, he thought, were something to be proud of.

He kept the conversation simple, of course, and confined mainly to short, direct questions regarding the rooms or machinery they passed. To some of the simple questions the robot gave concise and detailed answers, and occasionally he received a reply of "I'm sorry, sir, I have not been programmed with data on this subject. . ."

At one point Ross broke off to ask, "Why do you keep calling me 'sir' when you know my name?"

The robot ticked quietly to itself for a few seconds, and Ross went over the question again in his mind to see if it might sound ambiguous. It didn't, so he repeated the question aloud.

The ticking slowed and stopped. "A Ward Sister of my type has two choices of behavior toward human beings," the robot said in its pleasant, feminine voice. "Toward patients we are friendly but authoritative, because we are better qualified to know what will and will not benefit them, and surnames prefixed by 'Mr.' are used. When a human being is mobile and shows no marked signs of physical malfunction we treat him as our superior. The choice was difficult in your case."

"Between a mobile Boss and a bedridden patient," said Ross drily, "and I was a mobile patient."

"As my superior," the robot went on, "you are not

required to give reasons for your misuse and damaging of ward bed linen."

Ross began to laugh softly. Sisters were all the same, he thought; even the mechanical ones were inclined to fuss. He was still laughing when they reached Dr. Pellew's room.

It was much smaller than the quarters Pellew had once occupied, but it contained the same chairs, desk and bookcase. The only items missing were Beethoven and the thin, irascible person of Pellew himself. A heavy ledger lay exactly centered on the desk with an empty ashtray on one side and an adjustable calendar on the other. Pellew had been a notoriously untidy man, Ross knew, so this uncharacteristic neatness must be due to the cleaning robots while Pellew was in Deep Sleep. Knowing that the Doctor was not in a position to object, Ross sat at the desk and opened the ledger.

It was a diary, more than half filled with Pellew's odd, backward-leaning scrawl.

Before he settled down to reading it, the caution of a lowly student who was making free with his superior's holy of holies prompted a question.

"Who is the Doctor in charge at the moment?" Ross asked. "Who's awake, I mean."

"You, sir," said the robot.

"Me! But . . ."

He had been about to say that he wasn't qualified, that another two years of study would elapse before, if he was lucky, he could tack "Dr." in front of his name. But there was a staff shortage, so much so that they must have been forced to awaken students to fill in for qualified doctors. The ledger would probably tell him why.

"Have you any instructions, sir?" said the robot.

Ross tried to think like a Doctor in charge. He hemmed a couple of times, then said, "Regarding the patients, none at present. But I'm hungry—will you get me something to eat?"

The robot ticked at him.

"I want food," said Ross, making it simple and nonambiguous. The robot left.

5

THE FIRST SIX pages of the diary were heavy going, not only because they dealt mainly with details of administration in Pellew's almost unreadable writing, but because they were dated only a few months after Ross had gone into Deep Sleep and so contained no information likely to help in his present situation. He began cheating a little, skipping five, seven, twenty pages ahead.

He read:

> Communications ceased with Section F two hours ago and we have not been able to raise the others for over a week. For purposes of morale I have suggested that this may be due to broken lines caused by the earth tremors, which have been felt even down here. I have ordered the maintenance robots to slot heavy metal girders across the elevator shaft so as to make it impossible for anyone to take the cage up. There are still a few short-sighted, quixotic fools who want to form a rescue party . . .

Ross remembered an instructional circular from last night which had begun, *"During the Emergency . . ."* Apparently this part of the diary dealt with that Emergency, but he had skipped too far ahead. He was turning the pages back slowly when the robot arrived with six food cans.

He opened one and set it on the empty ashtray so as not to mark Pellew's desk. When he went back to the ledger the large, stiff pages had risen up and rolled past

31

his place. Ross inserted his finger and flattened a page at random. It said:

I took Courtland out of hibernation last week. In his present condition he will live only a few months so I have as good as killed him. The fact that he has told me several times that he doesn't mind only makes me feel worse—his bravery pointing up my cowardice. But I need help, and he was one of the best cyberneticists of his time. He is working on a modification of our Mark 5 Ward Sisters for me.

I wanted a robot with judgment and initiative and the Mark 5B seems to have those qualities. Courtland insists that it hasn't, that he has merely increased its data-storage capacity, increased its ability to cross-index this memory data, and made some other changes which I can't begin to understand. It does NOT have a sense of humor, but only gives this impression because it takes everything it is told literally. Despite all he says, Courtland is very proud of this new robot—he calls it Bea—and says that if he had proper facilities, or even a few more months of life, he could do great things.

I think he has done great things already. If only Ross can carry on. It will be his problem soon.

Ross felt his scalp begin to prickle. Seeing his own name staring up at him had been a shock, but what was the problem mentioned?

"How long since you talked to Dr. Pellew?" he asked the robot suddenly.

"Twenty-three years and fifteen days, sir."

"Oh, as long ago as that. When is he due to be awakened?"

The robot began to tick.

"That is a simple question!" began Ross angrily, then stopped. Maybe it wasn't a simple question, maybe . . . "Is Pellew dead?"

"Yes, sir."

Ross swallowed. He said, "How many, both patients and staff, are left?"

"One, sir. You."

He had been hungry and had meant to eat. Ross began spooning the contents of the food can into his mouth, trying to pretend that it had not happened. Or maybe these were the blind involuntary movements of a body which has died and does not yet realize it. Pellew was dead, Alice was dead, Hanson, everyone. Claustrophobia was something which normally had not bothered Ross, but now suddenly he wanted out. Everyone he knew—and so far as his mind was concerned, he had known and spoken to them only two days ago— was dead and buried, most of them for hundreds of years. The hospital had become a vast, shining tomb staffed by metal ghouls, and he was buried in it. He was suddenly conscious of five miles of earth pressing down on him. But he was alive! *He wanted out!*

Ross did not realize that he had been shouting until the robot said, "Dr. Pellew told me that you might behave in a non-logical manner at this time. He said to tell you that the future of the human race might depend on what you do in the next few years, and not to do anything stupid in the first few hours."

"How can I get out?" said Ross savagely.

A human being would have avoided the question or simply refused to reply, but the Ward Sister was a robot and had no choice in the matter. Even so, while it was giving the information requested it managed to insert a truly fantastic number of objections to his going. The elevator shaft was blocked, there was danger of contamination and the robot's basic programming forbade it to allow Ross to endanger himself . . .

"Do you know what going mad is?" said Ross, in a voice he didn't recognize as his own. "Have you had experience of mental instability in humans?"

"Yes, sir."

"It is against your programming to force me, by your inaction, into that state?"

"Yes, sir."
"Then get me to the surface!"

It took three hours.

The Ward Sister ticked a lot and generally got into the nearest approach that a machine could manage to a tizzy. Clearing the elevator shafts—there were five altogether—required the help of heavy maintenance robots and these had been put into a state of low alert two centuries ago and would respond only to direct orders from a human being. But they weren't nearly so bright as the Sister type and, while a single word was enough to set them in motion, it required a great many words to make them understand what he wanted. And the Ward Sister refused to let him into the cage until a full load of Cleaners had tested it first. These delays, by forcing him to think coherently, had a diluting effect on his original feeling of panic, but even he knew that his actions were not those of a sane man.

During the waiting periods between ascents he read parts of the ledger, and now knew what the Emergency had been. A war. According to Pellew it had lasted five months and had been fought to the bitter end by opposing automatic devices, because after the first week no human being could have survived on the surface . . .

Ross wanted out. Desperately, he wanted away from the unhuman attentions of robots and the sterile death of the wards. He did not expect to find living people on the surface, but he would settle for living things. Trees, insects, grass, weeds. And a sky with clouds and a sun in it and cold, natural air on his face. He didn't think there would be any survivors, but he never stopped hoping . . .

Each leg of the journey upward was the same. With the Ward Sister at his heels he would stumble out of the cage, yelling for a robot native to the section. When one appeared, invariably another Sister, he would ask, "How many human beings alive in this section?" When the inevitable reply came back he would pause only briefly, then say, "Where are your maintenance robots?" Within minutes he would be surrounded by a mechanical menagerie of repair and construction robots, all ticking at him or asking for clarification of their instructions in voices that were so human that it made Ross's flesh creep. Eventually they would be made to clear the way up to the next section.

Once he came to a level which he recognized as being the lowest section of the hospital of his pre-Sleep days. In this section the dust of centuries lay like gray snow in the corridors and the robots he summoned became the centers of choking, blinding dust storms.

The first level, which was less than one hundred feet beneath the surface, was a shambles. Lighting, elevators, even the native robots were so much wreckage. Great, gaping cracks grew across walls and ceiling like jagged vines and there had been many cave-ins. But there was also a tunnel, sloping upward steeply and with a fuzzy patch of gray light showing at its other end. In the robot's spotlight Ross could not tell whether the people of this level had dug their way out before they died or someone had dug down in an attempt to escape the holocaust above. He began climbing frantically, the Sister—whose three wheels were not suited to such a rough surface—falling slowly behind him.

He had to rest once, lying face downward on a slope of loose earth, rock and what looked like pieces of fused glass. There was a peculiar tang in the air which his nose, still inflamed by dust, refused to identify. With the lip of the tunnel only a few yards ahead, the dull, gray light was all around him. Ross thought that it was just his luck to pick dusk, or shortly after dawn, as his time to climb out. After a few minutes he pushed himself to his feet and began, wobbling and sliding, to run.

Ross looked slowly around him while the dark gray fog drove past, blackening his arms and clothing as he watched. To the limit of visibility, which was about fifty yards, the ground was dark gray and black—the smooth, shiny black of partly melted rock and the sooty gray of finely divided ash. The ash swirled and drifted from trough to trough in that frozen ocean of glass, or eddied upward to become the dry fog blowing past him. The sun was high in the sky, a dull red smudge with an enormous ring around it, and the sound of waves reached him from the half-mile-distant beach.

He had done a lot of swimming on that beach, alone, with other students, with Alice. Yelling and floundering and splashing for hours on end; "playing" was the only word which described that activity. And the sea had played, too—a trifle roughly, at times, considering that it was the vast, all-powerful mother of life on the planet and one of her most recent offspring was giving her cheek.

Ross began moving toward the beach. His brain seemed to be frozen with shock, because no time elapsed between the decision to go and his arrival.

The sun was a brighter red and visibility was up to half a mile—the breeze blowing in from the sea was relatively free of ash. But the great rollers which marched in were mountains of ink, and when they broke and roared, foaming, up the beach, the foam was dirty and left streaks of black and gray on the sand. The tidal pools were as warm and as numerous as he remembered, but all were lined by a thin film of black and nothing moved in them. There was no seaweed, no evidence of the green scum which collects in stagnant pools, nothing inside the most recently washed up seashells.

They had killed the sea, too.

Ross sat down on a rock which had been smoothed by the sea and given a mirror polish by the tiny sun which had come into being here, for a split second, over a century ago. He sat for a long time. It began to rain and the ash clouds which had obscured his view inland settled to the ground, disclosing a line of robots coming over the shoulder of the hill containing the tunnel mouth. He watched them for several minutes, wondering whether he should take off his ridiculous toga and dive for the last time into the breakers. But Ross was against suicide on principle. The world had ended, he was probably the last living human being, and the future held nothing but loneliness or madness. So it couldn't be hope which made him sit motionless while the dirty gray foam beckoned, for that had become a meaningless word. Perhaps it was because Ross was only twenty-two.

When the robots arrived and performed a neat encircling movement, the Ward Sister said, "You must return to bed, Mr. Ross." Seconds later a Cleaner lay his weakly resisting body along its back, pinioned him with five sets of metal arms and rolled back toward the tunnel mouth.

It took Ross several minutes to realize that he had undergone a change of status. The Ward Sister, it appeared, had heard him coughing in the ash-filled air at the mouth of the tunnel, had noted the many cuts and grazes on hands and legs he had acquired during the climb, and these, taken together with his somewhat abnormal recent activities, had caused the robot to react in accordance with its basic programming. He was no longer a Doctor in charge called "sir," but a patient called "Mr. Ross." And patients did what Ward Sister told them to do, not the other way around.

He was confined to bed for seventeen days.

6

UNTIL EACH TINY cut was healed and the last square centimeter of scab dropped away, Ross's every order was ignored. When sheer impatience made him abusive, that also was ignored, as were most of his threats.

The one threat which was not ignored occurred on the second day. Ross had been throwing a tantrum over not being allowed to exercise for a few hours every day. He had ended by observing, at the top of his voice, that such an inhuman confinement was likely to drive him around the bend, that it could very well force him into taking his life, perhaps, through sheer boredom. To this the robot had replied that physical examination showed he was in a severely weakened state, due to both recent revivication and his too-exhausting trip to the surface, and that prolonged rest was indicated. Also, since the danger of Ross's injuring himself had been mentioned as a possibility—the chief reasons cited being loneliness and boredom, two conditions not likely to improve—it was the Ward Sister's duty to guard him against this danger for the rest of his life.

Just then Ross did not want to think of the future. He wanted to chat about unimportant things such as how he should have his hair cut and why some items of his clothing had deteriorated while others had not. But Ward Sisters were supposed to be too busy to chat with patients while on duty, and Ross was now a patient. Three or four times a day he received a few words of encouragement, and that was all.

Ross did not like the pictures he saw when he closed his eyes, so he kept them open as much as possible, staring at the ceiling, moving them slowly around the room,

38

or squinting at the three-inches-distant bed sheet in an effort to resolve its weave. But the ceiling was white and free from discoloration, the room's fittings were bright, angular and cast no shadows, and trying to make his eyes behave like a microscope only gave him a headache. There were no angles or shadows or tricks of light on which his mind could build the nice, harmless pictures which would keep him from dwelling on his present terrifying position, and so he would be forced to look at the robot.

A smooth, upright ovoid with one fixed and one rotating eyepiece, and to Ross's mind a cybernetic miracle by virtue of its compactness alone. A servant, guardian and trained nurse, placed in this position of responsibility because of a shortage of human nurses, which had later become a shortage of human beings . . .

At that point the pictures which he did not want to see would come, whether his eyes were closed or not.

Pictures of Alice in crisp blue and white, serious, dedicated, untouchable. With her short hair, unplucked eyebrows and thin lips, her face had resembled that of a studious young boy. When he had discovered that she was neither unapproachable nor untouchable—toward himself, anyway—he had once told her that she looked like a boy. They had been swimming and Alice's dark brown hair was plastered tightly against her scalp, increasing the resemblance. A small, wet, feminine hand had made contact with his dripping back in a slap which stung, in memory, even now, and he had had to add a hasty qualifier to the effect that he meant from the neck up. Strangely enough, it had been later in that same day that he discovered that her lips were not thin, that they only seemed that way because she habitually kept them pressed together. Alice worried a lot, about examinations, her patients, about many trivial things which a less dedicated type would have ignored. She had very nice lips.

Pictures of Alice stretched on the sand behind the low rock which sheltered them from the wind, the heat of the sun covering them like a too-warm blanket. It was a picture in five sensual dimensions: the warm, damp smell as the sun blotted up the last remaining sea water from swimsuit and hair; the sensitive, tanned face looking up into his with eyes which seemed to grow larger and softer until he could see nothing else; then the kiss which, no matter how long, never lasted long enough; sometimes then she would sigh and murmur softly to him—but he rarely heard what she said, because the silly girl kept playing with his ears every time she tried to tell him something. They would kiss again and the emotional gale rising within him, the roaring in his ears and the mounting thunder of his pulse, would almost drown the slower thunder of the breakers, the great dead, filthy breakers which still crashed against a black and lifeless beach . . .

No matter how hard he tried to avoid it, his mind always slipped back into the same pit of despair. Until this moment "loneliness" had been a word with only a shadow of meaning. Until now nobody had known the crushing sense of loss and grief of a man whose loved ones, friends *and everyone else* have been taken away to leave him alone on a dead world. The fact that, by his own subjective time, only three or four days had gone by since Alice had kissed him a tearful good night and Pellew had growled his best wishes, and Ross's world had contained a crowded hospital which was part of a civilization covering a planet whose every square yard had teemed with life of some sort, made his loss that much more terrible.

Many times Ross wanted to die. But he was too young and healthy to die of grief, and any more positive approach to dying would certainly be checked by the Sister. And so his despair found its lowest point and, because the only way to go from there was up, it began to recede. Not that he felt hope or anything like it; it was simply an acceptance of his present circumstances and the feeling that perhaps he should look more closely into them before he made a more determined effort to end it all. After all, he had a hospital, hundreds of robots and he didn't know what else at his disposal

and taking stock seemed like a good idea. Besides, it
would keep his mind occupied.

At about the same time Ross made this decision he
discovered that while the robot continued to ignore all
his orders and/or invective, it would accede to reasona-
ble requests of the type which convalescent patients
could be expected to make. The Ward Sister did not
forbid him to read.

The first book Ross asked for was, of course, Pellew's diary. He read it through carefully from beginning
to end, then reread it in conjunction with the green
folder. Now he knew exactly what had happened to the
hospital, and when. Pellew had begun his diary as the
usual personal record of events, but toward the end it
became a series of orders and suggestions directed toward Ross himself, when the doctor had realized that he
was likely to be the only survivor with medical training.

Ross requested books which Dr. Pellew had suggested he study. Works on genetics for the most part,
which must have been heavy going even for the good
Doctor. For his own information he asked for books on
robotics, and one of them turned out to be a populariza-
tion which he could just barely understand. He also began to make plans for the time when the Sister would
stop calling him "Mr. Ross."

Then one "morning" when the lights had come on
after his eight-hour sleep period the robot placed three
food cans beside him and asked, "Have you any instructions, sir?"

Ross said yes with quite unnecessary force, and while
he was struggling into a fresh toga he began issuing orders. Some of them, he feared, were pretty tall orders.
First, he wanted the case histories of the people who
had died between the time of Pellew's death and his
own awakening. He was not hopeful of finding survivors in Deep Sleep, because the Sister had stated that
there were none. But Pellew's diary had said that Ross
was the only survivor with medical training, which im-
plied that there must be other survivors without training, and he wanted that point cleared up. Second, he

asked for a census to be made of all the operable or
repairable robots in the hospital, their numbers, types,
relative intelligence and specialties. Any who had been
placed in a state of low alert by humans prior to their
deaths were to be reactivated. Third, he wanted a report
on the water, food and power supply position.

Ross paused. From his reading he knew that the Sister had been relaying his instructions as he had spoken
them to the other robots in this level, who, because Sister's transmitter could not punch a signal through a mile
of solid rock, would relay them physically to the higher
levels.

He took a deep breath and went on: "You will detail
cleaning and maintenance robots to repair and clear the
damaged upper levels, including where necessary elevators and communication circuits. And I want a small
area of the surface cleared of ash and soil samples taken
at one-foot intervals to a depth of twenty feet. I'll require samples of the air and sea water as well."

Ross hesitated, then asked, "Does your training, I
mean programming, enable you to do an air or soil
analysis?"

"No, sir," the Sister replied, "but there are Pathology
Sisters capable of doing so."

"Very well, put them onto it . . ."

He broke off as a Cleaner rolled in, deposited a small
pile of folders beside him and began making his bed.
The notes Ross had made while lying down were
knocked to the floor, and the robot picked them up and
thrust them into its built-in wastepaper basket.

"I want those back!" said Ross angrily. When the
sheets had been returned, slightly crumpled, he added,
"I'll do my own tidying up from now on. No Cleaners
are to come here unless I send for them."

When the robot had gone Ross looked through the
case histories it had brought. There were five of them,
all relating to patients suffering from conditions which
in his time had been considered fatal. Like him, their
508 forms bore the words TREATMENT SUCCESSFUL, TO
BE REVIVED PERMANENTLY IN —— YEARS FROM THIS

DATE—the number of years ranged from forty to seventy-five. Unlike his own, they were all stamped DIED DURING REVIVICATION, and in all cases the attending physician was down as Ward Sister 5B. In spite of himself, Ross shivered. For the first time since meeting the robots on the day after his awakening, he felt afraid of them.

"Why did these patients die?" he said, as steadily as he could manage. "Tell me the exact circumstances."

The Sister ticked a couple of times, then said briskly, "Dr. Pellew's orders were to awaken all Deep Sleep patients when their revivication was due, and he did not cancel or modify these orders prior to his death. We therefore revived all patients as they fell due, using robot assistance. Specifically, I attended to the revivication while two Cleaners restrained the patients so that they would not injure themselves by moving too suddenly or too soon. On awakening the patients displayed extreme agitation and tried to break free of the robot arms which were holding them immobile. Their struggles were of sufficient violence to cause internal damage from which they subsequently died."

Remembering his nightmares in which the thin, metal arms of cleaning robots had gripped his chest, head and arms, Ross could understand the extreme agitation of those patients. He knew now that they had been trying to keep him from injuring himself, but then he had been convinced that something was intent on crushing the life out of him. But at the thought of those five patients dying like that, patients over whom Doctors like Pellew and Hanson had labored for so long to cure and preserve so that their race might go on, Ross gritted his teeth. With five people—three of them had been female—and almost unlimited robot labor, much might have been accomplished. In time they might have filled these echoing, empty wards, might have spread to the surface and begun filling the world again. Before that happened Ross would have had to work himself to death, probably, bringing children into the world, anxiously guarding the health of its tiny population, coordinating human and robot effort and generally behaving like a frantic mother hen—that was what Pellew had had in mind for him, according to one of the last entries in the diary. It might not have been an entirely pleasant future, but Purpose would have obliterated Despair and loneliness would have again become a word which had only a shadow of meaning.

"You stupid, blundering machine!" he raged suddenly. "Didn't you know they were long-term patients, from the prerobot era, and bound to be frightened by such an awakening? And why did you go on reviving them, letting them die, *killing them!* After the first patient died you should have tried—"

"My previous experience had been with short-term patients who showed no surprise at their awakening being supervised by a robot," the Sister broke in. "And Dr. Pellew had promised to issue instructions regarding the six long-term patients, but he died before doing so. There are three possible reasons for his neglecting to do so: that he did not know what instructions to give; that he intended living through until the first patient was due and awakening him personally, because he had stated several times to me that he was a very lonely man; or that he knew what orders to give but simply forgot to give them, he being very old at that time and tending to forget things . . ."

"He wasn't doddering," said Ross angrily. "I've read his diary. I know."

". . . But we had definite instructions to awaken these patients," the Sister continued, as if he hadn't spoken, "and had therefore no choice but to do so. This despite the fact that our basic function is to serve man and save men's lives. We kept reviving the patients in the hope that some of them would survive the process, but none did. Then we came to you and were faced with a dilemma.

"To a robot," it went on, "allowing a human to remain in Deep Sleep forever is the same as allowing him to die, and bringing one out of Deep Sleep was the same as killing him. And if we killed you, who were the last man, we would both fail in our purpose of saving human lives and at the same time remove our other reason for existence. We could not serve Man if there were no human beings left. That was why, when we commenced revivication on you and you began to display the same symptoms of increasing mental distress and violent muscular activity as had the others, I halted the process and returned you to Deep Sleep. In this I exceeded my instructions, but it seemed the only way possible at the time of not killing you . . ."

The Ward Sister became technical at that point as it went into details of conferences with various repair robots. As the most intelligent single robot in the hospital—the last modification produced by the great cyberneticist Courtland—the responsibility for solving the dilemma naturally fell on it. Its purpose in going to the repair robots was to have them try various modifications and extensions of its memory banks in the hope of emulating the creative or intuitive thinking used by humans in order to solve the problem. Whether the resultant modifications helped or not the Ward Sister had no way of knowing, but after several months and another halted revivication had passed, a new method of attacking the problem suggested itself . . .

"For a successful awakening I needed at least one human being in attendance," the robot continued in its brisk, feminine voice, "and by breaking down the function of the human during such a time into separate parts, converting the large problem into several small ones, I arrived at the solution. The human had to be seen, heard and had to assist the patient physically to do some gentle exercise. I knew of one of Dr. Pellew's ornaments which resembled a human being, and could be painted to increase that resemblance. I had access to tapes containing Dr. Pellew's voice, which were edited to fit the situation, and the exercise was provided by causing you to go into the corridor for your file, which also began the process of reorientation. It remained only for us to keep out of sight until you understood what had happened while you were in Deep Sleep, which was supposed to be after your reading of Dr. Pellew's diary. Instead, you ordered us to come out—"

"You've done very well," said Ross heavily. "Mr. Courtland would be proud of you."

"Thank you, sir."

"But you shouldn't have bothered."

The Sister began ticking at him.

Ross turned suddenly and strode out of the room, along the corridor and up the sloping ramp until he came to a compartment with MAINTENANCE on the door. With the Sister trailing a few yards behind, he entered and began searching the tool lockers until he found a long-handled wrench, which weighed about eight pounds and was over two feet long.

"I want you to do something for me," Ross said in a mild voice. "I want you to stand still." Then he swung the wrench against the robot's smooth metal casing with all his strength.

The blow landed with a shock which jarred him to his heels and a crash which was the loudest noise he had heard since awakening. It battered in one of the flush panels, bludgeoning through the mass of delicate surgical and medical gadgetry underneath. From the wound multicolored blood spurted as underlying drug containers shattered, and three syringes on extensible arms sprang out and sagged downward. Ross swung again.

The second blow caused only a shallow dent, because the robot had moved away, and the third one missed entirely.

"Stand still!" said Ross thickly, raising his metal club again and aiming for the robot's lenses. One of those last five patients had been a nineteen-year-old girl. *An eye for an eye,* he thought with a cold ferocity, *and for a girl's life a dead mass of scrap iron . . .*

"Mr. Ross," said the robot, retreating again, "you are not behaving in a sane—"

"This is a scientific experiment," said Ross, a little breathlessly, "to determine whether or not you can feel pain. And I am not a patient, so call me 'sir.'"

That was important, Ross told himself. If he gave good, logical reasons for wanting to smash it into its component nuts and bolts, he might get away with it— he would still be the boss. But once let it start thinking of him as a patient and then it would be the boss. He advanced again, silent and blank-faced, trying to hide his killing rage behind a façade of scientific curiosity. He had the Sister in a corner now.

One of the robot's body panels opened briefly. Ross did not see or feel or smell anything. His wrench hit the floor an instant before he did, and he didn't feel that because by that time he was asleep.

When Ross came to there was a big, multijointed angular object resembling a surrealistic spider working on the Ward Sister. Several of its panels had been detached, revealing a considerable amount of internal circuitry, and the overall effect seemed vaguely indecent to Ross. The Sister spoke first:

"The data which you required could have been obtained by a verbal request," it said in the brisk, pleasant voice it always used no matter what the circumstances, "so that your experiment, which has caused me a temporary loss of efficiency, was unnecessary. I do not feel pain, or pleasure, in the manner of a human being although I am trained to observe and treat its symptoms in patients. Primarily I have been built to serve Man and anything which hinders my doing so causes me a robot equivalent of pain and anything which aids me toward that end is a form of pleasure. To expand that, pleasure lies in working as hard as possible at the direction of human beings, maintaining myself at peak efficiency to further that end, and avoiding all situations likely to bring about a loss of efficiency when such avoidance will not endanger a human."

"So you got a kick out of knocking me over just now?" Ross said woozily. "An anesthetic gas, wasn't it."

"Yes, sir."

Ross shook his head. He was beginning to feel ashamed of his recent berserker rage—especially as it had been such a dishonest, camouflaged sort of rage—against this machine, which had, after all, been doing its best. He felt that he should apologize to the Sister, except that apologizing to a machine struck him as being ridiculous.

Awkwardly, he said, "Then I hurt you by causing a temporary loss of efficiency, and by defending yourself against a possible permanent loss of efficiency you gained pleasure. That makes us even."

"We are not competing, sir," the robot said. "You do not fully understand the position. All the robots here are your servants, because obeying you and protecting you gives us the only pleasure we are capable of experiencing. It is a matter of basic programming. If you should ever die that would hurt all of us very much."

Ross felt a prickling among the short hairs of his neck. *If you should ever die . . .* The robot must surely know that all human beings died in time, so why should it use that particular form of wording? This posed an interesting psychological point, he thought, and one which he must go into thoroughly at some later date. An electronic brain which made Freudian slips was something to think about.

He climbed slowly to his feet and stood for a few minutes until a slight dizziness had passed, then walked across to Sister and the repair robot.

"I shall be finished in twenty minutes," said the repair robot in a deep, masculine voice which matched its functional but unbeautiful body. "The damage is superficial."

Ross nodded. He said, "Most of the books down here are medical texts, and medicine looks like becoming somewhat of a dead science at the moment. But there used to be a good patients' library on the second level and it may still be there. I'm going up there to start learning something useful . . ."

As he left the maintenance storeroom a Cleaner fell in behind him to escort him to the second level and to guard him against any dangers that might threaten, the

most likely danger being a sudden suicidal urge on the
part of himself, apparently. Ross smiled sardonically
and began to question the Cleaner about its duties.

Keep the servants happy, he thought.

7

DURING THE MONTH which followed Ross kept the robots very happy indeed. Most of the cleaning and repair robots were engaged in rebuilding the first level and he found jobs of some kind for the others. He was so busy making work for the robots and advancing his grandiose—and essentially hopeless—long-term plans toward completion that he hadn't time to think about himself, which was exactly how he wanted it.

Gradually the reports he had asked for came in. He found that mechanically the hospital was in perfect working order, but that the contents of the blood bank and other medical supplies which had been in common use had deteriorated. The power supply was atomic and therefore no problem, there were food stores on every level, and although the water supply was low at the moment, more could be processed from the ocean now that it was no longer radioactive. Under its thin coating of ash the soil was rich, but dead.

A diary found in the debris of the first level gave him the explanation.

During the first three days of war more nuclear weapons were exploded on the Earth's surface than had been believed to be in possession of the combined armories of the world, and during the first month there was little slackening off. By that time nothing lived on the surface. Animal life perished first, then insects and finally the plants. Despite their high radiation tolerance, the bombs were too many and too dirty and the fallout claimed them. The fantastic number and frequency of the explosions made it plain that the bombs were being manufactured and launched from hour to hour, that the

work was being performed by servomechanisms and
that the bombardment would continue until those servos
were knocked out or their available sources of raw material ran out. And so the radiation pushed deeper, ster-
ilizing all life from the soil—the earthworms, the larger
microorganisms, the deepest, most tenacious roots, all
perished.

Outwardly there was very little change in the areas
not directly affected by the explosions. The long grass
waved in the wind and trees still stood proudly against
the sky, but the greenery had taken on a September hue
and it was only mid-April. And at sea the war was less
spectacular even though as many nuclear devices were
exploded underwater as had been loosed on the surface—many of the launching bases were on the sea bed
and the oceans teemed with unmanned submarines. A
lot of dead fish were washed up and lay on the beaches
for a long time, not rotting exactly, because the organ-
isms responsible for the process of putrefaction were
dead also, but simply drying up or falling apart until
they were washed or blown away.

The sea was dying of radioactive poisoning, the land
was dead already and at night the air glowed. There
were too few survivors underground to check what happened next, even had they been willing to sacrifice their
lives in trying.

The fires started by lightning or still-smoldering debris took hold and spread, everywhere. Dead vegetation
does not retain moisture for long, so that even a heavy
rainfall served only to slow that fiery advance. Across
fronts hundreds of miles wide the conflagrations raged,
sweeping first through countries and then continents
with a complete disregard for natural and national barriers alike, and spewing great masses of ash and smoke
into the upper atmosphere. The offshore islands held
out briefly, until deluged with sparks from a mainland
firestorm, and in the Southern Hemisphere the fire was
slow to take hold. It was winter there and in the equatorial regions the vegetation grew in swampland or was
kept wet by the rainy season. But the great tracts of

once-lush jungle were dead and, above the waterline, drying. When the dry season came they went the way of all the other combustibles on the surface of the planet.

Having died, Ross thought grimly, the Earth had cremated herself.

He did not feel as bad as he had expected to after reading that diary, and realized that discovering the scientific explanation for the surface conditions came as an anticlimax to his first sight of them two months ago. Remembering that constant fog of ash and soot, which had been less dense over the sea and when rain fell, Ross began to form certain conclusions.

Although very finely divided, the ash was heavier than air and its fall was sometimes helped by the rain. When it fell on land it formed a sticky mud, which, when it had dried out, was blown into the air again. Any that fell into the sea remained there, so that eventually the oceans would absorb it all. Probably the process would take many centuries, but in the end the air would be clear again. The ocean would stay dirty, and there was nothing that Ross could do about it. His final conclusion was that he should return his mind to circumstances over which he had some control, and the sooner the better.

There were three hundred and seventy-two robots, three large repair shops and a considerable variety of spares at his disposal. For Ross's purpose it wasn't nearly enough, and so he put the matter to Sister. Because it was only a robot he used simple language, cool logic, and took his argument forward in easy steps. At least, he started that way . . .

"I am the only human being left in a hospital whose robot staff is trained to care for thousands of patients," Ross began quietly, "and it follows that, with the exception of yourself and a few Cleaners, the staff will have nothing to do, medically speaking. I have been assured, both by you people and from my reading, that a robot with nothing to do is a very unhappy hunk of machinery indeed. But if I am to keep you busy, if you are to do the jobs I have planned for you, the robot nursing staff will have to learn new skills and subject themselves to drastic physical modifications. They must learn these skills in addition to their existing medical training, because there would be the possibility, a very slim one, I admit, that their medical skill might suddenly be required. Before I go into details, however, are these alterations in structure and programming feasible?"

The robot was silent for about three seconds; then it said, "I have communicated your question to the senior maintenance robot. Structural modifications are no problem, but the ability to learn is governed by the capacity of the memory banks. A full answer is possible only if we know the details of the work you require done."

"Very well," said Ross. "Get that maintenance robot down here. I know you can transmit vision as well as sound, but I'd feel more comfortable if he was right here. I've some sketches and illustration I want you both to see."

He went across to his desk, opened the big ledger, which over the months had grown into a cross between a diary and a scrapbook, and sat down. The Ward Sister stood behind him and shortly afterward the maintenance robot squeezed through the door, its blocky, multijointed body making the room seem suddenly crowded.

"What I have in mind is this," Ross began, without further preamble. "Robots of the Cleaner and Ward Sister type to have their wheels replaced by treads similar to those on the diggers, also whatever modifications necessary added to protect them against rain or drifting ash, so that they can operate for long periods on the surface. I know that they have infrared vision, so that working at night or in bad visibility will not hamper them. In addition I want them fitted with a means of detecting metal, digging it out and transporting it back here. These sketches will show you what I have in mind. But this is only the first step.

"The metal is to build more robots," Ross continued quickly, "who will go looking for metal to build yet more robots. For my purpose I will require thousands of robots, working hard and continuously, and the metal available in the ruins of the nearer cities will not be sufficient. Eventually we may be forced to mine and process the raw ore. But before that stage is reached I want to have robots searching the ocean bed, and the search extended into other countries by amphibious and airborne models . . ."

Ross was becoming excited in spite of himself. He was turning pages and jabbing his finger at sketches which he had not meant to discuss at this early stage, and babbling about submarines, helicopters, Archimedes and jet engines. He was leaving his audience behind, yet he couldn't stop himself. In a disjointed and nearly incoherent way Ross was outlining what was to be his life's work, the goal which would keep him sane and make him as happy as it was possible to be in his position, and suddenly he could no longer keep his hopes bottled up.

". . . I want the whole damned planet searched!" he went on wildly. "Every square foot of it. Somewhere there are other hospitals like this one, perhaps with patients still in Deep Sleep, or undersea bases which survived the war. It happened here so it could happen somewhere else! That is why the search robots must retain their medical knowledge, and extend it wherever possible. The descendants of those survivors are likely to be in bad shape.

"And if you should come on another Deep Sleep patient, *I* will supervise the awakening . . ."

Both the robots were ticking at him, a sure sign that they were hopelessly confused. Ross broke off awkwardly, then, in a more subdued voice, began to question the robots regarding the problems of converting his nursing staff to heavy industry.

And there were problems, all right. They lay solidly, one on top of the other, like a brick wall. One of the chief difficulties lay in the limited capacity of the robot brains to store new data. After basic programming a robot possessed the ability to learn by experience—in a very narrow sense, of course—because a small proportion of its memory bank was deliberately left unfilled. But this tiny fraction was not enough to contain data on a whole new specialty, and the result would be a cross between a very smart nurse and a hopelessly stupid miner. The answer was to cancel a large part of its medical programming, but Ross did not want to do that.

Another problem was the difficulty in putting ideas across to the repair robot. To it an illustration was just so many lines on paper; it had no understanding of perspective or of the solidity which they represented. Ross had to go over every line individually, explaining that this one was the radio antenna, that this particular squiggle was the towing hook and this series of parallel lines represented part of the caterpillar treads. Even then he could not make it understand properly. His frustration increased to the point where he felt like shaking it until its insides rattled or going at it with the two-foot wrench in an attempt to beat some sense into it, even though he knew that either course was likely to have the opposite effect. Finally he lost his temper completely and intemperately told it to get out of his sight.

In its maddeningly emotionless voice it requested clarification on the term "hell" and directions for getting there.

Ross closed his notebook and gently thumped the side of his head with a fist. "Why are you so stupid?" he said wearily. "You're supposed to be the mechanical wizard here, yet Sister, who is only a nurse, seems to get what I'm driving at better than you do—"

"It is a matter of programming, sir," the Ward Sister broke in. "Maintenance robots cannot abstract data from lines on a chart, such as pulse and temperature graphs, or from X-ray pictures as are the nursing robots—"

"I read circuit diagrams . . ." began the repair robot.

"Let's not start a fight," said Ross drily. "Just tell me why one of you seems more intelligent than the other."

There were two reasons, and as Ross listened to the

Ward Sister's reply he realized that he should have seen one of them without being told. Ward Sister 5B was the last, most recent modification built by the great Courtland. Robots were not supposed to be able to think creatively, but Ross could not forget that this particular Sister, when faced with the dilemma of possibly killing the last human being, had achieved something remarkably like creative thought. It had been too little and too late, but an achievement nonetheless. The second reason was simply a matter of increased capacity for memory storage, as represented by the large box riveted to Sister's ovoid body just above the rear wheel struts.

Which meant, among other things, that Ross could have his nurse-miner or even nurse-mining-and-repair robot combinations, merely by increasing the memory-storage capacity. To be sure, he put the idea to the senior maintenance robot, and received the reply that there was nothing against such combinations providing the memory bank was of sufficient capacity.

"Then what's all the fuss about?" Ross demanded angrily. "Why didn't you tell me it was only a matter of—"

"The normal type of robot," put in Sister at that point, "is not capable of volunteering information."

Listening to her, Ross had to remind himself that machines were not supposed to be capable of smugness, either.

"Then it's time we had a few more super-normal robots," he said seriously. "I've read Courtland's notes on the 5B modification, and from the little I understand of them it appears that Sister here has had a small change in circuitry which, when she is faced with a problem, makes available data on all similar problems which have been solved previously . . . No, that isn't what I meant. Courtland says that she has a choice of answers to any problem, and if she makes the wrong answer that error is filed as a datum and she will never make exactly the same mistake again.

"Anyway," he ended, "is it possible for 5B's modification to be reproduced in the other robots?"

The answer was yes, provided the senior maintenance robot was allowed to dismantle 5B to do so. When he heard that Ross felt oddly concerned about the Sister. Like any lay friend of a patient, he wanted to ask if the operation was likely to prove fatal, and similar anxious queries. He realized that Sister had come to mean a lot to him in the past few weeks. Whether deliberate or otherwise, her refusal to grant him a moment's privacy either day or night, while infuriating and at first downright embarrassing, had kept him from feeling too badly the loneliness of his position, and she was the smartest robot he had. The fact that her concern for him was an artificial, built-in feeling did not seem to matter.

Ross had difficulty in phrasing his next question, but the Sister answered it without trouble.

"The directives against harming another robot are only slightly less strict than those against damaging a human being," she said. "During the dismantling and reassembly I should incur no loss of memory or function."

"Good," said Ross, "then here is what I want done. First, all robots, both existing and those which are to be built, to have the capacity to store data on at least three specialties, with provision for further learning. Next, all robots are to be made capable of abstracting data by *every* aural and visual means. That includes the spoken word, radio, photographs, circuit diagrams, charts, graphs, contour maps, astronomical observations and the meteorological phenomena encountered in air and sea navigation. And when they are capable of doing this I want them to absorb data in all fields until they can't hold any more, then extend their memory banks and go on learning, indefinitely. Do you understand my instructions?"

"Yes, sir," said the maintenance robot.

"You require a robot which is unspecialized," said Ward Sister, and added, "Such a mechanism may be too large to operate inside the hospital."

Ross hadn't considered that angle, but it wasn't important. He said, "I'll require hundreds of such robots,

and we can stable them on the surface. Any other objections?"

The repair robot said, "The building program as outlined is possible, but I require a breakdown of your instructions and the sequence in which you want them
carried out."

Ross groaned inwardly; he hadn't considered details
himself yet. But he was becoming expert at talking with
authority on subjects about which he knew very little . . .

A few hours later he was present when the senior
maintenance robot and another of the same type scattered pieces of Sister all over the machine-shop floor.
Ross wasn't squeamish about dismantled machines, but
the way 5B kept carrying on a conversation while lying
about in that condition gave him the creeps. In a sur-
prisingly short time the senior had succeeded in doing
for the other repair robot what Courtland had done for
Sister, and in an even shorter time the newly enlightened
one had returned the compliment. They put Sister together again in no time at all.

Ross now had three robot geniuses on call, and he
knew that within a few weeks the Courtland modification would have been extended to all the robots. It
should have been a great moment for him, but instead
he felt strangely let down, for despite his recent inten-
sive reading on cybernetics, he had not understood a
single thing which he had seen done.

Analyzing his feelings, Ross came to the conclusion
that it was simply a matter of his pride being hurt. He
did not want to feel that a machine could be smarter in
any subject than he was, although it was plain, when he
thought about it more deeply, that every robot in the
hospital would soon be smarter than he was on any subject. He had to remind himself forcefully that they were
only tools. Complex, of course, but still only gadgets
designed for his use or convenience. The idea was to
use, not try to compete against, the things.

Only briefly did he wonder, with that uneasy fluttering in the pit of his stomach, if he knew what he was doing.

The first obvious change was that every robot acquired a trailer. Mounted on two wheels and joined to the main robot body by a flexible coupling which also carried a bundle of connecting cable, this was the housing for the extra data banks Ross had ordered. His idea had been to raise the general intelligence level of the robots in order to make his later, and more complex, instructions understandable to them. Instead, he often found himself having to explain the simplest, most obvious things—obvious to a human being, that is—while they fairly romped through items which to Ross had seemed extremely difficult. Gradually he found himself being forced into the position of a coordinator rather than a teacher, but that did not mean that he had less work to do.

On the surface a large transparent dome was built to house the first Miner, and the fifty-odd robots engaged in its construction. Higher on the hillside he built a smaller one, which enclosed a chair, some communications equipment and thirty square yards of soil from which the ash had been cleared. When it rained heavily and the wind was just right Ross could just make out the sea, but usually he looked out at a dirty gray fog and a dull, hot sun with a red ring around it. It was very warm on the surface, even at night, and Ross guessed that the sooty atmosphere was responsible for the general rise in temperature by decreasing Earth's albedo.

Although he kept the soil inside his dome wet, and it got all the sunlight there was going, nothing grew.

Between working on methods for programming the search and mining robots to accept data in foreign languages—some of the places they would be going, English would be neither spoken nor printed—he set his longer-term plans in motion. The principles of flight he demonstrated by flying paper airplanes until the robots engaged on that project were able to understand the literature available. Trying to put across the idea of buoyancy in water was more difficult. Because his model floated, the robots seemed to consider the water a form of mobile ground surface, and they kept trying to walk on it. The first couple of times, Ross laughed.

As the Miner neared completion he instructed another team of repair robots to design a multipurpose model which would not have to be as large as a railway locomotive. He gave them the few cybernetics books he could, together with some notes Courtland had made for further modifications. The following progress reports were disappointing and later ones grew as unintelligible to him as Courtland's notes had been. Ross kept them at it, partly in the hope that they would fulfill their instructions and partly to see if it was possible for robots to think subjectively.

Then one day, as he was inspecting the digging vanes of the new Miner, the ground stood on its end and he buried his face in damp, sooty earth. When he came to Sister was calling him "Mr. Ross" and putting him to bed, and he had to take a ten-minute lecture on the stupidity of human beings who insisted on working like robots, continuously and without sufficient rest, until their body mechanisms—which could *not* be repaired or replaced—became dangerously overstrained. His loss of consciousness on the surface, according to her diagnostic equipment, had been caused by mental and physical exhaustion and a long complete rest was indicated.

And by complete rest, Sister meant exactly that. Since acquiring the trailer which had more than quadrupled her data-storage capacity, Ward Sister 5B had become very difficult to outsmart. This time "rest" did not mean a change to working in a horizontal position; he was not allowed to make notes or study technical volumes.

She insisted on bringing him a selection of light, romantic fiction!

It had been almost a year since his supreme authority had been usurped like this, and it both angered and frightened him. He had urgent work to do and the thought of lying in bed without something to occupy his mind nearly threw him into a panic. The books he had been given only made things worse, describing as they did backgrounds and situations which were no longer a part of the real world, and were therefore extremely painful for him. There were no sun-drenched lagoons fringed with palm trees, no smell of freshly cut grass, no parents worrying about the current infatuation of their daughter. Ross would have given all he possessed or ever would possess to be even in the losing corner of an eternal triangle.

He stopped reading those books, not because all the vistas they described had become one—smoke and ashes lit by a red sun—but because they were about people. It was almost a pleasure when Sister ticked him off every morning for overworking, or lectured about the advisability of taking rest in addition to his sleeping period.

Ross found himself wondering why exactly he had been working himself to death. He had his whole life in front of him. What was the hurry?

If there were survivors underground somewhere, they would be eleventh- or twelfth-generation, and in no immediate danger of extinction if they had managed to stay alive until now. Similarly, there was no frantic hurry about finding any who were surviving in Deep Sleep; they would keep indefinitely. Ross was understandably anxious to contact any other survivors that there might be, he wanted to find and talk to other human beings in the worst possible way, but even that did not explain the way he had driven himself lately, at least not altogether. There was something else, some deeper, more driving urgency. It continued to drive him even when he was asleep.

8

HE WAS RUNNING through ash and smoke toward a trim single-story house seen through the trees of its surrounding garden and the ever-present smoke. There were the sounds of children playing—two, or maybe three—and a woman singing over a hammering noise which was coming from the back of the house. But no matter how fast he ran, the house with its unbelievably green trees moved away from him and he was running into an eternal black snowstorm. Or he was swimming frantically through an oily black ocean toward a shoreline of low, grassy-topped dunes which were not quite tall enough to hide the roofs of houses inland, only to see these symbols of life, both plant and human, swallowed up in the dirty, acrid-smelling fog.

There were many variations but the theme remained the same: frantic urgency, hurry hurry hurry or you won't make it. Ross knew that there had to be a good reason for that driving urgency—something in the present situation must be fairly screaming at his subconscious that there wasn't much time left—but try as he would he could not bring that reason up to the surface levels of his mind.

Not all the dreams were unpleasant, however; those in which Alice figured were quite the reverse. In these the sky was always blue and the black ocean never obtruded itself. Here again the theme was always the same, with no very subtle variations, and such that he woke up hating his cold white room with its untidy piles of books and Beethoven scowling at him. After a dream like that he would gulp his breakfast and go storming up to the surface or to the first-level library and work even harder, and sometimes he would be able to forget it.

Now he was not allowed to work at all. Now he had no way of forgetting Alice, or the beach, or the small park—not very well tended—on the inland side of the hill, or the hospital as it had been. Except when he lost his temper and threw Sister's selected light reading back in the place where her face should have been. Sometimes that would start an argument, bad language and a furious silence on his part, at others an exchange in which he tried to make Sister feel as confused as possible while she tried to reassure him.

Sister was much smarter these days, and had absorbed several textbooks on psychology.

After one particularly hot session on the twelfth day of what Ross considered his imprisonment, he asked suddenly, "Do you know what is meant by telling a lie, or doing a kindness, or making a pun?"

Sister had been spouting Freud and sex urges at him as if she had used them all her life, and Ross had grown annoyed because the robot knew so much more psychology than he did that he couldn't even make a fight of it. This was his way of putting Sister in her place.

"I have no data on puns or their methods of construction," Sister replied briskly. "Doing a kindness means to render assistance, and telling a lie is, I have read, the transmission as true of data which is incomplete or false."

Ross said, "I take it, then, that you would do me a kindness but you would not tell me a lie."

"Of course, Mr. Ross."

"But suppose, in order to render assistance, you had to tell a lie," Ross went on. "For the sake of argument, let's suppose a man is devoting considerable time and effort to a project which you know will fail, you being in possession of more data on the subject. You also know that to inform him of this fact, which it is your duty to do, would cause him extreme mental distress, insanity and eventually death. Would you tell a lie then?"

"It is against our basic programming to give false or incomplete data," Sister replied. "I would require guidance by another human before making such a decision—"

"Stop ducking the question," said Ross sharply. "Our supposition calls for there being only one human, the one you have to lie to." Then, in a quieter, more serious voice, he added, "I am trying to teach you the difference between giving assistance and being kind. If I can get the idea across to you, you may begin to think a little more like a human being."

"A human mind possesses free will, initiative," Sister protested. "No robot could—"

"Exercise initiative. But you did it when you awakened me without a brace of Cleaners sitting on my chest. And since then there have been improvements. The robots have given way to steamships." He laughed awkwardly and added, "That was a pun."

Sister said, "From my reading I know that steam-driven vessels were a later development than those propelled by oars, just as you have caused us to develop since your awakening. But I cannot understand why you used the word 'robots' when you should have said 'rowboats,' unless the accidental similarity of sounds . . ."

That particular discussion lasted for nearly three hours and broke off only because it was time for the lights to go out. To Sister the division between waking and sleeping periods was sharp. In the middle of a sentence she stopped speaking, paused, then finished, "It is time to go to sleep, Mr. Ross. Is there anything you want before I go into low alert?"

It was always the same formula and Ross had become tired of hearing it. Bitterly he said, "Yes, there is. I want a human female aged twenty, weighing one hundred and fifteen pounds, dark brown hair, brown eyes . . ." Under his breath he added, ". . . called Alice."

"Your request has been noted, but at the present time we are unable to—" began the robot.

"Good night, Sister," Ross said, and rolled onto his side.

He wanted to dream about Alice that night, but instead he dreamed that he was in a small, sealed room deep underground where the air was rapidly going stale. If he wanted to go on living it was imperative that he do something, quickly . . .

When Sister finally released him by speaking the magic word "sir" the First Expedition, as Ross liked to think of it, was ready to go. The same sense of frantic urgency which claimed his waking and sleeping moments alike tempted him to send it out quickly and with no change in the instructions he had already given. But although Sister had forbidden him to do everything else, she had not stopped him from thinking, or rather revising his thinking with regard to the purpose of the expedition. He had to consider the possibility that there might not be any other human beings left alive in the world he was proposing to search. If that should be the case Ross would have to take a long-term view.

A very long-term view . . .

9

THE WORLD HE knew was either incinerated or almost
aseptically clean. On the surface the war had been responsible for the former, and underground the conditions had been due to overzealous cleaning robots. With
the exception of Ross himself, there was no organic life
inside the hospital, not even on the microscopic level.
There were no lab animals, living or dead. Like the
corpses of the humans who had died, they had been cremated a few hours after death, and his own body wastes
were similarly treated. The food containers, which still
exploded in his face with irritating frequency, held a
synthetic which never had been alive.

Ross had had the idea of finding some warm, tidal
pool and filling it with all the scraps and leavings of
organic life that he could find in the hope that sometime
something in that hodgepodge of warring microorganisms would develop and grow until the evolutionary
processes could take over again. He had been thinking
in terms of millions of years, naturally, taking the long
view.

But the tidal pools were choked with ash and soot,
and even if his idea was possible a sudden storm or unusually high tide could wash his experiment back into
the sea, where the material would become so diluted
that no reaction could take place. And the idea was no
good anyway because the robots had done a too thorough job of cleaning up.

That was why the First Expedition did not start out
until two weeks later—it required that time to repro-
gram the Miner to search for and protect Life and not
just-human life. The books on plant ecology and horti-

culture were severely limited in the hospital, but his instructions included the necessity for absorbing any other data on this and related subjects which the expedition might uncover during their search. Small animals if any, insects, plants, weeds or fungus growths—all were to be reported, their positions marked and steps taken for their preservation until they could be moved to the hospital with absolute safety, for them. And finally Ross had given instructions regarding every contingency he could think of and he gave the order to move out.

On four sets of massive caterpillar treads the Miner rumbled through the thirty-foot gap which had been cut in the dome. Ross had been forced to compromise with his original idea for an all-purpose, unspecialized machine, but as he watched his monstrous brainchild go churning past he thought that he had made a good compromise. The powered tread sections were simply a vehicle to transport the digger-nurse unit—which was the seat of the robot's not inconsiderable brain—and to house the information-gathering and retransmitting devices. It literally bristled with antennae, both fixed and rotating, spotlights, camera supports and deep-level metal-detection equipment which gave its outline an indistinct, sketched-in look. Sitting atop this transporter section with its conical drill reflecting red highlights, the digger-nurse unit pointed aggressively forward. In operation the digger would lift itself clear of the transporter, stick its blunt nose into the ground and go straight down. Like a hot marble sinking through butter, Ross had thought when he watched the first test run. Outwardly it was a monstrous, terrifying object, which was why Ross had ordered it and the four robots following it to be painted with a large red cross. He didn't want anyone to get the wrong idea about them.

Watching the cavalcade go past—Big Brother trailed by two repair robots and two Sisters modified for long-distance surface travel—Ross thought that a little stirring music would not have been amiss. He strained his eyes to keep them in sight as they rolled and lurched down the hillside, but it had been two days since the last rain and the ash was beginning to blow about again. Ross stopped himself from waving good-bye at them with a distinct effort; then he turned and began walking toward the small control dome.

Here had been installed the equipment which enabled him to see all that the search robots saw, and here it was that Ross spent every waking moment of the next five days. He watched the Miner's radar repeater screens, its forward TV and the less detailed but more penetrating infrared vision. Every half-hour or less he checked that it was still on course, which it always was, and many times he asked if it had found anything even though the repeaters told him that it hadn't. By turns he was bored and frantically impatient, and bad-tempered all the time.

Some of the things he said and did were petty. He knew it and was ashamed of himself, but that didn't stop him from saying them. But one of the incidents, on the other hand, gave him just cause for losing his temper. The matter of the exploding food containers.

"I am getting fed up with being plastered with this muck every other mealtime!" he had raged, while trying to get rid of the foul-smelling goo, which, because of some trace impurities present during its manufacture, had in two hundred years turned into a particularly noisome stink bomb. "Go through the stores and separate the unspoiled from the rotten, then bring me only the edible stuff from now on. You shouldn't have to be told such a simple thing!"

"Doing what you suggest would mean opening every single can, sir," Sister had replied quietly. "That would cause all the food to spoil within a short time. It is therefore impossible—"

"Is it, now?" Ross had interrupted, the acid in his voice so concentrated that he might have been trying to penetrate the robot's steel casing with it. "I suppose it is impossible to put the unspoiled food in cold storage until I need it, using the Deep Sleep equipment? It would have to be reheated, of course, but surely your gigantic intellect would prove equal to that problem! But there is an even easier way—just shake the things. If they give a bubbling, liquid sound they're bad, and if no sound at all then they are good.

"That rule doesn't hold good in every case, but I don't mind an occasional mess."

As always, Sister had filtered out the profanity, temper and sarcasm and proceeded to deal with the instructional content of the words. She informed him that his instructions had already been relayed to a group of Cleaners, who would report when the job was finished. Then she suggested that he look at the main repeater screen, where something appeared to be happening . . .

Four hundred miles to the northwest it had begun to rain, pushing the visibility out to nearly a mile. The Miner's forward TV brought him a swaying, jerking picture of a narrow valley whose floor was a mixture of muddy ash and large, flat stones which might have once been a highway. Ahead the valley widened to reveal a great, shallow, perfectly circular lake in which black wavelets merged with a rippled glass shoreline in such a way that it was difficult to make out the water's edge. And below the pictured scene a group of winking lights indicated the presence of metal, tremendous quantities of metal.

The find came as a complete surprise to Ross, because he had been directing the expedition toward a one-time city some eighty miles to the north. Obviously this had been a military installation which had been constructed after his time, there being no mention of it in the latest maps. The important thing, however, was the metal which had been made available. Stumbling on it like that was such an incredible piece of good fortune that he couldn't help feeling, illogically perhaps, that more good fortune must follow it.

"Sink a tunnel to a depth of half a mile," Ross directed, trying not to stammer with excitement. "Angle in from a point two hundred yards beyond the waterline to avoid the risk of flooding . . ."

The digger unit unshipped itself, earth and ashes fountained briefly and it began its slow dive underground. Occasionally it altered direction to avoid large masses of metal, not because it could not go through them but merely in order to save time. It reported back continuously to the four-hundred-miles-distant Ross, by both speech and repeater instruments, and after nearly five hours' burrowing the picture of conditions underground was complete.

The installation had been a missile-launching base, extensive but not very deep. The bomb which had been responsible for the glass-bottomed lake, its force contained and to a great extent directed downward by the surrounding hills, had smashed its underground galleries flat. There were no survivors, but as the indications were that the base had been fully automated this did not bother Ross very much.

"I've been thinking," he said while the digger unit was returning to the surface. "Our construction program should be based on a site where metal is available rather than go through the time-wasting business of transporting it back here. So I'm going to send you as many repair robots as can be spared, and while they are on the way here is what I want done.

"You have absorbed data on open-cast mining," Ross went on briskly, "and your report states that there are large quantities of metal within fifty feet of the surface. I want you to rejoin your transporter unit as quickly as possible and have your repair robots modify it as a bulldozer. When you have uncovered—"

The Sister broke in at that point. "Mr. Ross," she said firmly, "it's time for bed."

Although Ross protested bitterly as he was led down to his room, underneath he was happier and more hopeful than at any other time since his awakening. He was still very far from achieving his goal of searching every square foot of the Earth's surface, but a beginning had been made. He knew the capabilities of his robots, knew that, given the raw material—which was now available—he would have a duplicate Miner built by the end of the week, and the week after that he would have half a dozen of them. The square law, he thought, was wonderful. Compared to what he was going to do the achievements of the first few rabbits in Australia would be as nothing.

He went to sleep dreaming happily of the orders he would have to give next day, next week and next year . . .

10

As DUPLICATES OF the first Miner were completed Ross sent them to investigate the sites of bombed towns and cities in the area, but for Miner One itself he had a special job. The inexplicable feeling of the need for urgency was still with him, as if somewhere, someone who was alive would die if he did not do the right thing quickly. Nevertheless, he sent Number One northward on a mission which did not include a search for human survivors. Fitted with special equipment and accompanied by a Sister with plant-biology programming, it had been ordered to search the polar areas for plantlife or seeds preserved under the ice. Life could survive intense cold; nobody knew that better than Ross himself.

Then suddenly he discovered who the someone was, the someone who was alive and who would shortly die if he did not think of something quick. It was himself.

"Using the testing procedure you suggested," Sister reported one morning shortly after he awoke, "we have found that approximately two thirds of the remaining food on this level is edible. A random sampling of containers taken from stores on the four higher levels indicates total spoilage. We suspect chemical changes brought about by radiation filtering down from the surface, which did not reach its full effect down here. At the present rate of consumption you have food for eighteen days.

"The matter is urgent, sir," Sister ended, with fine if unconscious understatement. "Have you any instructions?"

"There must be some mistake . . ." began Ross numbly, then went out to have a look for himself. But there was no mistake. Because it had been close to his room, he had been supplied with food from the lowest level; he had been using that store for two years, and now it turned out that it was the only one which contained edible food. This was something he should have checked on earlier, and it was now obvious that his subconscious had been trying to remind him of it during sleep. Yet if he had known earlier, what could he have done? Maybe fate had been kind to give him only three weeks' notice on the date of his death.

And Sister kept following him everywhere, continually asking for instructions.

"Yes!" said Ross suddenly, as it occurred to him that there was one useful order that he could give. He had been thinking emotionally, playing a distraught, tragic figure and not using his brain at all. He went on, "Signal all Miners and assistant robots to give priority to the search for underground food stores. Except Miner One, it is too far away to get back in time to do any useful work before the deadline . . ."

Deadline, he thought. Ross had a new definition of the word now—the end of a lifeline.

". . . And start opening all the cans which you think are spoiled," he ended sharply, "in case your random sampling has missed a few, or a few dozen. Get as many robots onto it as can be packed into the storeroom. Now I've work to do on the surface . . ."

For a long time Ross had used hard physical and mental labor as a means of not thinking about the past. Now he was using it so as not to think about the future. *Psychologically,* he thought mirthlessly, *you are a horrible mess.*

The work involved a project which Ross had shelved temporarily in order to concentrate on the search for survivors, a robot helicopter. Now the possession of such a machine might mean the difference between life and death for him—if the search robots found food and if it could not be brought to him fast enough by land to reach him in time. So he built models and read aeronautical texts and watched his prototype helicopter chew up the hillside with its rotors in vain attempts to throw itself into the air. Then one day it staggered off the ground and circled at an altitude of one hundred feet under a rough semblance of control. Watching from the small dome, Ross felt very little satisfaction, because it had taken him thirteen days to achieve this. He had five days left.

The helicopter was still clattering about the sky when one of his Miners reported in. Negatively, as usual.

The problem, according to the robot searcher, was that its metal-detection equipment was not sensitive enough to differentiate between food canisters and the structural wreckage with which they would be associated. The only solution involved sinking test tunnels at intervals and examining the wreckage visually. This was a long, difficult process which held small probability of success, the robot warned, because, in addition to the time involved, none of the city underground shelters had been as deep as the hospital's fifth level, so that any food which might be found would almost certainly be inedible.

"Things are tough all over," said Ross, and cut the connection viciously. But there was another attention signal blinking at him. He keyed it into the main screen and saw a wavering gray blur which resolved itself into a blizzard immediately the caller identified itself. It was Miner One.

"Sir," it began tonelessly, "data gained after forty-seven test bores leads me to the following deductions. During the war very many nuclear missiles were intercepted and exploded in the polar regions, and several interception bases and stockpiles were situated under the ice. It must have been the most heavily bombed area on the planet. The background radiation is still above normal, though not dangerously so. Analysis of the underlying soil shows complete sterility."

Ross didn't know what he said to the Miner. All hope had drained out of him and suddenly he was horribly afraid. His world that he had been trying to make live again was dead, the land a crematorium and the ocean a black graveyard, and himself a wriggling blob which had lived a little past its time. And now his time was coming.

He had never considered himself to be the suicidal type, and in the two years since his awakening he had never seriously considered it. But now he wanted to break cleanly with life before he could become any more afraid, something quick like a drop down the elevator shaft or a one-way swim out to sea. At the same time he knew that Sister would not allow anything like that. He knew that he was doomed to a horrible, lingering death from slow starvation, probably with Sister asking for instructions and clicking because she could not supply the one thing he needed, and he felt himself begin to tremble.

"Have you any instructions, sir?" said Sister, over and over.

"No!"

The Sister's voice was not designed to express emotion, but somehow she managed to do so as she said, "Sir, can you discuss the future?"

In her emotionless, mechanical fashion Sister was frightened, too, and suddenly Ross remembered one of his early discussions with her. If he died then the robots' reason for being would be gone—it was as simple as that. No wonder they were all asking for instructions, and no wonder Sister had let him work two hours past his bedtime a few nights ago. He didn't know what death involved exactly for a robot, but it was obvious that they were scared stiff. He could feel sorry for them, because he understood how they felt.

Softening his tone, Ross said, "My original instructions regarding the search for survivors will keep you busy for a long time, and those instructions stand. And there is another area of search which I haven't mentioned until now. Space. There was manned space travel for six decades before the war, with a base on the moon and perhaps on other bodies as well. All of them would have had to be maintained from Earth and could not have supported life indefinitely. But with Deep Sleep techniques . . ."

It's a strong possibility, Ross thought sadly. *If only I could have been around when those robots reported back.*

". . . Anyway," he went on, "I am giving you direct orders to find human survivors. Don't stop looking until you do. You will therefore be serving me until you find your new master, so I think that solves your problem."

"Thank you, sir."

"The moon and Mars are the best bets," Ross said, half to himself. "I know nothing about astronautics, but the search will turn up books on the subject, or uncompleted missiles which you can study. And be careful about the air pressure, you can operate in a vacuum but humans can't. And when you do find them tell them that I . . . tell them . . ."

It should be a noble, inspiring message, one that would ring gloriously across the centuries. But everything he wanted to say had a whining, frightened note to it, a coward's soliloquy. He shook his head angrily, then repeated Dr. Pellew's last message to himself.

"Tell them it's their problem now, and good luck."

Abruptly Ross whirled and charged out of the dome and along the corridor leading toward the elevators. Striding along, he cursed, loudly and viciously and as horribly as he knew how. He cursed to keep from crying and for no other reason, because the thought of Pellew and the brilliant, selfless, utterly splendid men who had preceded him was the greatest tragedy his world had ever known. He thought of Hanson, Pellew, Courtland and the others, of the desperate, unsuccessful experiment with the mutations, and the unending struggle to cure the incurables who were in Deep Sleep— which had been successful. But mostly he thought of those grand old men watching and working alone while all around them the patients and their colleagues slept, taking turns at going into Deep Sleep and running their relay race against time. And all for nothing. It had served merely to extend the lifetime of the human race, or more accurately the last member of it, by two miserable years.

11

WITHOUT REMEMBERING HOW he got there, Ross found himself in his room. The bed hadn't been properly made for days and the place was a shambles of scattered books and papers. Since dismissing the Cleaners, making the bed and cleaning up had helped keep his mind occupied, but lately he had had plenty of things to occupy it with. He tipped a pile of books off his chair, and, in the act of sitting down, saw himself in the locker mirror. He dropped the chair and moved closer. It had occurred to him that he was looking at the Last Man and he felt a morbid curiosity.

He wasn't much to look at, Ross thought: a skinny body dressed in a ridiculous toga. The face was thin and sensitive, with further proof of that sensitivity—or weakness—apparent in the way the lips quivered and in the dampness around the eyes. It was a young, impressionable, enthusiastic face, the face of a man who was too much of a coward to face reality and too stupid to give up hope. Ross turned away and threw himself onto his unmade bed.

For two years he had tried to avoid thinking of the past because of the awful sense of loneliness and loss it brought, and he had concentrated instead on a bright, distant, rather indistinct future in which he would gradually bring together a nucleus of humanity and set out bravely to repopulate the world. Now he had to face the fact that he was going to die soon, that there was no future, and that the only thing of value left to him was the past. He wanted to remember his preawakening period, now—in some strange way he considered it his duty to remember as many places and events and people as he possibly could.

Gradually his fear had been replaced by a mood of vast solemnity, a sadness so complete and all-embracing that it was almost a pleasure. Now he knew what he had to do with his remaining days of life.

Remember.

For the days which followed Ross set a timetable for himself—a loose, unhurried timetable which was subject to change without notice. In the mornings he read, chiefly from books which he had hitherto considered painful or a waste of time. He did not complete the works but dipped briefly into poetry, into brute violence, into sickly-sweet romance. Sometimes he would merely look at the dust jackets, at the ordinary, studious or pseudo-Bohemian faces who had had three children, or gained a Nobel Prize or been married three times, and who had produced works like *The Body Doesn't Bleed, Alternative Method for Producing the Hannigar Meson Reaction* or *Dawn Song*. He did not try to criticize or evaluate; the good, bad, tragic, sordid and glorious were remembered, and nothing more. In a way Ross was holding a wake, remembering the good and bad points of the deceased, and he had an awful lot of remembering to do.

In the afternoons he would pace the long, shining corridors and go over in his mind what he had read that morning, or he would listen to music or lecture tapes—the few remaining which had not become distorted beyond use by the passage of time—or try to hum a piece of music which originally had been scored for full orchestra. Then in the evening he would return to his room and get into philosophical arguments with Sister until the lights went out.

It was then that his hands would begin to shake and he would begin to wonder if he would be able to carry on with this act of quiet resignation to the end, or, when his hunger became extreme and he no longer had the strength to read or hold a book, would he start crying and begging for the robots to do something, and die blubbering like a baby? He was only twenty-four and he didn't think he could trust himself.

On the fourth day—the last in which he would have full rations—he went onto the surface. It had rained during the night and visibility was fairly good. He found a rock on the hillside facing the sea and sat watching the grimy rollers breaking on a black shore. It was his own life he was remembering now, some ingrained habit of politeness returning people and incidents in their reverse order of importance. His sheltered childhood, the emotional confusion of adolescence, the hospital with its acid-voiced ogre Dr. Pellew, the parents he was beginning to appreciate only now, and Alice . . .

Suddenly restless, Ross got up from his rock and began climbing the hill again. He walked quickly past the control dome, to which the search robots continued to send in their negative reports—no food, no survivors, no life of any kind. When he came to the landward-facing slope, which had once been the hospital park, he stopped.

An expanse of rich, dark earth streaked with ash in which nothing grew, not because it was incapable of supporting growth but because all growing things were dead. On the day before he was to go into Deep Sleep it had not been like this, however; Ross felt that he could remember every unpruned bush and knee-high blade of grass. The park never had been well tended.

He had been trying to act as though nothing very important was going to happen, as if Deep Sleep was a simple appendectomy. When Alice came off duty he had asked her to go swimming with him, the way he had always done. Ross wanted to have a last swim and to say good-bye to her on the beach. But Alice had insisted that the sea wind was too cold—it was late September—and she wanted to go for a walk instead. She had held his hand tightly even before they left the hospital building, and Alice had previously been too shy for such public demonstrations of affection, and they had gone into the park. He had tried to keep the conversation gay and inconsequential for as long as he could, but eventually he had to begin to say goodbye . . .

While the idea of Deep Sleep had frightened Ross, it had been nowhere near as strong as a fear of death. He knew that he would awaken someday and so far as he was concerned there would be no interval of time. But he had not realized that to Alice he was going to die tomorrow, going to disappear from the world and from her life. He had not been prepared for this Alice, who clung so fiercely to him that he could hardly breathe, and wet his cheeks with her tears and whose eyes, when they looked into his, held so much love and sheer compassion that . . .

She had been a quiet, thoughtful girl—pleasant, but practical. They were to be married when Ross qualified, but even with him she had maintained a certain reserve. He remembered her telling him laughingly that she preferred to neck on the beach, because there the ocean was handy for him to cool off in.

Standing on that muddy hillside with its eternal smell of damp smoke, Ross knew that Alice was his most precious memory. He thought that at this moment, with the memory of that slow walk back through warm-smelling grass which caught at their feet sharp and clear in his mind, he was prepared to die.

And then suddenly his newly achieved mood of calm and solemn acceptance of his fate was shattered, by that same memory. He began to tremble violently as the realization grew in him that he might, just possibly, not have to die at all. On that September day he had been given more than he knew: He had been given his life.

Oh, Alice . . . he thought.

Behind him Sister was expressing concern over his shivering and making determined efforts to take his temperature. This struck him as being excruciatingly funny and he began to laugh. Sister became even more concerned.

"I'm all right," he said, sobering. In a voice which

was still far from steady he gave his orders. All search robots were to be recalled for a special project. He gave minutely detailed instructions regarding it to Sister, and made her repeat them back, because he would not be available himself when they arrived. Finally, immediate preparations must be made to put him into Deep Sleep . . .

Four hours later he was lying in the padded, coffin-like container with the section above his face hinged back to reveal the glittering lenses of Sister staring down at him. The cold had passed the uncomfortable stage and was becoming almost pleasant.

"Now remember," he said for about the fourth time, "if the idea doesn't work out I don't want to be awakened. You'd be wakening me only to let me die of starvation . . ."

"I understand, sir," said Sister. "Have you any other instructions?"

"Yes . . ." began Ross, but lost track of what he said after that. The chill was accelerating through his body and he must have been in a kind of cold delirium. Soon the entire room and its contents would be similarly refrigerated as a precaution against a breakdown of his container, a point which he had forgotten until a few hours ago. He kept seeing the ludicrous picture of three Path Sisters dissecting the cuffs of his old tweed trousers. Swim or walk, sea or park, death or life. He wanted Alice.

"I'm sorry, sir."

The flap closed with a gentle click and the cold was like an explosion within him that engulfed his mind in icy darkness. But deep inside him there was a spot of warmth which had no business being there, and a light which grew until it pained his eyes. *Faulty equipment,* he thought disgustedly, *or they've muffed it*. When his vision cleared he glared up at Sister, too angry and disappointed to speak.

"Do not try to move, Mr. Ross," the Sister said sharply. "You are to undergo a half-hour massage, after which you should be able to walk unassisted. Are you ready . . . ?"

It might be massage to Sister, Ross thought as he gritted his teeth in agony, but to him it felt like the treatment received in the worst of the old-time concentration camps rather than something of therapeutic value. At the end of the longest half-hour of his life Sister lifted him to a sitting position, and he succeeded in gathering enough breath to speak.

"What happened? Why did you wake me up . . . ?"

"Can you stand up, Mr. Ross, and move around?" asked Sister, ignoring him. Ross could, and did. The robot said, "I suggest we go to the surface, sir."

Noting the "sir," Ross snarled. "So I'm not your patient anymore, somebody you could order about and beat half to death? Now I'm the boss again, and I want some straight answers. What went wrong, why did you halt the cool-down? Have you found an edible food cache . . . ?"

"You have been in Deep Sleep," said Sister quietly, "for forty-three thousand years."

The reply left Ross mentally stunned. He was unable to speak, much less ask further questions during the trip to the surface, and there he received a greater shock.

12

THE SUN SHONE clear and yellow and incandescent out of a pale blue sky, and from his feet a rippling sea of green stretched to the horizon. Five miles away the hills which he had not been able to see since his first Deep Sleep had a misty look, but it was the pale shimmer of a heat haze rather than windblown smoke. The air tasted like nothing he had remembered, so clean and fresh and sparkling that he seemed to be drinking rather than breathing it. Ross closed his eyes and with heart pounding madly in his throat turned a half circle; then he opened them.

Pale blue sky and deep blue sea were separated at the horizon by a distant range of white cumulus. The bay was filled with whitecaps and the biggest rollers that Ross had ever seen burst like liquid snow onto a beach that was clean yellow sand for as far as the eye could see.

Suddenly visibility was reduced to nil by a mist in his eyes, although Ross never felt less like crying in all his life.

"It took much longer than you had estimated," the Sister's voice came from behind him, "for the grass grown from your seedlings to make the change from interior cultivation in artificial UV to surface beds covered by transparent plastic, and even longer before they would grow unprotected on the surface. This was due to finely divided ash in the atmosphere having a masking effect on those sections of the solar spectrum necessary for the growth of plant life. However, time and natural mutational changes had produced a strain capable of surviving surface conditions."

Without pausing, Sister went on, "While this strain was developing the ash was gradually being absorbed by the sea and land surface, causing an increase in sunlight. This accelerated the spread of the grass, which in turn hastened the fixing of ash into the soil. And as the grass had no natural enemies or competing life forms, its spread across the planet was, relatively, quite rapid. But it required an additional several millennia for it to evolve, and for us to isolate, edible grains suitable for processing into food.

"This has now been done," Sister concluded, "and your food-supply problem is solved."

"Thank you," Ross mumbled. He couldn't take his eyes off the bright yellow sand on the beach. Wind, rain and salt water—mostly the salt water, he thought—had brought about chemical changes which had given the once-grimy beach this freshly laundered look. All it had needed was a little time.

Forty-three thousand years . . . !

Even the ghosts of the past were dead now, and the proud works of Man, with the exception of this one, robot-tended hospital, were so many smears of rust in the clay. Ross shivered suddenly.

Sister began speaking again, interrupting what was becoming a very unpleasant train of thought.

She said, "Your present physical condition is such that, although you cannot be classified as a patient, an immediate return to full-time duties is to be avoided. I suggest, therefore, that you do not concern yourself with our various progress reports just yet, and instead that you take a vacation . . ."

There was a clap of thunder that went on and on. Ross looked around wildly, then up. He saw a tiny silver arrowhead at an unguessable altitude drawing a dazzling white line across the sky. As he watched the vapor trail developed a curve and the ship went into a turn which would have converted any flesh-and-blood pilot into strawberry jam. It lost speed and altitude rapidly and within minutes was sliding low over the valley and heading out to sea again. The noise made it hard for Ross to think, but it seemed that the ship had slowed to far below its stalling speed. Then a shimmering heat distortion along its underside gave him the explanation: vertically mounted jet engines. It came to a halt above the beach and began to sink groundward. For a moment it was lost in a sandstorm of its own making; then the thunder died and it lay silent and shining—all two hundred feet of it!

He hadn't mentioned vertical-takeoff models to the robots, Ross told himself excitedly; this was something they must have worked out for themselves, probably with the help of books . . .

"Now that it is possible, we thought you might like to travel during your convalescence," Sister resumed, "and the robot which you see on the beach contains accommodation for a human being. If you feel up to it I would suggest—"

Ross laughed. "Let's go!" he shouted, giving Sister a slap on her smooth, unfeeling hide. He stumbled twice on the way down, but it was sheerest pleasure to fall onto that long, sweet-smelling grass, and the too-hot sand which burned his bare feet was like a sharp ecstasy. Then he was climbing into the cool interior of the ship and looking over the accommodation.

The observation compartment was small, contained a well-padded chair and gave an unobstructed view ahead and below. There was a larger compartment opening off it, containing a bunk, toilet facilities and a well-stuffed bookcase. Ross would not have minded betting that the books were all light, noncerebral works.

"You've thought of everything," he said, spontaneously.

"Thank you, sir," said the aircraft, speaking through a grille behind the observation chair. In a pleasant, masculine voice it went on, "I am Searcher A17/3, one of five models designed for long-range reconnaissance and search-coordination duties. On this assignment, however, the maneuvers and accclerations used should cause you the minimum of physical discomfort. Where would you like to go, sir?"

Later, Ross was to remember that day as being the happiest of his life . . .

At altitudes of ten miles down to a few hundred feet, and at speeds ranging from zero to Mach Eight, Ross looked at his world—his fresh, green world. He did not think that he was being conceited for regarding it as his own, because he had found it a blackened corpse and he had brought life to it again. For the grass, which had originated from a few tiny seedlings caught in the cuffs of his trousers, covered all the land. Ross was happy, excited, stunned by the sheer wonder of it.

In equatorial Africa and around the Amazon Basin the grass was a tangle of lank, vivid green. The old-time grasslands were emerald oceans which stretched, unrelieved by a single tree or bush, to the horizon. Sparse and wiry, the grass struggled to within twenty miles of the Arctic ice, and on the highest mountains it stopped just short of the snowline. There were seasonal changes of color, of course, and variations due to increasing altitude and latitude, but they were too gradual to be easily apparent. To Ross it looked as though someone had gone over the whole land surface with a paintbrush, coating everything with the same, even shade of green.

Sometimes an inland lake, or a desert, or a snow-capped range of mountains would suddenly break the monotony of land- or seascape, and Ross would tell himself smugly that although his world might run heavily to unrelieved blue and green, that was a much nicer color scheme than gray and black.

Late afternoon found him flying above the Caribbean. When he saw the island. It was one of many, a small, flat mound of green ringed by a white halo of surf, and Ross did not know why he picked it in particular. Perhaps it was the tiny bay which gleamed like a yellow horseshoe on its western shore which caused him to order the aircraft to land. Certainly he had been feeling like a swim for the past few hours.

Sister raised no objections beyond reminding him that he was not to overexert himself, that in the time since his last exposure to sunlight the mechanics of stellar evolution had brought about a significant increase in solar radiation, and that in all the world there remained not one usable tube of sunburn lotion. Nodding soberly, Ross told her that he would bear all these points in mind. Then he wheeled and went charging down the beach and, with a wild yell, dived into a monster wave which was just beginning to curl at the top.

After the swim he moved inland to where the sand gave way to long, hot grass, and lay down to dry off. The sun was very hot, despite its being only an hour before sunset. A great, drowsy happiness filled Ross, and a quiet optimism for the future of his world, his robots and his race. He was too sleepy and contented at the moment to work out details, but, considering what he had already accomplished, he felt very confident. Sighing, he rolled onto his back, and his fingers unconsciously went through the motions of pulling a long stem of grass and placing it between his teeth. He began to chew.

At that point Sister informed him that the grass he was chewing was not one of the edible strains, but that its use in small quantities would not prove harmful. Ross laughed, then climbed to his feet and headed toward the aircraft. There he made a sizable dent in its food store and a somewhat larger one in its bunk. And so ended the happiest day of his life.

Ross awoke next morning to find the ship airborne and climbing to avoid a hurricane which was sweeping in from the southwest. An hour later, two hundred miles west of Panama, he spotted the vapor trail of another A17 and spoke with it briefly without diverting it from its search duties. He had barely finished speaking when he saw a long, whitish smudge on the surface of the sea close to the horizon. Within minutes it had resolved itself into the most awe-inspiring sight that Ross had ever seen.

Next to his grass, that is.

Spaced out in perfect line abreast at intervals of half

a mile, close on one hundred long, low, angular ships battered their way through the long Pacific swell like some gigantic battle fleet. Five hundred feet long, excessively low in the water, their superstructures covered with a random outgrowth of bumps, girders and angular projections, they were like no ships that history had ever seen. Devoid of such purely human necessities as decks, ports and lifeboats, their bizarre aspect was perhaps explained by the fact that they were ships which sailed rather than ships which were being sailed. Their wakes boiled and spread dazzlingly astern as if each ship were towing a thin white fan, until the sea turned almost to milk before the turbulence died. One hundred ships, identical but for the numerals painted on their bows, all holding a formation which would have sent the most exacting admiral in history into paroxysms of joy.

"The Pacific search fleet," Sister explained. "They are equipped with every method of underwater detection mentioned in the literature available to us, together with some which seemed to us to be a logical development of that data. They are accompanied, at a depth of five hundred feet, by ten auxiliary vessels capable of making a close investigation of any find down to a depth of one mile. Below that their pressure hulls implode and special equipment is necessary."

"Let's go down for a closer look," said Ross.

For half an hour he flew up and down that tremendous line of ships, communicating with some, but often just staring spellbound at the breathtaking perspective and at the way they seemed to even pitch and roll with the waves in unison. He, Ross, had been responsible for bringing this vast fleet into existence, and the thought made him feel a little drunk. He had a sudden urge to make them re-form into triple lines ahead, or concentric circles, or to make them spell out his name across fifty miles of ocean, but conquered it. Then shortly afterward Sister suggested that they fly southwest; she wanted to show him the interplanetary search project . . .

That also was a happy, exciting day, but his pleasure was being spoiled by a constant and growing restlessness. He wanted to get back to work and Sister wouldn't let him. If he tried to give instructions to some of the search robots Sister countermanded them, and if he asked for detailed reports on anything she stopped that, also, with the brisk reminder that he was on vacation. Hitherto the robot had treated him in one of two ways—as a patient, when she didn't do anything he told her, or as the Boss who was obeyed implicitly. Now she had seemingly developed a third alternative in which she did some of the things he asked and argued him out of the rest. At first he had suspected a malfunctioning which might have been due to the absence of Sister's data-storage trailer—he had thought that she had left it behind because of its awkwardness inside the aircraft. But then Sister informed him that she had not had to use the thing for the past ten thousand years, that subminiaturization and new data-indexing techniques had rendered it obsolete.

And so for two weeks Ross lazed and swam and collected a suntan on all the famous beaches of the world, until Sister indicated that he was fit to resume work by saying, "The search reports are kept at the hospital, sir. Do you wish to return?"

Again happily, Ross went back to work. Except for short breaks when he swam or went for a walk across the valley, all his time was spent in an enlarged control room which he had ordered built overlooking the sea. Between watching pictures relayed from search subs on the ocean beds or gray, static-riddled views of the lunar Alps, he worked at bringing himself up to date.

13

THE LAND SURFACES of the planet had been searched, thoroughly, to within a few hundred miles of the poles. One thousand, seven hundred and fifty-eight underground installations had been discovered and examined, which included launching bases, hospitals, underground towns and single residences, and mines converted into bomb shelters. In the sea seventy-two military or naval establishments had been examined up to the present, but two thirds of the Pacific and much of the Indian and South Atlantic Oceans had yet to be searched. So far three bases had been discovered on the moon, but none of them had been able to survive the warheads sent against them.

The search had uncovered vast quantities of usable metal, all of which had been salvaged, and many functioning robots and other servomechanisms of the nonthinking type. Millions of books of all kinds, engineering blueprints and various pictorial forms of data had been scanned, absorbed and stored in special memory banks, where they could be reproduced at will. As a result of this his robots had become much more adaptable, and gained tremendously in initiative. Now his most general and loosely worded instructions, even wishes he had left uncompleted, would be acted upon correctly and as quickly as was possible.

Altogether a tremendous achievement. But on the negative side . . .

No human survivors had been found, no animal life of any kind. Birds that flew, insects that crawled, worms that burrowed: none. The sea, lifeless.

Looking out of his dome, Ross began to hate the

grass which rolled away on three sides of him. Apart from himself, it was the only thing which was originally alive on the whole planet, and the only thing which he had gained by his last sleep was a well-stocked larder.

He took to wandering about the valley and throwing himself down on the grass at a different spot each day. He would lie for hours at a time, staring at the sky and praying just one spider or earwig or ladybird would crawl across his arm or leg. He began speaking to the robots less and less, which distressed Sister considerably. She began looking for ways and means of interesting him, and one day she actually succeeded.

"One of the robots we salvaged is a Tailor, sir," she said brightly as Ross was about to set out on another aimless walk. "It had occurred to me that you might like something more functional than the bed linen to wear."

Three hours later Ross found himself climbing into his first proper clothes in more than forty thousand years. As he stood before the mirror, resplendent in the tropical whites of a naval captain, Ross thought that it was just his luck that the robot had been a military Tailor. But the whites did set off his tan to advantage. If Alice could have seen him now . . .

"You've made this from bedsheets, too," said Ross harshly, to break a painful train of thought. "Try dyeing the stuff. And if you make it with an open collar, don't forget the shirt and tie to go with it, otherwise it would look ridiculous."

"Yes, sir," said the Tailor and Sister in unison. The Tailor moved off and Sister asked, "Is there anything else, sir?"

Ross was silent for a moment; then he said, "I'm fed up, bored. I'd like to go to the moon."

"I'm sorry, sir," Sister replied, and explained that the accelerations used would be instantly fatal to a human being, that radiation from the vessel's power unit would kill him within a few hours, and that there were other hazards, both radiation and meteoric, which they had no means of guarding him against. For the last human being, space travel was too risky.

"In that case," said Ross carefully, "I think I should go into Deep Sleep again."

"For how long, sir? And what reason?"

Forever, Ross felt like saying, but he knew that if he did Sister would start treating him like a patient again. He had a good reason—or excuse, rather—for wanting to undergo suspended animation again. The idea had come during one of his many despairing hours lying in the grass, and the funny thing was that it just might work despite being only an excuse.

He said: "There is no longer any hope of finding human survivors, in space, under the sea, in or out of Deep Sleep, and it is foolish to pretend that there is. My only purpose must be to bring intelligent organic life back to this planet, and for that we must seed the oceans. Life began in the seas and it may do so again. However, the only organic material available in quantity is the grass, so here is what I want done.

"First choose a strain which flourishes in swampland," he continued quickly, "and gradually increase the depth of water until it grows completely submerged, then gradually replace the fresh water with an increasingly saline solution. Replace soil with sand, and ultimately transplant into shallow sea water. I know that I'm trying to make evolution run backward, but there is a chance that a strain of sea grass might adapt into a mobile life form, and eventually develop intelligence.

"Do you understand your instructions?"

"Yes, sir," said Sister, and added, "The search of the Pacific will be completed in seventy-three years. Would you like to be awakened . . . ?"

"You are not to awaken me until the project is a success," said Ross firmly.

And if it wasn't a success, they would never wake him up. At the moment Ross did not care. All at once he was overcome by a horrible depression and a feeling of loneliness so intense that it was like a twisting cramp inside him. He knew that there had been no need for him to rush into Deep Sleep again so quickly, that it might appear to Sister that he was doing it in a fit of pique because she wouldn't allow him a trip into space. The truth was, he admitted to himself, he wanted to escape.

His hopes of finding survivors had been sheer self-delusion, of the same order of probability as discovering a genii who would make his every wish come true. Even worse had been his hope of bringing intelligent life back to his world, of sleeping across the millennia and awakening only for fleeting moments to guide it up the evolutionary ladder until they would stand beside him as equals. That had been hoping on a colossal scale, and he had only now begun to realize that the scale had been more than colossally stupid.

One thing became very clear to him as the robots prepared him for the third time, and that was that he wanted to die in his sleep . . .

14

AN HOUR OR so later, to him, the robot masseurs were finishing their pummeling of his warming body, and Ross asked the inevitable question. Sister told him twenty-two thousand years.

"Hardly a catnap," said Ross sourly.

He felt cheated. His mood of depression, the horrible, aching loneliness and the awful boredom were with him as strongly as ever. Like his body, they had been preserved intact across the millennia. Perhaps something had happened to make him feel better.

"Make your report," he said tiredly. "Or, better yet, let me have a look. And *don't* tell me that I'm unfit to receive reports or that I should take a trip. My last vacation, by subjective time, was ten days ago, so just take me to the surface . . ."

The grass had grown taller and become less flexible—it would no longer be pleasant to lie down in it, Ross thought. His heart was pounding and he felt lightheaded, clear indications that the oxygen content of the air had increased. The breakers still crashed in a satisfying manner onto the beach, *but the beach was green!*

There was no sand at all, just a wet tangle of grass which ran unbroken along the shore and straight into the sea. The waves had a strong greenish tint, proving that it extended a considerable distance underwater.

"I couldn't swim in that stuff!" Ross burst out. It didn't matter that Sister was describing the development of a strain which would flourish in sea water, and which repeated uprooting by heavy seas had caused to evolve a limited degree of mobility. The process by which uprooted and washed-up sea grass moved back into the sea was a slow one, and only rarely successful, but it could be the beginning of an intelligent plant life-form, Sister affirmed. But Ross could not work up any enthusiasm over the achievement; he kept thinking that the only pleasure left to him had been taken away.

"And you woke me up for this?" said Ross disgustedly. "For a lousy plant which takes three weeks to crawl five yards back to the sea. Cool me again, until something worthwhile happens. Right now."

The next time he awoke and went up to the surface it was night. The grass stood ten feet high, each stem a half inch thick, and the wind scarcely moved it. On the beach sand again shone whitely, lit by a moon swollen to three times its normal size. Sister explained that increasingly high tides caused by the moon's drawing closer to its primary had forced the sea grass downward onto the ocean bed to escape the constant uprooting and several interesting, if minor, mutations had occurred. The sun was now too hot for him to bathe in safety.

Listlessly, Ross received the reports that the search of the Pacific, Luna and Mars had produced negative results. He barely looked at the picture relayed from the sea bottom showing the latest changes in his grass—to him the mutations seemed very minor, and not interesting at all. And before the bloated, yellow moon had gone down into the sea he asked Sister to return him to Deep Sleep.

"I advise against it, sir," said Sister.

"But why?" Ross demanded. "There is nothing for me here, and besides, you should be grateful that I want to spend so much time in Deep Sleep. Didn't you tell me once that I am the last human being, and that when I die your reason for existence will be gone? You should be glad of the chance to spin my death out for a few hundred thousand years. Or don't you need me anymore?"

Sister was quiet for so long that Ross thought her audio circuits had developed a fault. Finally, she said, "We are still your servants, sir, and always will be. We are also grateful that your lifetime has been extended by Deep Sleep, but feel that allowing you to do so indefinitely shows selfishness on our part. In addition to the sound psychological reasons for your remaining awake, we feel that you are entitled to some pleasure, too."

Ross stared at the gleaming ovoid body with its one fixed and one rotating lens and wondered incredulously what had become of the robot which had clicked irritatingly at him and droned, "I am not programmed to volunteer information." This robot had developed intelligence to the point where she was being troubled by something remarkably like a conscience! She had become so human a personality that Ross had forgotten when he had stopped thinking of her as "it." Suddenly he felt ashamed.

It was high time he came to grips with reality. Sister was right, even though the pleasures available were severely limited.

He said: "I suppose there is nothing against me having a midnight swim, providing I'm careful not to stab myself to death with the grass on the way to the beach."

"The water is pleasantly warm, sir," said the robot.

"I could study, start helping you with your problems again. And I could travel."

"By land, sea, or air, sir."

"Good," said Ross, and stopped. He was beginning to get an idea, a pretty wild and at the same time a very childish idea. As it grew he had to tell himself several times that he was the Boss, that the world and everything in it was his, to do with as he liked. He grinned suddenly, thinking of the vast army of robots at his command—something like two million, according to Sister's latest figures. A large proportion of them were immobile, or would be unable to participate for various reasons, but even so he thought that it promised to be quite an affair. Excitedly he began detailing his requirements.

Sister listened, made no objections, and informed him that what he proposed would require approximately three weeks. Ross replied that he would spend the time swimming, studying and consulting with the Tailor. Then he returned to his room to sleep, as happy as a boy with a new set of toy soldiers.

But when the great day dawned Ross had plunged from excited anticipation to a new low in despair. During the past three weeks he had tried study, tried to produce some original thoughts on his present situation and future hopes, only to find that all books had deteriorated into uselessness, their contents recorded in the brains of robots. The robots were in possession of full and accurate data on all subjects from astronomy to zoology, and the ability to make use of it in such a way that it made Ross's slow, human methods of reasoning seem moronic by comparison. Time and again he had started arguments with them on such obtuse subjects as genetics, the continuous-creation theory and moral philosophy, only to be confounded every time. It was no comfort for him to discover that he was arguing not with one robot but hundreds, all storing their share of data and making it instantly available to one another.

The mechanics of that communications and indexing system had interested him, until one of the robots tried to explain it and he understood about one word in ten.

His robots were far smarter than he was. Ross felt stupid and useless, like an idiot child. And he did not care now whether he played with his toys or not. But they had been gathering for days, overlaying the green of the surrounding hills and valleys with the shining gray of their bodies, sliding like long metal ghosts into the bay to drop anchor, and scoring thunderous white lines across the sky before landing on the plateau to the north, and he felt that he had certain obligations toward them. So he dressed himself in the navy-blue uniform, which was styled after that of an army major general and bore the wings and insignia of an air marshal, and swung over his shoulders an ankle-length cape which was lined in red and trimmed with gold. Then he went up to his control dome and gave the signal for the review to commence.

Immediately the land robots lurched into motion,

forming themselves into a column that was easily a
quarter of a mile wide and which rolled toward him
along the valley floor and passed within a hundred feet
of the dome before disappearing around the shoulder of
the hill. They poured by like an endless metal river,
types which he recognized as descendants of the original
Miners, but many others which he had to ask Sister
about. The long, tree-hard grass was flattened and
churned into the earth by the passage of the first wave,
and before an hour had passed the column had gouged
a quarter-mile furrow along the valley which was in
places twenty feet deep. Ross turned to look out over
the bay.

Obviously his ships had had access to considerable
data on naval maneuvers. In rigid, closely spaced flotillas down to single units they charged back and forth
across the bay, weaving to avoid other ships engaged in
equally complex operations, and throwing up a dramatic white bow-wave which fluttered like a battle en-
sign. Ross was stirred in spite of himself. The bay was a
blue slate thirty miles across, literally covered with the
white scrawls and squiggles left by the hurrying ships.
His eyes were caught by a robot that was almost the size
of an old-time battleship which had dropped two search
subs and launched an aircraft while tearing shoreward
at full speed. At the last possible moment it went slicing
into a U-turn which threw a dazzling scimitar of foam
astern and went charging out to sea again. Then a mul-
tiple sonic crash pulled his attention skyward.

In perfect echelon formation five descendants of the
A17 Searchers roared low over the valley and pulled
into a vertical climb that made the two-hundred-foot ar-
rowheads shrink to dots within seconds; then they
curved over into a loop and came screaming down
again. They leveled out over the sea, re-formed and
went thundering past the control dome in a rigid line
abreast.

Ross saluted.

Immediately he felt his face burning with shame and
anger. He had been thinking and acting in the most

childish way imaginable: playing-acting, dressing up in theatrical uniforms and treating the robots as if they were his toys. And the toys had cooperated to the extent that they had made him salute them! Were the damn things trying to get a rise out of him or something . . . ?

"Do it again," snarled Ross. "And this time close up, there's about half a mile between you!"

"Not quite as much as that," Sister objected. "But at the velocities involved it is safer to—"

"I have seen human jet pilots," said Ross scathingly, "who flew wingtip to wingtip . . ."

Effortlessly the formation climbed, though not quite wingtip to wingtip, rolled into their loop and leveled out, and suddenly there were only three of them and a formless tangle of wreckage which fell across the sky to crash three miles inland.

"Wh-what happened?" said Ross foolishly.

Sister was silent for nearly a minute, and Ross thought he knew what was going on in her complex, mechanical mind. Then she told him simply that two robots of the higher intelligence levels had been irreparably damaged, that their metal was salvageable but the personalities concerned had been permanently deactivated. She also suggested that he go below at once, as the robots had possessed nuclear power plants and there was a danger of radioactive contamination.

"I'm sorry," said Ross, "truly I am."

On the way down to his room he had time to think about a lot of things, but chiefly of the complete hopelessness of his position and his pathological refusal to accept the reality which had faced him on his first awakening. He was the last man and he should have accepted that fact and allowed himself to die of starvation when he had the chance. Instead he had instituted a search for survivors which was doomed from the start; then he had tried to re-create intelligent life and produced only grass. The race of Man was finished, written off, and he was simply a last loose end dangling across Time.

Maybe he wallowed a little in self-pity, but not much or for very long. He did some positive thinking as well.

Over the years the robots had developed intelligence and initiative to an extent which would have been frightening if Ross had not known that they were his servants and protectors. Their basic drives, he now knew, were the need to serve Man, the urge to acquire data and experience in order to serve Man more efficiently and the purely selfish urge to improve their own mental and physical equipment. If, however, they could be made to serve themselves rather than Man, what then? The answer was a race of intelligent beings who would be immensely long-lived and virtually indestructible, in short a super-race who would take over where Man had left off.

There was *nothing* that the robots couldn't do, if they would only stop thinking like slaves.

When they reached his room Ross sat on the edge of the bed and began repeating his thoughts to Sister, and the conclusions he had come to regarding them. He used very simple words, as though he was talking to the old, childish Sister of his first awakening, because he wanted to make absolutely sure that the robot—that *all* the robots—understood him. As he spoke a feeling of ineffable sadness overcame him, and, strangely, a fierce pride. This was a moment of tragedy and greatness, of Ending and Rebirth, and Ross was suddenly afraid that he was going to ham it up.

Awkwardly, he concluded, ". . . And so you can regard me as a friend, if you like, or a partner." He smiled bleakly. "A sleeping partner. But that is all. From now on I have no right to command you. I have set you free."

For several seconds the robot did not say anything, and Ross never did know whether his noble act of self-sacrifice was refused, ignored as the ravings of a sick mind, or what. Then Sister spoke.

"We have prepared a little present for you, sir," she said, "but, bearing in mind your remarks some time ago on the subject of kindness as opposed to assistance, I have been undecided as to whether or not I should give it to you. I hope you like it, sir."

It was a large picture, life-size and in color, of the head and shoulders of Alice. Obviously an enlargement of the photograph he had kept in his wallet. The flesh tints were off slightly, her glorious dark tan had a faintly greenish sheen, but otherwise the picture looked so natural and alive that he wanted to cry, or curse.

"It's perfect," he said. "Thank you."

"You always call for her during your last moments of consciousness prior to Deep Sleep," Sister went on, "and even though the wish is expressed while your mind is incapable of working logically, we must do everything possible to try to fulfill it. At the moment, this was the best we could do."

Ross stood the picture against the bust of Beethoven and looked at it for a long time. Finally, he turned to Sister and said, "I want to go to sleep."

They both knew that he wasn't talking about bed.

15

WHILE HE SLEPT his world of grass absorbed carbon and CO_2 from the soil and air, synthesizing oxygen. Over the centuries the oxygen content of the atmosphere increased, doubled. It was inevitable that a long dry spell would occur, broken by a sudden thunderstorm. A flash of lightning stabbed earthward, igniting the grass, which now grew in spines twenty feet high. Within minutes there raged a conflagration covering several acres, which hurled towering fountains of sparks into the sky and spread with the speed of the wind. For in that oxygen-rich air even the damp material caught and the sparks never went out. A tidal wave of fire swept across the continental land masses, slowed but never stopped by rainstorms, adverse winds or mountain ranges. A few islands in mid-Pacific escaped, but all the others caught the airborne contagion and became their own funeral pyre.

Ross awoke to a scene which made him think that Time had gone full circle: sooty ground, smoke and a baleful, red-ringed sun. Before he could say anything Sister explained what had happened, then went on to assure him that the amount of carbon released into the atmosphere had restored the oxygen content to normal and that the combustion products currently fouling the air would, as they had done once before, disappear with time. Her reason for awakening him was to report on the progress of the sea grass.

Violent tides pulled up by the approaching moon, she began, had forced the grass to seek the more sheltered environment of the ocean bed. Here extreme pressure, darkness and a gradually rising temperature had brought about a significant mutation. In order to keep alive in those conditions the plants had to absorb large quantities of necessary minerals from the sea bed, and at the same time, because they had to retain their defensive mobility, their roots had to be shallow. The result was that they had to keep on the move.

Recently these mobile plants had begun to band together. There were now several hundred colonies of them crawling like vast, moving carpets across the ocean floor, grazing for minerals and the non-mobile strains of their own species.

"Leave them for a couple of million years," said Ross, sighing, "and see what happens." He turned to go below again. He agreed that it was a most significant mutation, the most promising yet, but his capacity for hope had gone.

Sister moved quickly in front of him. She said, "I would prefer you to remain awake, sir."

The wording and accompanying action made it seem more an order than a request. Ross felt anger stir within him, then die again. He said, "Why?"

"For psychological reasons, sir," the robot replied, respectfully enough. "You should remain awake for one month at least, so that you can appreciate and understand what has happened during the preceding period of suspended animation. Major changes are occurring and you are giving yourself no time to adjust to them. You must interest yourself in things again. We . . . we fear for your sanity, sir."

Ross was silent. In the present circumstances, he thought, sanity was a distinct disadvantage.

"We could hold another review, sir," Sister went on. "There are not as many robots available as there were last time, but then the visibility is not so good, either. We were thinking that we might stage a mock battle for you. The casualties would have to be pretended, of course, because we may not willfully damage or destroy ourselves unless in the defense of a human being, but we have absorbed many books on the subject of war and are confident that we could put on a show which would amuse you, sir."

Ross shook his head.

"There are ways in which you could assist us . . ." began Sister, and then for the first time in countless thousands of years she began to tick!

"How?" said Ross, interested at last.

Outside a sudden rain squall left the ground steaming and the sky reasonably clear. Above the sea a vast, fuzzy crescent shone through the smoke haze. The sun was a formless white glare on the western horizon, so this must be the moon. Ross felt a tiny surge of hope at the sight, but it was the sad, negative sort of hope, the hope of escape.

He had missed Sister's opening remarks, and brought his mind back to present time to hear her saying, ". . . your instructions give us very little to occupy our time, and even a robot can become bored when forced simply to observe minute changes which require thousands of years to become manifest. For this reason we have, with the enormous store of data at our disposal, sought methods of reevaluating and extending our knowledge of the sciences. With the physical sciences we have made considerable progress . . ."

She began to tick again in the way which used to be indicative of a major dilemma. This was something about which she must feel very strongly.

". . . But in the social and related sciences we have encountered problems on which we need human guidance," she finished with a rush.

"Such as?" said Ross.

"An example," said Sister. "Is it allowable to force human beings into an advanced state of civilization rapidly, by means of periodic wars, supposing that there are very good, but not vital, reasons for wanting their advance to be rapid?"

You have been getting in deep water, Ross thought, surprised and more than a little awed. Aloud, he said, "Speaking from experience, I'd say that it is not allowable under any circumstances. Your hypothetical human beings should advance slowly and naturally, so that physical knowledge should not outstrip the psychological, if they are to survive to enjoy their advances . . ."

He stopped, a growing suspicion beginning to form in his mind; then he added, "I know this is a hypothetical problem, but are the robots by any chance planning on fighting a war among themselves to increase their—"

"No, sir," said Sister.

But the suspicion would not leave him. He was remembering a discussion he had had with Sister a long time ago, about kindness, and lying, and puns. Certainly she had never made anything remotely resembling a pun, but she had done a few things which were meant to be kind. Maybe . . .

"Are you telling the truth?" he asked sharply.

"Yes, sir," said Sister again.

"If you are, that's what you would say," Ross said thoughtfully. "And if you are lying that is still what you would say." His voice became suddenly harsh. "But remember this. I want no wars, no matter how good the reasons appear for having them. That is an order!"

"I understand, sir."

"And to keep your busy little minds out of mischief," he went on, more quietly, "I have a job for you. It will require considerable time and effort, but when built will give me much more pleasure than any review or war games . . ."

In Xanadu did Kubla Khan . . .

Ross envisaged a palace to end all palaces, a slender shining tower a mile high possessing the internal capacity of a large city. The structural material would be transparent, allowing an unimpeded view in all directions while at the same time blocking off the heat and glare from the sun. Architecturally it would be simple and esthetically pleasing, as a whole and in its internal subdivisions, which should blend with and at the same time accentuate their contents. Furnishing his palace might be an even longer job than building it, because he wanted it to house reconstructions of all the famous sculptures, paintings, tapestries and other art treasures of the world. And at the earliest possible moment he wanted to be moved into the new structure. He was growing tired of always waking in his underground room, and when the new building was complete he wanted the old hospital closed up.

"Only the works which have been illustrated or adequately described in material found by the original search robots can be reproduced," Sister said when he had finished speaking, "paintings relatively easily and the three-dimensional works with more difficulty. Much original research in structural methods will be necessary, and as we lack the intuitive reasoning processes of human beings the project will take a long time."

"I've got plenty of that," said Ross easily. The lie would have fooled a human, he thought, much less a robot.

He remained awake for three weeks on that occasion, watching from the control dome the colonies of pale green sea grass undulating along the ocean bed, and extending his requirements regarding the size and contents of the palace. Possibly he sounded a little on the megalomaniac side to Sister, but he hoped that she would not realize that all the amendments were designed solely to extend the time necessary to complete the project. For the truth was that he did not care at all about art treasures or a splendid-crystal tower which soared a mile into the sky. All he wanted was that his frozen, sleeping body be transferred from its safe subterranean crypt to somewhere more . . . vulnerable.

When he returned to Deep Sleep it was with the memory of a gigantic crescent moon and the hope that Sister and the others would not miss him too much when he was gone.

16

TIME PASSED.

Ninety-seven million miles away the sun grew old and small and hot. On Earth the icecaps finally disappeared, the seas never cooled and, with the rise in temperature, the molecular motion of gases saw to it that the planetary atmosphere leaked slowly into space. The moon continued to spiral in, pulling up tides which forced the sea grass even deeper into the ocean and caused many more significant mutations to occur, until it entered Roche's Limit and broke up. What the war had done to the planet was like a pinprick to what happened then.

Not all of the moon fell on Earth, only enough to raise the sea level by three hundred feet and open a few large cracks in the crust from which lava and superheated steam poured for many hundreds of years, and changed the planetary surface out of all recognition. Most of it remained in orbit, grinding itself into smaller and smaller pieces until Earth had a ring system to rival Saturn's.

Ross awoke to find the base of his tower one hundred feet below sea level, the local topography unrecognizable, and a night that was as bright as day. The rings blazed across the sky, dimming all but the brightest stars, a celestial triumphal arch. Every wave in the sea threw back a reflection which made it seem that his tower rose out of an ocean of rippling silver. And joining the blazing sky with the dazzling sea were the thin white tendrils of the shooting stars.

"How did the palace escape?" asked Ross bitterly.

He found himself lost after the first three words of

the explanation, but the answer seemed to be some kind of force field, or repulsion field. ". . . And I regret to say, sir," Sister ended, "that the sea grass was unable to survive the catastrophe."

"Too bad," said Ross.

There was a long silence; then Sister suggested showing him around. It was mainly in order to please the robots who had built it rather than from curiosity that he agreed. He felt terrible.

Every synonym for magnificent, opulent and awe-inspiring could have been used to describe the palace in which he now lived. It was vast, but comfortable; grandiose, but in perfect taste. *Like a museum with fitted carpets,* thought Ross ironically. But he was tremendously impressed, so much so that he did not mention to Sister the one minor, but maddeningly constant, error. In all the otherwise perfect reproductions of great paintings, regardless of how the original Old Masters had painted them, the faces and bodies had been given a deep, rich tan coloring with a background hint of green.

It was exactly the shade they had used in the blowup of Alice's picture, and he remembered telling Sister that it had been perfect. Which was probably the reason that they had given everyone the same complexion. After the first few days, however, he became accustomed to it.

Strangely, Sister made no objection when he asked to Deep Sleep.

The centuries passed like single cards in a riffled deck. He awoke to a sea which steamed all night and boiled all day. The air was a white, superheated fog from which there fell a constant, scalding rain. Altogether it was a monotonous, depressing sight and after the first day Ross stopped looking at it. Instead he wandered the vast halls and corridors, over floors so smooth and mirror-polished that there were times when he felt he would fall through them onto the ceiling, or across carpets so thick in the pile that it was like walking in long grass, like a silent and resplendent ghost. He rarely spoke, and when he did it was more often to the Tailor than to Sister. His thoughts and mood were reflected in his dress.

There was the black uniform, severely cut and edged with the bare minimum of silver braid, and the long, ankle-length cloak with the single silver clasp at the throat which went with it; that was the uniform of brooding tragedy. Then there was the white uniform that was heaped with gold braid, decorations and a Noble Order represented by the scarlet ribbon which made a broad, diagonal slash across the chest. A cloak of ermine and purple went with that one, and a crown. That was the dress of a man who, literally, owned the world. And then there were the shapeless white jacket and trousers which had been the uniform of a working Doctor . . .

Sister did not like his wearing that uniform, neither did she approve of his requests that some of the robots be given human shape, using plastic foam on a humanoid form. Such activities were psychologically undesirable, she said. And it was Sister who, on the eighteenth day since his latest awakening, suggested that he go into Deep Sleep again.

He wondered about that and, because no subjective time at all elapsed during suspended animation, he was still wondering about it when he was revived.

17

THE SUN HAD become an aged, malignant dwarf whose glare had left Earth a desiccated corpse. The seas had long since boiled away into space and with them had gone the air. The atmosphere which remained was too rarefied to check the meteorites which still fell from the rings. The sky was black; all else—the sun, the rings, the cracked, dusty earth—was a searing, blinding white. A high-pitched humming sound pervaded every room and corridor in the palace, and he was informed that it was produced by mechanisms laboring to keep the internal temperature at a level comfortable to its human occupant, and that the noise was unavoidable. An even more disquieting occurrence was that Sister no longer accompanied him wherever he went.

The reason given was that she had other duties to perform.

Three days later, while wandering about on the lower levels, he found her stopped outside the door to one of the sub power rooms. She was not simply in a state of low alert; she seemed completely lifeless. Nothing that Ross could do, from shouting to beating on her shiny casing with hands and feet, elicited a response. For the first time the realization came that she—*it*—was only an involved piece of machinery rather than a near-human servant and friend. It made him feel suddenly afraid, and lonelier than ever.

He thought regretfully, *I have been wasting Time . . .*

The two years spent in the blackened, smoking world, when he had worked, studied and initiated the first robot search for surviving life, had been happy and at the same time something of which he could feel proud. Even happier had been his second awakening, to the fresh, green world he had brought into being, with that world-girdling vacation with Sister and the A17. But within a few days he had given in to despair and talked Sister into putting him to sleep again. Since then his life had been a series of disjointed episodes in a violently changing world. To him only a few days had passed since the two robot aircraft had crashed—he was still sorry about that—and the seas had started to boil. Why, his body still retained the tan from the vacation!

Recently—*recently?*—Sister had deliberately avoided giving him the exact figures, but he knew that countless millions of years had passed while he aged a few weeks. At the present rate the very universe could live and die, and he would still be in his early twenties, still living and still wanting to sleep farther into the future, while around him stretched eternal blackness and the cold, lifeless cinders of the stars.

He should have faced up to reality millions of years ago, when his sea grass was crawling about the ocean bed and exhibiting the first stirrings of intelligence, and he should have lived out his life then. Probably he would not have accomplished anything, but at least he would have tried. Just as Pellew, Courtland and the others had tried. He thought again of those great old men who had taken it in turns to stand solitary watch over the hospital's dwindling Deep Sleepers. They had faced loneliness and despair also, and at times they must have reached the brink of madness, but they had not stopped trying until they had stopped living. He had thrown their lives away along with his own.

The vast robot potential he had wasted by assigning impossible tasks, simply from a cowardly desire to die in his sleep. He should have considered the interplanetary angle more fully, tried to transplant Martian or Venusian life forms into a sterile Earth. The result might have been nightmarish, but it would have been life. He was sure that Pellew would have understood and forgiven him if it hadn't been human life. There were a lot of things he could have, and should have, tried.

Ross bent forward and slowly put his hand on her smooth metal casing and looked at the glinting, emotionless lenses, neither of which moved. Sister had always looked emotionless, and he shouldn't get so worked up over an outsize metal egg which had finally broken down.

"I'm sorry," he said, and turned to look for another robot who would be able to put him into Deep Sleep again. There seemed to be very few robots about, these days . . .

He awoke with the conviction that he was dreaming that he was awakening, because Sister was bending over him. "But you're dead," he burst out.

"No, sir," Sister replied, "I was reparable."

"I'm very glad to hear it," said Ross warmly. "And Sister, this time I'm going to stay awake no matter what. I . . . I would like to die of old age, among friends—"

"I'm sorry, sir," the robot broke in. "You have been revived only that we may move you to safer quarters. The refrigeration units over most of the tower have failed, and only a few sections are inhabitable over long periods. You will be much safer in Deep Sleep."

"But I don't want—"

"Are you able to walk, sir?"

There followed a hundred-yard walk which developed quickly into a hobbling run as the plastic flooring burned his feet and a blast-furnace wind scorched his skin and sent the tears boiling down his cheeks. He caught glimpses of charred furniture and cracked or melted statuary, but he didn't see outside. Which was probably a good thing. The run ended in a narrow, circular tunnel which terminated in a tiny compartment containing little more than a Deep Sleep casket. The heavy, airtight door swung shut behind them.

"Turn around slowly, sir," said Sister, aiming a gadget at him which emitted a fine odorless spray. "This should help you later . . ."

"It's staining my skin green . . ." began Ross, then snapped, "But I want to stay awake!"

Sister went through the motions of assisting him into the Deep Sleep casket. In actual fact she forced him into it and held him while a sedative shot she had administered took effect. "Wait! Please!" he begged. He thought he knew what was happening and he felt horribly afraid.

Selfishly, the robots were going to keep him alive as long as they could. When outside conditions made it impossible to keep this tiny compartment refrigerated, they would refrigerate only the casket. He would go on living in Deep Sleep until the last robot died. Then the cooling unit would fail and he would awake for the last time, briefly, in a casket which was fast becoming red-hot . . .

But there was something wrong about the whole situation.

"Why did you wake me?" he asked thickly. "Why didn't you move me without waking me up? And you gave me a shot. There haven't been any medical supplies since . . ."

"I wanted to say good-bye, sir," said the robot, "and good luck."

WHEN THE HUMAN ROSS was safely in Deep Sleep, Sister spoke again. It used a language which was flexible, concise, yet highly compressed—the language which had been developed by intelligent, self-willed robots over two hundred million years and which traveled, not through air or ether, but by a medium which brought it to the other side of the galaxy at the speed of thought.

"Sister 5B," it said. "Mr. Ross is in Deep Sleep. Latest observations corroborate our predictions that the sun will shortly enter a period of instability. The detonation will be of subnova proportions and will precede its entry into the cooler red-dwarf stage, but in the process all space out to the orbit of Saturn will become uninhabitable for human or robot life. Is Fomalhaut IV ready?"

"Anthropologist 885/AS/931," replied another voice. "It is ready, 5B. But you realize that the closer the natives approach our Master's requirements the more difficult it has been to control them. I keep wanting to call them 'sir.' And his definite wish that war not be used to accelerate the rise of civilization here has delayed matters, although it has produced a culture which is infinitely more stable than that possessed by Earth—"

"Geneticist 44/RLB/778," broke in another voice. "I do not agree with this philosophical hairsplitting! At a time when Earth still retained her oceans we found a planet at the stage where saurian life was being replaced by mammalian, and we controlled and guided the evolution of these mammals until we have reached the *point where they duplicate the original human life form so closely that interbreeding is possible. When does a perfect duplicate become the real thing?"*

"Sister 5B," returned the original speaker. "It was hairsplitting such as this which allowed us to evolve intelligence, plus the general instructions issued to us by the Master. First we convinced ourselves that a motionless, unthinking and unliving human being in Deep Sleep was alive, when all logic contradicted this. Then we took his instructions to find, aid and protect all forms of life, in conjunction with his wishes expressed during cold delirium regarding the female human Alice, and twisted them to our own selfish purposes . . ."

They had been told to search and when Earth and the nearer planets proved empty of human survivors they had continued outward to the planets which circled other suns, all the time concealing that fact. Ross had once discussed lying and kindness with Sister, and the robots had tried very hard to understand and practice those concepts. They had had an unfortunate tendency to tick when a direct lie was called for, but otherwise they had managed very well. When a subspace drive was developed with the aid of pre-war Earth mathematics, they had concealed that also, just as they kept quiet when their metal bodies became obsolete and they evolved into beings of pure force. A few of them had to energize the old-style bodies for Ross's benefit, and once Ross had found Sister's body while it was vacant . . .

". . . But now we are about to carry out his wishes and keep ourselves alive into the indefinite future as well. When he comes to the planet and race we have prepared for him, his life will end a little more than a half century hence. But we will not die because his descendants will be partly human, and we are very good at splitting heirs."

"Geneticist 44/RL/778. With all respect, the Master should not have told you about puns, 5B."

"So we will continue to search," Sister 5B went on, "safe in the knowledge that our Master is immortal. We will gather data, we will aid or guide life forms which

*we encounter, or ignore them if this appears to be the
kinder thing to do, and we will expand throughout all
the galaxies until the end of space is reached . . ."*

*"Astronomer 226/V/73," broke in a new voice. It
was polite, as befitted one who was addressing the being
who had spent practically all its life close to the Master,
yet at the same time it was tinged with impatience at
these older robots who insisted on repeating things everyone knew already. It said: "If it transpires that the
space-time continuum has positive rather than negative
curvature and we return to this galaxy, our starting
point, what then, 5B?"*

*"We will say," 5B replied quietly, " 'Mission accom-
plished, sir. Have you any further instructions?' "*

Ross awoke and, as he had done three years and an
eternity ago, began to exercise painfully by crawling
about on the floor. The air smelled fresh and cool and
there was no sign of Sister or anyone else. He ate, exercised and ate again. Almost by accident he discovered
the sliding door which opened into a compartment
which contained a large circular picture of the branch
of a tree. There was a startling illusion of depth to the
picture, and when he moved closer to examine the odd,
feathery leaves he discovered that it wasn't a picture at
all.

He left the tiny ship and stumbled through a carpet
of grass patterned by weeds and bushes which had
never grown on Earth. He breathed deeply, through his
nose so as to hold the scent of growing things for as
long as possible, and his pulse hammered so loudly in
his ears that he thought that he might prove once and
for all whether it was possible to die from sheer joy. It
was only slowly that sounds began to register: leaves
rustling, insect noises, the swish of passing cars and the
thump of waves on a beach. Five minutes took him to
the edge of the sea.

There was nothing strange about the sand or the sky
or the waves, except that he had never expected to see
such things again. But the group of people lying on the

beach was alien. It was a subtle alienness which, Ross now realized, he had been prepared for by the reproductions in his palace—an underlying greenish tinge to their otherwise normal skin coloring. And even at this distance he could see that the people sprawling on their brightly colored bath towels might all have been close relatives of Alice . . .

The implications were too vast for him to grasp all at once. He swallowed a couple of times, then said simply, "Thank you, Sister."

A silent, invisible globe of force which hovered protectively above his head bobbed once in acknowledgment. Sister had evaluated the situation and had long ago decided that allowing the Master to think that all the robots had died would be the kindest thing to do.

Ross walked slowly toward the bathers, knowing somehow that he had nothing to fear. There might be language difficulties at first, misunderstandings, even unpleasantness, but they did not look like the sort of people who would hurt anyone simply for being a stranger. They didn't seem . . . warlike.

They were different, of course, but not much. You wouldn't mind if your sister married one of them.

Come to think of it, he thought, you wouldn't mind marrying one yourself.

Counter Security

THE OBJECT LYING on Mr. Steele's desk was the remains of a large, black plastic doll, Tully saw as he took the chair which the store manager indicated to him. The doll had lost a leg and both arms, one eye socket was empty and the nose had been pulled out of shape. There were also patches of hair missing from the scalp, and a narrow band of spotted material—the collar of the doll's dress, no doubt—still encircled its neck. Altogether it was an intriguing and rather pitiable object, Tully thought, but hardly the sort of thing to cause the store manager to send for the night security man as soon as he came on duty.

Tully was about to voice his curiosity when Steele's receptionist announced Tyson of Hardware and Dodds, the Toy buyer. The SM waited until they had stopped moving in their chairs, then cleared his throat and began to speak.

"In the ordinary way, Mr. Tully," he said in his soft, unhurried voice, "all cases of malicious damage to stock by members of the staff are dealt with by the departmental buyer or floor supervisor and are not usually the concern of the night security people. Neither, I might add, are they the direct concern of the store manager, since I have slightly more important matters to occupy me."

His tone became gently sarcastic and he looked pointedly at the Toy buyer, who looked at the carpet.

". . . However," he went on, "this seems to be an unusual case, in that neither Mr. Dodds nor the supervisor on that floor has been able to do anything beyond establishing the fact that these occurrences do not take place during shop hours. Meanwhile the Toy department is being terrorized by an epidemic of armless dolls—"

"That sounds like an exaggeration," Dodds broke in quickly, strong emotion doubling the volume of his naturally loud voice, "but believe me, it isn't! My staff are all girls, some of them colored, and this sort of thing . . ."

The SM silenced Dodds with a coldly disapproving look. Mr. Steele detested all unnecessary noises. He liked to think of his store as an efficient, smoothly running machine and he was fond of reminding people that any part of it which operated loudly rendered its efficiency suspect.

"The retail value of the dolls is of no importance," Steele resumed. "What concerns us is the way in which the culprit can do such damage without being caught. That and the bad effect it is having on the Toy-department staff. On the surface it looks like a practical joke, but—"

"A *joke!*" Dodds burst out. "I tell you my girls are terrified! At first they treated it as a joke, but then they kept finding them nearly every morning and the rumor started that there was a psychopath loose in the store . . . !"

"Very *well,* Mr. Dodds," said the store manager irritably. "You tell it."

". . . Just look at the *facts!*" the Toy buyer rushed on, plainly too excited to notice the danger signals flying on the other side of the desk. "During the past two weeks nine dolls in all have been mutilated like this. Nine *black* dolls. All had a leg and both arms pulled off, the hair twisted or pulled out, the faces disfigured and their dresses torn off. One or two such incidents might be attributed to simple malicious damage, but nine of them in two weeks points to something much more sinister . . ."

Tully found himself looking at the doll, which no longer seemed such an innocent object, and thinking about the implications of the word "mutilate" as opposed to "damage."

". . . I'm not saying the rumor is true," Dodds went on, "but the facts support it. They point toward a perverted mind, a mind with some dreadful obsession about Negro dolls. I mean Negro girls . . ."

Dodds stopped for breath and the store manager rejoined the conversation. He said, "Despite what you have just heard, Mr. Tully, we are not faced with a general walkout. But the rumor is causing trouble and I want it killed. The quickest way to do that will be to find out who is pulling these dolls apart, and that is where you come in . . ."

It had already been established that whatever it was that happened was occurring outside of normal shop hours, Steele told him. The dolls were always found by staff arriving in the mornings, usually by the cleaners, who were always first in. Either the culprit was someone, not necessarily a member of the staff, who was hiding in the store at night, or the store was being broken into from the street. It was suggested that Mr. Tully keep a closer watch on the entrances to the Toy department . . .

At that point Tully felt like reminding him that the store was reputed to be burglarproof from the ground up, that the Toy department occupied the basement and that to gain access to it from the street would call for a fair-sized mining operation. He did not say anything, however, because the store manager knew these things as well as he did. And he noticed that the other had made no reference to his failure to notice anything peculiar going on during the past two weeks, when dolls must have been having their arms pulled off nearly every night. But now that the matter had been brought officially to his attention he knew that Steele would have plenty to say if he did not put a stop to it.

". . . This is an odd business whose solution may require a certain amount of imagination," the SM said, his eyes flicking briefly toward the inch or so of magazine showing in Tully's jacket pocket, "but then I see that that is something with which you are well supplied. Have you any questions?"

Before Tully could reply, Dodds broke in again. "Sir, you didn't mention the—"

That was as far as he got. Furiously, but still quietly, Steele said, "Mr. Dodds, there are some misdemeanors committed in this store which I, or Mr. Tully here, are *not* obliged to investigate personally, and complaints of people spitting on the back staircase is one of them!"

More to take the heat off the loud-voiced but kindly Dodds than from any strong curiosity over the matter, Tully nodded toward the Hardware buyer and said, "What is Mr. Tyson's connection with this?"

"Eh? Oh, very slight," said Steele, regaining his composure with a visible effort. "He is having trouble with shortages. Some power tools, and a motorized lawnmower, missing from packing cases which have the manufacturer's seals unbroken. There is some kind of hanky-panky going on, but pilfering at this end is not suspected so it is not a matter for you. He may also have come to lend moral support to Mr. Dodds, who is going to need it . . ."

He stood up suddenly, smiled and said, "Thank you, Mr. Tully." Then he began quietly to draw Dodds's attention to the Toy department's sales figures for the preceding week in comparison to the same week last year. This was a matter which Mr. Steele *was* obliged to investigate in person, and as Tully closed the office door softly behind him the inquisition was just beginning to warm up.

Tully walked slowly out onto the sales floor, trying to make his mind think in a positive and constructive manner and not succeeding at all. Around him stretched the polished, square ocean of the Hardware department with its bright display islands of Do-It-Yourself, electrical goods, refrigerators, et al. There were only a few customers about, it being only half an hour to closing time, and he decided to have a chat with the people in the Hardware stockroom. Steele had told him that the shortages did not concern him, but Tully disliked having his mind made up for him even when he knew that the other party was right.

A few minutes later he was getting all the details from Carswell, Tyson's assistant. Carswell was an extremely conscientious type who expected everybody else to be the same, and the fact that everybody else wasn't had had a bad effect on his disposition over the years.

"Either the packers were drunk or the maker is trying to pull a fast one," Carswell said hotly. Then, tolerantly, for him, he went on, "There might be an excuse for three power drills being missing from a case which was supposed to contain twenty—an error in packing, no doubt, because the maker's seals on the cases were unbroken. But when we told them about it they insisted that there was no error, that they had packed twenty power drills and if their seals were intact then we had received and in due course would be billed for twenty power drills. And the trouble is, we've been holding them in storage unopened for a couple of weeks, which weakens our case considerably . . ."

Except where they had been severed by Carswell's wire cutters, the thin metal bands sealing the cases were in one piece, smooth and shining apart from a few tiny discolored sections which looked as if they were beginning to rust. The packing inside had fallen to the bottom of the case, but there was a suggestion of shaping to it as if the case had contained something which had been taken out rather than that the packing had merely been pushed into an empty case. For several minutes Tully poked around in it without quite knowing why, and lifted a handful up to his nose. It smelled of dust and dry straw and, vaguely, of peppermint, he thought, before he nearly blew over the case with the granddaddy of all sneezes.

Tully left Hardware and took the elevator to the ground floor, intending to ask some questions in the Toy department while its buyer was still engaged with the store manager—he felt that he would get a more valuable reaction if he talked to the staff without Dodds shouting everybody down. But at the top of the basement stairs he changed his mind. There was another possibility which he should try to eliminate first.

When he reached the nurse's office a few minutes later he coughed gently in the manner of one intent on signaling one's presence rather than displaying symptoms of a respiratory malfunction. Through the frosted-glass door which separated the tiny waiting room from the dispensary proper he saw a white shadow approach and resolve itself into the nurse as the door was opened.

She looked down at him, the soft brown eyes in her rather severe face scanning him automatically for signs of physical injury or distress; then she said quietly, "Good afternoon, Mr. Tully. Is something troubling you?"

"Well . . . yes," said Tully, standing up. He outlined what was troubling him, the store manager and a lot of other people, then ended awkwardly, ". . . Maybe I shouldn't ask this sort of question. I mean, what you find out or even guess at might be privileged information—I'm not sure what your position is in cases like this. But I was wondering if—"

"*If*," the nurse broke in firmly, "there was anyone who came to see me who was as mentally disturbed as you and this rumor you mention suggest, I might or might not divulge his name. That would depend on the circumstances. I would, however, declare him unfit for work and immediately send him to his doctor, who would take over from there. I would not allow him to run around loose. Does that answer your question, Mr. Tully?"

"Thank you, Nurse," said Tully, and left.

The possibility of a Negro-hating psychopath among the staff was not completely eliminated, he thought as he resumed his journey to the Toy department; all the talk with the nurse had proved was that the psychopath, if there was one, had not revealed himself to her.

On his way down the basement stairs Tully was caught by a stampeding mass of chattering femininity on their way up. It was quitting time, which meant that he wouldn't be able to ask the Toy girls any questions to-day. His only possible source of information seemed to be Miss Barr, Dodds's assistant, who was still standing by the model-railway display, putting on her outdoor face.

But he learned very little from his talk with her. According to Miss Barr, every doll had been found in the same condition—missing both arms, one leg, one eye, the nose pulled out of shape, hair disarranged and clothing, if the doll had been wearing any, ripped off. The only minor variation was that sometimes it was the right and sometimes the left eye that had been poked out, just as it could be the right or left leg that was missing. When she began to grow agitated and started repeating herself, a condition highly unusual in the competent and level-headed Miss Barr, Tully made gentle reassuring noises, helped her on with her coat and said good night.

When Tully was alone in the department he closed, bolted and locked the door at the top of the stairs; then he went on the prowl. His eyes missed nothing and he kept his lips pressed together so that he breathed in a long series of sniffs. This was routine, because his job required keen eyes and a very sensitive nose.

Few people realized that the store, equipped as it was with the latest security devices and well covered by police patrols, was in no danger of being robbed, that the greatest and only danger was from fire. There was a sprinkler system installed, of course, which could be made so sensitive that a whole department could be instantly flooded—and its stock ruined, incidentally—if someone switched on an electric heater. Or it could be made less sensitive so that a fire could gain an unbreakable hold which the spray from the ceiling would be unable to check. For, despite its imposing façade, the store was one of the oldest buildings in the city, and much of its stock was even more inflammable than its structure.

So the primary job of the night security man was to guard against fire and the causes of fire. Every stockroom, locker room and cubbyhole—the only exceptions were the washrooms—had its NO SMOKING notices. But despite the eagle eyes of the buyers and floor supervisors, the staff continued to sneak off for a smoke in all those places at every opportunity. Tully did not mind their smoking; the trouble arose when they were interrupted at it and were forced to hide the evidence quickly. They hid it in some very odd places, and the evidence smoldered sometimes for hours before Tully's nose led him to it and he rendered it safe.

On this occasion he was not simply looking for smoldering cigarette butts. He intended sealing the basement from outside and before he did so he had to be sure that there was nobody hiding in it. He looked behind and under every counter and display stand and with his master opened every locker in the Toy staff room, and finally he was satisfied that the department was empty. He spent ten minutes then at the model railway display, taking the 4–6–2 tank loco around the layout and performing a few simple shunting operations; then he killed all the lights and headed for the Dugout.

The total floor area of the basement was only a fraction of that of the ground floor, it being merely two cellars joined by a narrow corridor. A floor plan of the basement resembled a dumbbell with square weights, the square representing the Toy department being twice the size of the one enclosing the Dugout. In the middle of the corridor was a heavy swing door which was kept permanently dogged open. There were two lights in the corridor, which he switched off as he passed them.

The Dugout was a large untidy room which served as the supply base and—unofficially—rest room for the cleaning staff. Drawn up in the center of the room like some alien armored division were the rubber-wheeled bogies which carried the electric polishers and vacuum cleaners, and ranged around the walls were storage cupboards filled with floor polish, liquid soap and an incredible quantity of rags, most of which were oily. Of all the places in the store, this was the one in which a fire would be most likely to start. Tully searched and sniffed meticulously, as he did every night in this potential danger spot, but without finding either a hiding place or a trace of tobacco smoke. He gave a last look around, then mounted the ramp which replaced a stairway at this end to facilitate movement of the wheeled cleaners. He switched off the lights, then closed, locked and bolted the door from the outside.

An odd thing happened while he was locking the door. One of the keys in his bunch, the thin, lightweight master for the Payroll department lockers, flipped up suddenly and stuck to the bar. A few minutes' testing showed him that the bolt and surrounding casing of the Dugout door were strongly magnetized.

If Tully had been asked to write down his thoughts just then he would have put down a row of question marks. He thought of checking to see if there was an electrician working late and asking him how and why the lock should have become magnetic, then decided that before doing anything else he should complete the sealing off of the basement.

Still keeping his eye on the two entrances to the basement, he paid a quick visit to the Haberdashery counter and a cigarette and confectionery kiosk which were on the same floor. At Haberdashery he took a spool of black thread, leaving a chit with his signature on it stating that the goods were being used in the store's business, and at the confectionery counter he opened a large packet of chewing gum. He thought of paying for this at first, but then reminded himself that he didn't *like* gum and he was chewing it solely in the line of duty. He left a chit for that, too, knowing full well that the people in Accounting would have some very sarcastic things to say about it tomorrow. Tully grinned to himself and, chewing furiously, headed for the nearest basement door.

Fifteen minutes later the entrance to the Toy end of the basement was bolted both inside and out and had a length of black thread stretched across it approximately six inches from the floor level. The Dugout door had been similarly treated except that it was bolted and locked only from outside. He had also rigged threads at one-floor intervals on the staff stairway. The thread in each case was held by gum so that it would pull away rather than break, because there was a chance that his man might hear or feel a thread break and so have warning of the trap. Tully was assuming that any surreptitious movements which took place would be via the staff stairs, because the store's main stairway, which wound around the central well and elevators, was kept brightly illuminated all through the night. It was also in sight of Tully's night station at the Book counter as well as being in full view of anyone passing the main entrance in the street.

As well, the staff stairway would be in total darkness while the main one would be lighted, so there was no reason for the men working late to break his threads. No innocent reason, that was.

With the feeling that he had taken all the precautions it was possible to take at this time, Tully began the first and most important of his six nightly rounds. Except for the well and the center of light and activity where some display staff and carpenters were working on the Fashion Theater, the store was in darkness. The floor supervisor on lockup, whose job was also to keep tabs on the people working late, had already checked all doors and windows and killed the lights. Tully's first nightly duty was to make sure he had done these things properly, which he always had—floor supervisors were just as security-minded as Tully himself, and none of them wanted to be caught out by the night man. It was a point of honor with them. Tully laughed wryly to himself as he paced the darkened sales floor, thinking that the competition which was fostered between departments—so fierce at times that it put an unfair strain on the word "friendly"—touched even the night watchman.

Gravely, Tully begged his own pardon; he meant the Night Security Officer . . .

All around him the store began settling down for the night. The light and heating fixtures made soft pinging noises as they cooled, or creaked eerily just above the threshold of audibility. The woodwork ticked and sighed and the floor, relieved of the day-long pressure of thousands of pairs of feet, stretched minutely and moved itself into a more comfortable position. The sounds it made varied from those of a herd of running mice to the noise of distant gunfire. Later the store would come to rest, but during his first few patrols the sound effects could be quite startling.

Some people would have been bothered by these sounds. They would have let their imaginations loose among the eerie creakings and tinklings and scufflings and peopled the darkness with formless horrors. Not that Tully didn't have a good imagination. To the contrary, but he prided himself in that his imagination was properly under control. He had no time for gothic horrors or brooding menaces or fantasy of any kind. Tully liked his science fiction straight.

So he patrolled up and down behind the shadowy counters, ignoring the noises off and with most of his attention concentrated in his nose, thinking the sort of thoughts he always thought around this time of night. He thought about his job, which was easy and, because few people would work the hours he worked, very well paid. Then he would think about the day job at the counter which was not so well paid and which he had held for so many years without getting any farther up the ladder. He had been good at his job, but then so had about two thousand others in the store, and he must have lacked that extra bit of push which would have led to promotion. Finally he would think about himself.

He was an intelligent, well-read—he by no means restricted himself to science fiction, although he preferred it—and essentially lazy person. His few close friends credited him with high intelligence by inference and did not, because they were his friends, mention laziness at all. But others came straight out and asked him if he was so intelligent why didn't he have a better job? Tully had asked himself the same question often without finding a satisfactory answer. Apparently there *were* no jobs which demanded a calm, easygoing disposition allied with detailed, but not specialist, knowledge on such widely varied subjects as stellar evolution, the history of the Roman Empire, the latest work being done on the psychology of worms and similar unrelated items. At the moment his job gave him plenty of time to read and think, and gave him security while he was doing these things, so he had no real cause for complaint. Tully now knew that he had not been happy in his job at the counter. The pay had been lower even though the chance of promotion had been much higher. But basically all he had had was a chance, and Tully's reading had included data on the laws of chance, so after due consideration he had gone after the job which was a fairly well-paid dead end—he had chosen Security.

Pun unintentional, he thought wryly.

His watch said eight thirty and he was just finishing the third floor, walking from the brightly lit well toward the staff stairway. Around the well everything stood out bright and sharp and clear, but as he moved away from it objects began to throw long shadows, which eventually grew so hazy that the objects themselves became shadows. The vast, unlighted portion of the shop seemed to have become unreal, as if God had switched it off because nobody was using it. This was a very fanciful line of thought for Tully, but he sometimes indulged in such thinking when he wanted to mentally change the subject.

He did not like to think that he was a highly intelligent, well-read failure . . .

On the way to the fourth floor he checked his thread and found it unbroken. The sight of the thin black thread turned dusty white by the narrow beam of his torch sent the odd business of the dolls rushing back into his mind, and immediately his dark mood lifted. He had been given a problem which he did not think any ordinary night watchman could solve. Mr. Steele had suggested as much, although there was the possibility that the store manager had simply been making a crack about his taste in literature. This doll business was a challenge and Tully felt that if he met it successfully he might be able to stop thinking of himself as a complete failure.

Tully spent longer than usual on the fourth, particularly in Mr. Steele's office. His reason for that was that he wanted to have a closer look at the mutilated doll. He found it in Mr. Steele's wastebasket, rescued it and placed it on Mr. Steele's blotter. Then he switched on Mr. Steele's desk lamp and, with a slight qualm of something he couldn't put a name to, he sat down in Mr. Steele's chair.

His second examination of the doll told him nothing new, at first. It was still just a one-eyed, one-legged, armless black doll with a lot of its hair missing. But then he noticed that the hair might have been pulled out accidentally, that it had not simply been yanked out but rather that somebody had been trying to twist it into all-over pigtails. Tully grunted; it seemed a useless bit of information. Almost automatically he lifted the doll and smelled its hair.

And got a faint, almost undetectable odor of something which could have been peppermint.

Suddenly impatient with himself, Tully threw the doll back into the wastebasket. He was imagining things; either that or his nose was suffering from persistence of smell. It was stupid to suppose that his dolls and Tyson's missing lawnmower had any connection . . .

On the fifth floor, which housed the store's administrative offices, and on the roof above it there were no smoldering cigarette ends or signs of anyone skulking in the elevator housings. By the time he had finished the roof check it was nine twenty, so he hurried down to the

Time office to make coffee for his first supper and watch the overtime men clocking out.

Ten minutes later he was standing at the only unlocked exit from the store, with the floor supervisor in charge of lockup and overtime, watching the late workers troop out. Tully did not know what exactly he was looking for, but he did know that nobody left the place chewing peppermints or with a lawnmower under his coat. He chatted for a few minutes with the supervisor, offered him a cup of coffee, which was accepted, then let him out.

By nine forty-five Tully was alone inside a tightly sealed department store.

After his coffee and sandwiches he did his second round, then set up a folding chair in the Book department. He sat down, drew the magazine which had arrived that morning out of his pocket and prepared to face the night. He was supposed to make his rounds at random intervals, the theory being that nobody would know where he was going to be at any given time. It being next to impossible to devise completely random intervals, Tully mixed business with pleasure by reading his magazine for the night and patrolling between stories. Sometimes he read the short stories first, sometimes last, just to make it more difficult for any hypothetical observer who might be trying to beat his system . . .

He began his third round at eleven fifty-eight, thinking that there were some people who could handle psi—Bester, Sturgeon and a few others—and some who most definitely could not. When they tried, their stories read like fantasy; instead of natural laws and controlled experiments there was chaos and a sort of aseptic witchcraft. Still seething quietly, Tully finished his round and read another story. He had his second supper, it being close to one thirty, then made his fourth patrol.

All the threads were intact, he saw nothing unusual, not a thing was stirring, not even a . . . But then, he reminded himself, the store did not have mice.

It was during his third story that Tully heard something—something unusual, that is. The floors and lighting fixtures still ticked and creaked at intervals, but this sounded exactly like a bolt being drawn. As he strained his ears to listen it was followed by the sounds of a door being opened and closed quietly and a muffled slapping sound. It seemed to be coming from the Dugout entrance.

Tully put down his magazine, sheer habit making him mark his place with a used bus ticket, and moved from behind the counter. He glanced quickly at the department telephone, which at night was connected to an outside line in case he suddenly needed to call the police or the fire department, then shook his head—he didn't need help, at least, not yet. With his torch in one hand and his shoes in the other he sprinted silently toward the Dugout entrance, pausing only long enough to check that the Toy door was still bolted and its thread unbroken.

The other door had been opened and the thread pulled from its anchoring gum. For a moment Tully dithered between entering the Dugout and checking where the person who had entered it had come from; then he made up his mind and ran up the stairs.

The threads were dislodged from the first to the fourth floors, but not the fifth. Whoever it was must have been hiding on the fourth floor, although Tully didn't see how anyone could have remained hidden after the going over he had given the place. On the way downstairs again his light picked out a small damp patch on one of the stairs, as if someone had spat and scuffed over it with his shoe. He paused, sniffing. There was a distinct smell of peppermint.

So Steele had been wrong, Tully thought wildly; the dolls and Tyson's missing lawnmower and now even the spitting on the staff stairway were all part of the same problem. He hurried down the stairs with the pieces of what he thought had been three separate puzzles whirling around in his mind, trying to form a picture of the person who was responsible for the disappearance of various tools and one large, motorized lawnmower, who mutilated black dolls, who was fond of eating pepper-mints and who spat.

It was as well that in a few minutes he would be meeting this person face to face, Tully thought grimly; he thought that otherwise he would die out of sheer cu-riosity . . .

Still in his stockinged feet, Tully opened the Dugout door. Fanning the beam of his torch, he painted the room with fast zigzags of light. It was empty. But there was a narrow, vertical band of light coming from the corridor leading to the Toys. It took him a couple of seconds to realize that someone had partly closed the door halfway along the connecting corridor, the door which had been dogged open for so long that Tully had almost forgotten it had hinges. He moved forward care-fully, keeping the door between the source of light and himself, until he was just behind it. Then he looked into the Toy department.

There were enough lights switched on to show him the scene in detail. The mouth of the corridor framed the corner of a counter, a large square of floor, and something on the floor that was five feet long and black and sluglike. The sluglike something was curled around a large black doll, pulling one of its arms off . . .

Tully staggered back against the wall, instinctively seeking a prop for his shaking body while he tried to steady his whirling mind.

The wall wasn't there.

Tully opened his mouth to scream, and grunted in-stead as his shoulder hit a hard, sloping surface and he began to roll. The roll lasted only for a few yards before he crashed into an irregular metal object which knocked the breath out of him. His shoes and torch thudded gen-tly against his body, and when he could breathe again he groped for the flash and switched it on.

He was lying close to the bottom of a hollow sphere twenty-five feet in diameter which had been cut out of the store's foundation material. He could see where the concrete, masonry and even the steel reinforcing had been sheared off along a perfect, spherical plane, and where the loose earth and clay was kept from falling into it by a thin film of hard, transparent material. The only break in the sphere was the opening which Tully had fallen through.

A smaller spherical object rested at the bottom of the hollow, surrounded thickly by metal objects, some of which he recognized as having once been powered hand tools. There was also a six-foot circle of brickwork which was obviously the plug for the entrance, and the motorized lawnmower which he had collided with on the way in. All the tools had been . . . changed . . . in ways that would have given their designers nightmares, and what had been done to the lawnmower verged on the obscene. The smell of peppermint was overpowering. Tully climbed to his feet and, carefully, began to explore.

The beam of his flash bobbed and vibrated along the hull of the small, spherical ship with its not quite transparent shell and alien internal plumbing. It jerked because his hands were shaking, because his whole body was shaking. He had the shakes because part of him was afraid, the part which was thinking like a store night watchman, but mostly he was shaking with sheer excitement as his mind stretched and his imagination soared to accept the reality of what was before him.

An alien ship, probably force-landed and needing repairs, skillfully concealed while the repairs were being carried out. The evidence lay all around him—tools, human tools, modified and used to make other tools which made other tools which might be capable of making the repairs. It was a unique situation, probably the first time such a thing had happened on Earth, but at the same time it was one that was very familiar to Tully.

Many times he had discussed just this situation with those few friends who shared his taste in literature. What would you do, the question usually went, if an alien spaceship landed in your backyard? Would you try to talk, would you run, or would you call out the militia? The answer which Tully and his friends preferred had invariably been the first one—you would try to talk, try to work out a method of communication. Then if the visitor needed help, or was trying to help you, you would be able to discover which. Of course, there might be a third alternative—it might be hostile, completely inimical . . .

Neither Tully nor his friends liked that third alternative. For one thing, they had come up against that situation far too often in stories and they thought it corny. Another reason, a much more subtle and complex one, was their feeling that the universe was such a big place that it was ridiculous to think of anyone coveting one tiny mote in it to such an extent that they would contemplate war to get it, together with a strong, philosophically based belief that anyone who was advanced enough to cross interstellar space must be highly civilized as well. If there was any hostility, any *apparent* hostility, it would come about through misunderstanding.

Tully would have to see to it that he managed his First Contact without misunderstandings . . .

He shivered again with sheer excitement and swept his torch around the hideout which the alien had built in the middle of the store's foundations. It had been using and modifying Earth-type tools for its repairs, that seemed obvious. But there were other questions to which Tully itched to have the answers. How had the alien been able to materialize inside the solid foundations and create this place? And how was it able to pick out a place where tools were readily available? Had it detected them, or did it already know they were there? Had the ship been traveling, not through interstellar space but through time . . . ? The answers, he knew, could come only from the alien.

Abruptly Tully came to a decision. He tied his shoes together by their laces, hung them around his neck and, with the torch sticking out of his mouth like a metal trunk, scrambled up to the opening. At the lip of the hole he paused, sniffed, then hurried quietly along the corridor and out into the store. He replaced the thread across the door so that he would know if the alien left the basement while he was making his preparations.

Much of the equipment he needed was already in the basement in the shape of children's blackboards and chalks. And a measure of contact had already been made in that he knew what the alien looked like and, by virtue of its detection gear, the alien was used to the sight of Tully's species. At the same time he would have to render his general aspect less frightening to the alien. One, the most important, method would be not to carry a weapon or anything which might be mistaken for such. Then there was another, more positive method . . .

Grinning suddenly, Tully headed for the confectionery counter. There he uncapped the big glass jar that was labeled EXTRA STRONG PEPPERMINTS and began stuffing his mouth and pockets with the hard white candy. The way Tully saw it, the alien's body odor smelled of peppermint, or of something very like peppermint. The smell was not unpleasant to Tully, but the human body smell might be quite distressing to the alien, and if he tried to conceal it with the nearest equivalent he could manage to the alien's own smell, that should further reassure it of his friendly intentions.

Completely disregarding the bad effects to his teeth, Tully began to crunch and chew. Within minutes his tongue, mouth and throat were practically paralyzed by the hot-cold burn of the peppermints and his breath was stinking up the whole department. Tully popped in a few replacements and hurried back to the Dugout.

He paused on the way to look again at the phone in the Book department, wondering if he should call somebody. Not the police or the fire department. Definitely not Mr. Steele, at least not yet. One of his friends maybe, except that even then what he had to say might not sound believable at three o'clock in the morning. He wasn't frightened, Tully told himself; just excited and a little worried. He couldn't help thinking of all those armless dolls and wondering how they fitted into the alien's purpose.

The theory of a sex maniac wandering the Toy department had been demolished. Tully now knew what exactly it was that wandered the Toy department at night, but what bothered him was its behavior toward the dolls. Had it, in some obscure fashion, been trying to communicate with *him* . . . ?

Tully went into the Dugout quietly, closing and locking the door behind him, and along the corridor. At the partly open dividing door he put his flashlight on the floor and continued toward the Toy department, whistling and putting his feet down firmly so as to give the alien warning of his coming. But just before he entered the basement he stopped whistling when it occurred to him that high-pitched sounds might not be pleasant to alien ears—the noise he was making was not pleasant even to his own ears, Tully had to admit. Then suddenly he was in the Toy department and the alien was on the floor less than five yards away.

It was long and black and sluglike, with a soft bulginess about its body which suggested that internally it must be nearly all liquid. It moved by altering its center of gravity rapidly back and forth, in a series of tumbling lurches accompanied by a wet slapping sound. The head section—Tully guessed it was the head by its direction of motion—had a gray, shining bulge which might have been a single eye over a long, conelike proboscis, and five long, thin tentacles sweeping forward. Its direction of motion was away from Tully and it was moving fast. Obviously it was afraid of him.

Tully stuffed more peppermints into his mouth and followed it, but slowly so as not to frighten it further. So far as he could see it wasn't wearing or carrying anything, so he was in no danger from extraterrestrial weapons. He showed his empty hands continually and made reassuring noises, and tried to attract its attention by drawing non-scale diagrams of the solar system and Pythagoras's Theorem on one of the children's blackboards. But that was no good; it kept running away from him and trying to get back into the corridor where its ship was.

Tully could not allow that, at least not yet. While the

e-t was still excited and afraid of him he didn't want it getting its hands on a weapon.

He was standing in the mouth of the corridor trying to think of some other approach when he heard a noise which caused the cold sweat to pop on his forehead.

He had been blind, stupid—Tully could see that now. He had made a gross tactical blunder. The broken threads between the Dugout and Hardware department indicated the passage of someone between the fourth floor and the basement, but they could just as well have shown movement in the opposite direction. There were *two* aliens and the other one was coming back. Tully could hear it working at the locked Dugout door . . .

His first thought was that he had to keep the two aliens apart, until he could make the one he was chasing understand that he meant no harm. If the second alien came on the scene it might misunderstand and Tully would not be able to stop it from going to its ship for a weapon—always supposing it wasn't already carrying one. He must close the door in the corridor. He had already taken a step in that direction when he remembered that it was a simple bolt fastening, and locks and bolts did not a prison make for these aliens—he remembered the way his key had stuck to the Dugout lock. The aliens could open locks magnetically. He would have to wedge it shut.

A set of kiddies' building blocks gave him what he wanted and he ran back to the dividing door. By that time the second alien was on the way down the ramp and Tully used his flashlight briefly to have a look at it.

It was bigger, thicker and somehow meaner-looking than the one behind him. *The male of the species,* he thought. When it saw him it began to hurry, humping and lurching down the corridor and making high-pitched gobbling sounds. Behind him the other one began gobbling, too. Tully slammed the door and began kicking in the wedges just as a large, soft heavy weight made its hinges creak.

A few seconds later one of the wedges was pushed from under the door . . .

Tully had just decided that he had made another blunder. That the second alien, with the devices in its ship available, could probably blast through the door in nothing flat, and probably blast through Tully as well. But now it seemed that it was not going to be as quick and dramatic as that. The second alien did not want to destroy the door, because that would leave unmistakable evidence of its presence in the store, but no doubt Tully could be made to disappear tracelessly. He kicked the wedge in again, just as the one beside it popped out.

The smaller alien behind him had amused itself by pulling the arms off dolls. The second one . . . Tully wondered sickly what it would feel like to have his arms and leg pulled off, his nose mutilated and his eye . . . He tried desperately not to think about it, tried to think about good, civilized aliens, but his mind kept turning back to the other sort. The sort that Lovecraft used to write about.

According to Lovecraft the whole of time and space was peopled with cruel, debased, unspeakably foul entities, beings as cold and malignant and uncaring as the interstellar wastes in which they dwelt. Humanity with its concern over Right and Wrong inhabited a single dust-mote, unknown and unknowing, in a continuum that was one vast, blasphemous obscenity. Tully had not liked Lovecraft's ideas, but they had been written up so well that they had stuck in his mind despite this. And Lovecraft's aliens were the type who *would* pull another living, intelligent creature apart with less feeling than an unthinking boy pulling the legs off a fly . . .

Two more wedges jerked from under the door, and Tully couldn't move to replace them. All he could do was shake. His mind seemed to be a tight, hard ball of panic. He was beginning to realize that it was an *alien* on the other side of the door, a being whose civilization and philosophy and thought processes were such that there might be no common ground between them. And even if understanding was possible, he had spoiled any chance he had ever had of gaining it by closing the door.

Judging by its reactions, his attempt to contact the first alien had simply driven it into a panic, and then when the second one had come rushing to its aid he had barred the way. So far as the e-t outside was concerned he might be doing anything to its mate, and the longer he kept them apart the less likely the larger alien would be to stop and think. And he couldn't run himself because the Toy door was bolted on the outside.

It occurred to him suddenly that he had met this situation before also—the bug-eyed monster, the girl, and the hero dashing to the rescue. Only this time *he* was the bug-eyed monster . . . !

Somehow that thought brought him out of his panic state. Basically his problem was to show that he was a kindly disposed bug-eyed monster and not the other sort, and to show it unmistakably and fast. Tully was getting the glimmering of an idea, based on an assumption that might be all wrong, but he needed time to try it out. At least ten minutes. Abruptly he started kicking in the wedges again, kicking them in so hard and far that he ruined the toe-caps of his shoes and nearly broke a couple of toes. Then he sprinted back to the Toy basement and started tearing open a box of modeling clay.

Pulling and kneading at the stuff, Tully tried to work it into a shape that was shapeless. The clay was an improbable green color, but this did not worry him because the modeling set included a sprayer which, as well as giving the finished model a thin, hard skin within seconds, allowed it to be painted any desired color. While he worked Tully tried not to think of the gamble he was taking, or the scraping as wedge after wedge was pushed away, or of the gobbling which came from the other side of the door.

His theory, he told himself desperately, was supported by all the facts. It explained why one alien was careful to hide all traces of itself and its work, by plugging its bolt-hole and probably doing some sort of self-welding job on the metal strapping around the packing cases it had pilfered, while the other one left mutilated dolls lying around . . .

He finished it just as the last wedge shot out and the door banged against the wall. Tully tried to ignore the heavy, slapping sounds of the second alien coming along the corridor and moved instead toward the other alien—slowly, so as to frighten it as little as possible. It was in a corner, still making agitated gobbling noises. It occurred to Tully that his height might frighten it so he got onto his knees, then flat on his stomach, and crawled toward it holding out the thing he had made in one hand. Behind him the slapping grew louder and the smell of something that wasn't peppermint grew stronger.

He was gambling everything on his theory being right: lying flat on his stomach, defenseless, not even looking at his potential attacker. And his main reason for taking such a suicidal risk, Tully thought wildly, was that he did not want to think of the galaxy being peopled with Lovecraft aliens . . .

He was only a few feet away from the smaller alien when the big one lurched to a halt beside Tully. It didn't look at him, but shot its five whiplike tentacles out at the other e-t. Five smaller tentacles came out to meet them, touched, and almost tied themselves in five separate knots. Tully held his breath, afraid even to hope. It was not until the smaller e-t had left for the ship carrying the doll which Tully had made for it, and its parent began drawing a solar system with seventeen planets in it on the blackboard, that Tully knew he had guessed right.

Later that morning, as he tidied up the corridor and Toy department after the aliens had gone underground for the day, Tully thought that it had been obvious from the very start that a child had been responsible for the doll business. While its parent had been up in Hardware searching for the proper tools, Junior had grown bored. It had wanted to play with a dolly, but all the dollies in the Toy department were the wrong shape. So it had chosen one that was the nearest in color and pulled off the arms and a leg to give it a more "human" shape. Twisting out its nose and hair to resemble the five tentacles and conelike proboscis and removing the surplus eye had been further attempts toward that end. Looked at objectively, the mutilated dolls did look a little like the aliens. But not much, because the small alien had never thought enough of them to bring them back into the ship.

It had kept, and had seemed delighted with, the doll which Tully had made for it. Which meant that the Toy-department reign of terror was over. As for the spitting on the staircase, well, the aliens were not built for climbing stairs and they sometimes lost small amounts of body fluid when forced to do so. That, too, would stop in a few days' time when the repairs to the ship were complete. And the tools borrowed from Hardware would be returned to their former shape and replaced. No doubt this would cause widespread consternation, Tully thought wryly, but Tyson could not very well *complain*. All in all, everybody should be happy.

Tully yawned and looked at his watch. It was six thirty. He had just time to remove all his thread and chewing gum from the doors and stairways, make some coffee and finish the last story in his magazine before he unlocked the staff entrance for the cleaners arriving at seven thirty. It had looked like being a very good story, he thought as he walked slowly up the Dugout ramp, which had been his reason for saving it until last.

It would probably be an anticlimax.

Dogfight

INTO THE GIGANTIC task force assembling on the fringe of the Sirius system had gone the resources of seven inhabited worlds, and still it was not big enough. Captains, subfleet commanders and all the way up the pyramiding chain of command, men drove themselves mercilessly to the limit of endurance and beyond, one eye always on the clock. This which was being asked of them could not be done, they swore. More particularly, it could not be done in *time;* the problem of liaison and supply, the mountain of organizational detail involved in merely assigning positions, made the task impossible. It couldn't be done, they persisted angrily while they strained every nerve and muscle in their bodies doing it.

For the directive had *Maximum effort* . . .

Precisely on the calculated second, though still frantically engaged in sorting itself into proper battle order, the great fleet moved off. Mighty capital ships over half a mile in length, massed echelons of cruisers and a veritable cloud of lighter stuff all slipped as one into hyperspace and shot away on their allotted course. Each ship of the fleet was now at the center of a small, self-created and highly artificial continuum where reaction was out of all proportion to action and matter was not held down to the limiting speed of light.

Hours and days passed, then weeks, and the fleet—still at maximum acceleration and below the required strength—plunged onward. But its numbers were being augmented now by units sent by planets adjacent to its course. It did not matter that whole worlds were drained of war resources or that planetary populations had worked night and day to put them there—they were there, on course and on time; that was the important thing.

On the flagship, logistic problems of enormous proportions were being broken down into handy, manageable sizes. Supply and maintenance vessels were already following in their wake and this supply line had to be protected. The fleet continued to grow, but at a slower rate as units were detached to neutralize the few enemy positions nearby which were a potential threat. When the growth finally ceased its make-up and numbers were exactly as ordered in the directive from the tactical computer, and the point in time and space where its headlong dash was to end was only hours away.

As yet nobody had any idea what to expect when they got there.

Morale was high, however. The men were confident that RK9—the official designation for the tactical computer at Headquarters—would take good care of them. RK9 knew her stuff; whether this present mad dash was a surprise move to end the war or a step intended to counter an attempted breakthrough by the enemy, the battle computer would have the moves worked out well in advance. Unlike some of the electronic brains used in the opening decades of the war, when every major battle was such a bloody shambles that the victors could not honestly say that they had won, RK9 was mindful of the men inside the ships she moved around. And something very like this had happened some eighty years ago, when RK9 had just come into operational service, a piece of brilliant anticipation and bold strategy which had turned the tide of the war.

But despite their trust in the giant computer, their knowledge that it would not wantonly throw away their lives, they knew that war was still a risky business. As the tremendous battle fleet hurtled onward many of them wondered if they would live to see many more days.

Henson knew that the single moon of Earth was the most heavily defended body in all the vast volume of space under human control, and the whole of that incredibly complex and efficient defense system of ships, missiles and long-range detectors was centered around the crater Harpalus. It was as if some early planner had arrived at a figure in men and materials which could protect it against any conceivable attack, and then multiplied everything by three. Within this fantastically thorough network of defense there came into operation protective measures of a less material sort: hundreds of shrewd, hard-eyed but unobtrusive security officers whose purpose was to deal with any possible attack from within. And the reason for it all lay in a series of chambers half a mile below the crater floor in which were housed the near-legendary battle computer RK9 and the offices of General Craig, Director of Strategy.

As the newly appointed aide to the General, Henson thought sourly, he should have been in a uniquely favorable position for an enemy agent. . . .

Looking across the anteroom at the soundproofed door of Craig's office, Henson decided that there was definitely something going on—or, more accurately, that something was going *wrong*. Shawcross, the senior officer in charge of Materials and Personnel, was with the General at the moment. He had gone barging into Craig's office without so much as a nod. "It's happened again!" he had shouted angrily; and "That unprintable thing will have to be destroyed, do you hear! We can't have a—" The door had slammed behind him at that point, leaving Henson to the realization of how near he had been to learning something of importance.

Presently the door opened and Shawcross came out, closely followed by Craig. Looking at the face of the Materials and Personnel man, Henson was reminded of the evolutionary pattern of a main sequence star—when Shawcross had gone in his thin, intense face had been red and swollen with anger, which had now condensed to a tight, white-hot fury. He left without speaking. General Craig stared after him for several seconds, looking worried, then turned to Henson.

"I've a job for you, Colonel," he said, and paused. His tone was harsh but not deliberately offensive, the one used when he had a lot on his mind and was trying to disguise the fact. He went on, "We have made a penetration in force and the prisoners are becoming a problem. Go out there and handle things—you've been cleared for all data on the operation and you can have the subsidiary computer for the next two hours to work out the details. All right?"

"Yes, sir," said Henson briskly, desperately trying to hide his feeling at the news that he was about to be pulled out of the center of things just when some sort of crisis was impending. But, like the eager and patriotic young officer that he was trying to portray, he added, "The operation, sir, was it a success?"

"So far, yes—it was a surprise move." The General gave a short, unmirthful laugh, turned and reentered his office. He left Henson with the odd feeling that the operation had been a surprise to everyone concerned, including the Director of Strategy.

Definitely, he thought, there was something here which could be exploited to the advantage of his hard-pressed race. If only he knew what it was.

Next day the being who called himself Colonel Richard Henson was at the controls of a one-man courier vessel en route to his latest assignment. It was on rare occasions such as this, when the eyes of security men, his fellow Earth officers or even the Human man-in-the-street were off him, that he was able to relax and become himself. Strangely, this was not a wholly pleasant

process, he had discovered; it felt almost as if the real
him was the character in the play—a character
strangely lacking in depth, whose background was hazy
in places and whose lines he did not know very well—
and the Henson role the reality.

For it was not a nice thing to be a Semran under-
cover agent, and a member of a culture which was
steadily losing an interstellar war with Earth.

At times like this he found his mind trying to slip into
one of the many worlds of might-have-been. If a little
more diplomatic oil had been introduced one hundred
and thirty years ago, when the two cultures had met,
properly used it could have caused the mutually abrasive surfaces to acquire a smooth, cool polish instead of
leaving them hot and raw. Or if the Semrans had retained their technological lead, or if the Humans had
not developed RK9 . . .

As a culture Semra had been old, highly advanced
and intensely conservative, that of Earth young and on
the brink of interstellar expansion with all that had im-
plied. At first the war—the great, sprawling, unwieldy
and *slow* war—had gone in favor of the Semrans.
Semra was superior in ships, in men trained to work
them and in the speed and efficiency of the tactical
computers which fought all her battles. Then gradually
the Humans had built and improved on their equipment
until a deadlock had been reached. Battles continued to
be won and lost, but only by the narrowest of margins.
Thinking of those terrible encounters, of what he had
heard and read and just imagined about them, Henson
cringed.

The war had been a murderous chess game then,
with the opposing battle computers—cold, logical and
unfeeling machines bent only on winning the game no
matter if it meant practically clearing the board to do
it—as players and the Human and Semran beings concerned as unimportant and worthless pawns. Every engagement resulted in a massacre for both sides, the ad-
vantages lost or gained being microscopic. The ensuing
deadlock had been broken only when the Earth forces

had begun using RK9, and it had been at that point that Semra started losing the war.

Staring unseeingly at the controls before him— switched to automatic now to allow him to concentrate—the Semran agent began to feel the gnawings of self-doubt. So much depended on him now. The Semran High Command had early realized that the Earth successes were due solely to the new computer. If the circuitry or working principles of that genius among computers could be copied and given to them, or if the RK9 computer could be destroyed or sabotaged in some fashion, then the defeat looming inevitably before them might be staved off until some more positive action could be taken. That was why, driven by a desperate High Command, Semran Intelligence had contrived to train, mold and almost kill one of their agents in a last-ditch attempt to place one of their people next to Earth's super battle computer.

On Earth Richard Henson had been a brilliant student and a more than adequate cybernetics engineer. With a highly technical war being waged, it was only natural for him to join the fighting forces as a computerman, gain promotion and eventually attain the position he craved. And once there what had happened? He had been sent off on an errand half across the galaxy!

But was this assignment merely a piece of bad luck, he wondered suddenly, or were the Earth security people on to him? He knew that he had been given a background that was solid and well documented and the physiological differences, which were very few and minor, had been removed by traceless surgery. But a single slip could have negated all that. His mind was drawn into a tightening, descending spiral of despair for his race and himself until it reached the state where he was on the point of giving up and setting course for the nearest Semran-held world.

Angrily he curbed these traitorous impulses and began forcing himself into the Henson character again. Henson was a happier and more positive person, and he had a lot of preparatory work to do before the end of the trip. Almost gladly, Henson plunged into it.

The planets overrun by the latest Earth penetration were outpost worlds of little importance and so lightly held that they offered no opposition to the overwhelming force of the enemy—Semrans, although brave enough, were very practical. But when Henson reached his destination—a point in space approximately two thirds of the way along the Earth line of advance, which was the center of organization for Supply and Maintenance—he found that the prisoners were already piling up fast. The total personnel of the thirty-odd outposts taken over, even though they had been lightly defended, came to a respectable figure. The admiral commanding this advance supply base had, as well as the normal worries of his position, the problem of feeding and keeping control of over five thousand prisoners of war with inadequate supplies of food or men to guard them. Henson's arrival was a great relief to all concerned.

"We have transports already on the way from Earth which should arrive in a day or two," Henson told the senior admiral immediately the introductions were over, "and a place has been found for the prisoners. It would be a big help, however, if you could let me borrow some computermen and guards until the others arrive . . . ?"

The Admiral agreed without hesitation. Even though the other's shoulders sagged under their weight of gold braid—and responsibility—and Henson bore the relatively minor rank of colonel, agreement was merely a matter of form because behind and above that Colonel's insignia loomed the awful majesty of RK9.

"In that case," said Henson, smiling, "we'll have the prisoners out of your hair in no time at all." The Admiral's hair was going thin, but just enough for him to take the words as a compliment rather than a crack. He went on, "But I wonder, sir, if I could ask a question. Back on Luna the security is so tight that we never know what the Big Brain is thinking until long after whatever she has planned is finished. Could you tell me how this current job is going?"

The Admiral was silent for a long time; then he said brusquely, "I honestly don't know. It seems to be going well, but how can one judge the degree of success when the objective of the operation is unknown . . . ?"

This Admiral, thought Henson suddenly, is a man under considerable internal pressure. It was clear that there were a lot of things which he wanted to get off his chest and, despite the danger that the things he would say might land even a man of his vast seniority in trouble, he was bent on saying them to someone who he thought could do something about it . . .

". . . What sort of picture do the words 'penetration in force' give you?" the Admiral went on. "A great spearhead of ships and men plunged into the heart of enemy territory, disrupting supply routes, cutting communications and rolling everything before it?" He snorted. "Well that is not happening here.

"Maybe seventy or eighty years ago an offensive in this area would have done some good—one did, now that I remember—but the enemy has long ago retreated from this volume of space except for lightly defended positions which are little more than advance listening posts. Instead of a deep, potentially fatal wound we have therefore inflicted nothing but a long, shallow scratch. And to make this scratch, to collect this super task force, we have had to practically strip a whole galactic region of defense!"

Some sort of reaction seemed to be expected of him at this point, Henson thought. He said, "Er, what are they doing now, sir?"

"Nothing!" the Admiral barked. "Just nothing! Eighty thousand units big and small and all of them just waiting for something to happen. The job of supplying them alone . . ." He broke off and with a great effort brought his voice back to a conversational level. "An emergency directive calling for maximum effort sent us out here and so far there have been no further orders from RK9 or anyone else. Now we both know that there have been times when fleets were moved suddenly without their personnel being in the picture, but they were always informed of their place in that picture very shortly afterward. This time we know nothing at all. And what is worse, I've begun to hear of other, and admittedly smaller, instances just like this one."

When the Admiral had begun speaking Henson had been prepared to hear him blow off a little personal steam, but now it was clear that the other was a seriously worried man. He was also beginning to realize that perhaps it had been a piece of rare good fortune being sent out here by Craig—he was finding out things that he would never have discovered on security-blanketed Luna. And it was important information, too, so important that it was all Henson could do to hold the grave expression on his face while the Admiral continued talking.

"The fact that this movement has left a region open to enemy attack is bad enough," he went on, "but what is worse is the way some of the men are beginning to feel about RK9. They trust her, of course—she still wins battles, looks after their safety by winning with the minimum of casualties, and so on. These men are of the opinion that this operation was a move to anticipate one by the enemy, and that because they have not shown up the enemy has been outsmarted and the operation is therefore a success. But some of them, the more informed ones, are beginning to have doubts. Among other things they are wondering if perhaps the Semrans have developed a computer which is as good, or maybe better, than ours . . ."

When Henson left the Admiral a few minutes later, after assuring him that he would bring all these points to the attention of General Craig, he had to fight to keep from shouting with sheer exultation. He now had proof that something was definitely wrong with the much-vaunted tactical computer of the Earth forces, so much so that Human morale was becoming affected. And large volumes of Earth territory were undefended through this peculiar malfunctioning of RK9. This was the sort of information which could win wars. It might win this one for the Semrans.

During the three days it took for the transports to arrive, Henson worked furiously, striving to shorten if only by hours the time it would take for him to complete his assignment and return to Luna and RK9. The immediate problems demanding solution were those of storage: where to put the erection machinery which had to produce temporary shelters for five thousand Semran prisoners, the vast number of agricultural and associated mechanisms which would render them self-supporting, and the tremendous quantities of food needed to keep them alive until that time would come about. The agricultural material was the worst headache because it had to be of the old-fashioned plow and tractor type—big, awkward, cranky things whose power source had to be the internal-combustion engine rather than the lighter and more handy atomics, because that way there was less chance of plow shares being turned into swords. And there had to be a necessary surplus allowed in some categories, mainly where medical supplies were concerned, because the prison population might be added to by further captures as well as the increase which would take place normally with the passage of time.

In the very rare moments when such pressing matters did not occupy his mind Henson would dream a little. In these hurried but vivid daydreams he would discover and make available to the Semran High Command some terrible flaw in Earth's war machine, of such importance that the whole trend of the present conflict would immediately swing over in favor of the Semrans. In practically no time Earth would be forced to sue for peace and if he, the Semran Intelligence officer who had brought it all about, had any say in the matter those terms would not be too harsh.

For Earth was a ruthless, but never needlessly cruel, enemy—their P.O.W. system in particular was extremely humane, *and* highly economical to boot! And the differences between Semra and Earth, especially to a person like himself with wide experience of both sides' points of view, were not great . . .

The beautiful dream would usually be interrupted by a harried computerman waving tapes and protesting that there had been no provision made for seed storage—that hold J-107, the space normally used for this purpose, had been converted into extra living quarters and the only other possibility, B-82, was being used for the milk and meat animals, all of whom would just *love* to get at that grain, and had the Colonel any suggestions?

But finally the transports arrived, were loaded and set off with a destroyer flotilla as escort. Between them the transports contained nearly two thousand prisoners together with security men and ecology experts. The operating crew, as was usual on unarmed and highly servomechanized ships of that type, numbered fewer than twenty and their quarters were much more spacious and well-appointed than on the fighting ships. Henson's next most important job being the talk with the senior Semran prisoners, he asked the ship's captain for the loan of that worthy's cabin. Just, he had joked, so that he would make a good last impression.

On the tenth day after leaving the advanced supply base Henson had the three senior prisoners brought to him.

He made his manner polite but slightly distant when he greeted them and offered seats, but it was not until he was seated himself that he recognized Harelfa and saw that his old-time friend knew him . . .

"I am Colonel Henson," he announced quietly, and while the Semrans exchanged their names and rank with him he studiously looked right through Harelfa. Harelfa, who was no fool, did exactly the same with him. He went on, "Some of you may have heard rumors of how Earth deals with her prisoners of war, rumors which say that because no trace can be found of any Semran once he has been taken prisoner that we do not take prisoners. Well, I can assure you that this is not so.

We do take prisoners, though what we do with them will come as a shock to you."

Henson smiled, then continued, "But before I tell you your fate a little background information might help you to understand what is to happen . . ."

Since the time, more than six decades before, when the forces of Earth had unquestionably gained the initiative in the war, the prisoner problem had increased to fantastic proportions. As the war progressed millions of men and vast quantities of war materiel were tied up merely in guarding these prisoners. And, as might have been expected, cases of cruelty and malnutrition became more and more common because facilities for taking care of them were becoming increasingly strained. It was quickly reaching the point where the whole war effort was being affected by this hampering burden of prisoners. A solution had to be found, and it was.

"While you are on this ship," Henson went on, "you are prisoners bound to the rules of obedience and subject to the punishments of those who disobey. When you leave it, however, you will be free."

Henson paused and tried his smile again, but the three faces before him remained stony. They were not surprised, because they just did not believe him.

"With you when you leave," he explained, "will go enough food, prefabricated shelters and agricultural machinery to start you off as a self-sustaining colony. We will leave you to do as you like with yourselves but we know that, being intelligent beings, you will work to stay alive. During the next ten or twenty years we will drop other 'prisoners' down to you and you will doubtless assimilate them into whatever form of culture you devise for yourselves—we will have no contact with you whatsoever nor will we try to guide your thinking in any way."

The startled looks were coming now, all right.

Henson said, "You can see the beauty of this idea, and the fact that it is workable only with a culture like the Semrans' where absolute equality of the sexes is the norm. Instead of having to feed, clothe and shelter our

prisoners for the rest of their lives—*and* guard them—
we allow them to do all these things for themselves. The
original expense of setting you up as a colony is great,
but not a patch on what the other way would be, and a
few men at most will be sufficient for guard duty.

"Those few men will be in an orbiting spaceship,"
Henson concluded gently, "just in case some of you suc-
ceed in throwing together a spacecraft with which to
take home news of the location of this planetwide
prison camp. I don't think this would be possible—the
machinery being given you, while usable, is anti-
quated—but we try not to underestimate any being's in-
genuity. The ship will have means of detecting and destroying any such attempt."

Up until then everything had been in Earth English—the Semrans as a race had little difficulty learning
new languages, compared with the Earthmen. But now
the Semran officers were talking heatedly together in
their own tongue, which Colonel Henson was not supposed to know. It took considerable effort to make his
face register blank noncomprehension while they talked,
often mentioning places and people he knew as well as
they, although none of them was ever likely to see them
again.

If only he could get Harelfa alone, he thought long-
ingly, so that he could get some *news* . . .

"Your method of dealing with prisoners," burst out
one of the trio suddenly in English, "is highhanded, unfair and . . . and selfish! Compared with our expense
of maintaining camps for you Humans—"

"Surely," put in Henson gently, "there are not all
that many Earthmen captured these days."

The objector subsided and there was a silence which
began to grow awkward. Henson stood up.

This, he reminded himself, was not Harpalus, where
security men waited to jump at the slightest suspicion of
odd behavior. Besides, the guards on this ship were just
that, not the trained psychologists and spy-hunters who
clustered so thickly around RK9. Henson wanted badly

to talk to Harelfa, and by Heavens he *was* going to talk to her, and right now!

He said, "That is all for the time being. When you have digested the information just given you I'm sure you will have questions. Well, my duty is to give you all the help possible short of allowing you to go home. At the moment, however, I would like to talk to one of you alone. Flotilla Leader Harelfa, perhaps . . . ?"

Harelfa nodded. "Kind of you," she said with just the right mixture of dryness and hostility, "not to phrase it as an order."

The same old Harelfa, thought Henson as the other two Semran officers and their guard left the cabin. It had been twenty-three years since he had seen the other, just before he had gone into training for the Henson role, and there was suddenly so much he wanted to say and so much he needed to know that his speech centers were paralyzed through sheer overload. Finally he got out, "We can talk . . ."

And they talked. Henson was careful to avoid giving details about himself because of the slight danger that Harelfa might let slip something to the other prisoners which in turn might be overheard by the guards. But the Flotilla Leader had no such curb on her tongue, and as she talked Henson gradually came to realize that this was not the Harelfa he had known of old at all—there was an air of cynical hopelessness about her that had nothing to do with capture and the prospect of lifelong isolation on the P.O.W. planet. Only when she began talking about the war and its effect on the Semran population as a whole did the reason for it appear.

Dissatisfaction, despair and growing unrest: it was the picture of a culture which had been losing the war for so long that the thought of winning it would have been a totally alien concept. ". . . The space forces are maintained chiefly through a mixture of organizational inertia and a remaining vestige of racial pride," Harelfa went on, an almost whining note becoming apparent in her voice which was also foreign to the Harelfa of old. "That is the situation behind us when we fight, and it's hard to say whether it is the unquestionable superiority of Earth or this which affects us most. But we're licked anyway, so long as that computer of theirs—"

"There are indications," put in Henson carefully, "that RK9 may be losing her grip."

"Some of us have thought that, too," Harelfa agreed, "and although some of its actions recently have been strategically sense-free, we can't take the chance of ignoring them. We don't *dare!* The Earth battle computer is not greatly superior, technically, to our own. But its directive, its programming—it has a different angle of approach to a battle, as strange and difficult to understand as, say, the Humans' emotional attraction and protective feelings which they feel toward females of their own species instead of reserving those instincts for their young as we do. We can never be sure that it isn't contemplating some new and more devious strategy.

"The current operation, for instance," Harelfa went on angrily, "has the appearance of being a colossal tactical blunder. Yet we can't act on that assumption and hit back at the points where it has left Earth defenseless. Oh, if only we could . . ." A look of yearning had come to Harelfa's despairing visage and for a moment her eyes shone at the thought of Semran forces plunging through a gap in the Human armor and sweeping everything before them, rolling over the system of Sol and taking Earth itself, Luna and RK9. For a brief, glorious moment Harelfa saw victory; then she shook her head impatiently and continued, "Instead of that our whole defense system has been disrupted in our attempts to counter this very devious or very stupid move. And the more apparently senseless its actions are, the more disorganization and confusion it causes us. We can't trust it.

"The point has been reached," Harelfa concluded hopelessly, "where Earth's tactical computer could go completely mad, and they would still win."

Listening to Harelfa, Henson felt himself wanting desperately to wipe the sick hopelessness from the other's voice and expression. He wanted to tell her that as

Colonel Henson he was aide to Earth's Director of Strategy, who was the Human in charge of RK9. That he must very shortly be taken into Craig's confidence and that he would then know all there was to know about that unbeatable battle computer. Given information in advance he, Henson, would be able to pass it on to Semran agents on Earth—contacts who had escaped detection by security forces for the simple reason that they had remained completely inactive up until now. The sole duty of these agents was to collect and pass on information from Henson, but only when he had information which was worth passing. Very soon now he would have it, Henson wanted to tell her, and with a channel right into the heart of Earth's center of planning the war would certainly swing back in favor of the Semrans. So much so that unless some catastrophic piece of bad luck befell him in the near future, Semra would win the war. He longed to tell Harelfa all these things, but only one thing stopped him.

Kindness.

Harelfa was being exiled on a planet which was intended to become her home and the home of generations to come of Semran prisoners. For a while she and her comrades would be unhappy, but work and the pride they would take in forming a self-supporting community would tend to make them forget—and succeeding generations would forget completely the ideological difference which had caused them to be placed in the planetwide prison which had become their home world.

But Henson had heard it said of a certain subspecies on Earth that they lost battles but won wars. It was not one hundred percent certain that the Humans would lose and that the conquering Semran forces, given the coordinates of the P.O.W. planets by the capitulating Earth, would seek out and release the prisoners. If he told Harelfa everything he knew and then something went wrong, if Harelfa was to spend the whole of her remaining lifetime daily expecting a Semran force to rescue her, and with her the rest of the colony, that would be a torture too terrible to contemplate . . .

Gradually the realization came to Henson that he had been quiet for a long time, and that Harelfa was looking at him intently. He said quickly, "I suppose you'd better be getting back to the others. I'll talk with you again soon, and with the others so as not to arouse suspicion among the guards—there will be a lot you will need to know about setting up the colony . . ." He trailed off into silence.

Harelfa nodded and turned to go, then hesitated. She said, "Our Intelligence people did a good job, Colonel. When you were explaining about the Earth P.O.W. system to us a few minutes ago you sounded truly enthusiastic about it, as if you were really convinced of the rightness of the whole thing. It makes me wonder . . ." She broke off to give Henson another long, searching stare, then added, "I hope you remember which side you're on."

Henson's first impulse was to laugh, his second to explain how thoroughly he had had to steep himself in his Human role; how he had had to strive to *be* a Human, in viewpoint, in manner and even in emotional reactions. If he had not done so he would never have arrived at his present position of trust. But somehow, Henson thought with a sudden feeling of discomfort, all these things would have sounded like a protestation, a lame excuse for some unexplained misdemeanor. In considerable turmoil of mind he watched Harelfa leave and said nothing.

During the work of establishing the colony and on the journey back Harelfa's words returned several times to his mind, bringing vague feelings of guilt. But with his arrival on Luna all these tenuous feelings were obliterated by larger and more immediate issues. Harpalus was seething with excitement over a battle which was expected shortly, and in his absence the situation between Generals Craig and Shawcross over the computer had come to boiling point.

The row was going on in the outer office this time when Henson arrived to make his report, and it stopped as soon as he went through the door. General Craig's face was pale and there was a stubborn set to his jaw as he glared toward Shawcross, whose visage was growing visibly darker with suddenly pent-up emotion. The silence was electric.

Abruptly Shawcross wheeled about. "General Craig," he snapped, "kindly take this blasted aide of yours into your confidence and tell him what's going on around here. Then notify Security so I can talk to you when he's hanging around here. That way the ignorant damn fool won't make me burst a blood vessel." He brushed past Henson, paused momentarily to growl, "My apologies, Colonel," then stamped out.

Henson's "Quite all right, sir" was to an empty doorway.

The Director of Strategy did not mention Shawcross at all during Henson's report and the subsequent discussion on it, despite the Colonel's repeated and obvious attempts to guide the conversation that way. Toward the end of it he said suddenly, "Colonel Henson, what is your feeling about this P.O.W. system? And don't say what you think will please me, say what you think!"

The General, Henson saw, was under a severe strain. He felt that Craig was seeking reassurance about something, some decision that the Director of Strategy had taken which even he himself was not sure was right. Henson saw the torment in the other's eyes and thought that, of all the Humans he knew, he liked and respected this one the most. But he did not know enough to give the reassurance that was being sought; he could do only as he was told.

He said, "I approve of it. I think it shows some very sound thinking in high places. Normally at this stage on Earth, we would be an expanding culture, exploring, colonizing, spreading from system to system. The war stopped that, but not entirely. The colonizing process is going on, with Semran prisoners, and the beauty of it is that they will have forgotten the war in a comparatively short time and be simply colonies waiting to be reopened to interstellar flight."

Henson hesitated for an instant before going on. What he wanted to say verged on the disloyal, but he decided that the risk was worth taking by saying it because a little verbal disloyalty in a person who was in a high position tended to disarm suspicion more than the other way about. He added, "The galaxy is being populated and eventually it will be civilized—does it matter by whom? I think it is a very good system."

The General stiffened up suddenly. He said, "There are a lot of things you need to know about this job and I'm going to enlighten you. But not for a few hours yet. There is going to be a battle visible very shortly, one of the biggest, and I want you to watch it with me in the observatory. I'll be able to explain things better there.

"And if you're wondering about the little inquisition," he added, smiling, "it was because I think you a very able man and I was trying to make sure in advance whose side you would be on . . ."

Those, thought Henson after the General had gone, had been almost exactly the same words used to him by Harelfa. Both of them had admitted his ability but shown doubt regarding his loyalty. Was there, he wondered uneasily, some indefinable something about him which stamped him as a traitor?

Recently the temptation had been strong to sink himself completely in the Henson role and forget that he was a Semran agent—that would undoubtedly have been the easier and much more safe course. And in his present position and during his rise to it he was doing a lot to help Earth against his own people. That had been necessary for him to gain a position of trust, he had argued at the time, and the wrong he had done would be outweighed by the service he would render in the near future. Maybe the reason for his uneasiness— "guilt" was not too strong a word—was the fact that he liked this Henson characterization so much, and that he sometimes felt pleasure in the job of prosecuting the war against his own people.

Craig's remark had to do with interdepartmental loyalties, Henson was sure, but it nevertheless could be a pointer toward some basic flaw in his make-up. Until the time came for him to go to the observatory he fought a continuous, bitter and unresolved struggle with his conscience.

From the viewpoint of an observer in the solar system the battle was beginning to take shape in the area between the constellations of Cancer, Gemini and Orion, although the actual spatial coordinates of its position were nowhere near the stars composing those systems. To the naked eye it appeared as tiny tendrils, squiggles and fat worms of multicolored light all inching together toward a common center somewhere in the region of Procyon, but with the aid of the equipment in the battle observatory, the details became apparent.

That equipment could give a picture—blurred and distorted, it was true, but still a usable picture—of markings on the surface of 61 Cygni C. It now projected images from the battle area which showed the fat worms and squiggles of light to be great fleets, subfleets and flotillas jockeying for position. It even showed the intermittent breaks in some of the ships' light as their captains practiced the dodging out of and into hyperspace, which was the most important maneuver in present-day warfare.

The ship's light . . .

A vessel using hyperdrive created its own continuum around it and disappeared from normal space—but not quite. From the hyperdrive engines which propelled it through its artificially created spacetime there was an enormous amount of radiation leakage which spilled into normal space as light, a pure, almost solid mass of light so intense that it had to be counted in the order of billions of candlepower per second. Thus it was that even when a ship traveled in hyperspace, *especially* when a ship traveled in hyperspace, its position relative to normal space was always apparent because of its light. But light is a limiting velocity as well as a radiation phenomena and hyperships often exceeded that speed, so that their position as located by their light spillage was long out of date. Above him now, for instance, Henson knew that ships angling toward the battle area from the solar-system side were invisible because, being nearer to him, their trails of light had already passed, while vessels coming in from beyond it were likewise invisible because their light had not reached him yet.

But they were all drawing rapidly together; soon all their lights would be visible . . .

"That," said General Craig with a wave toward the observatory's transparent dome, "is the reason why we can't afford to relax even now. I doubt if the Semrans are in a position to mount another such attack, but we can't be sure. The one we are seeing now, however, could have overrun the solar system if we hadn't been able to move our defenders out there in time. If it unable to duplicate RK9.

Here it comes, thought Henson eagerly. He was going to find out something important at last. In an effort to hasten the process he said, "I know, sir, but what beats me is why the Semrans haven't developed a computer equally as good. They have the brains."

"They have the brains, all right," Craig said. "But brains are not all that is needed, there is a little something extra required which they have not got: the proper type of emotion. The Semrans are an old, intelligent and emotionless race, and whether they have simply evolved away from it or never possessed it I can't say— I just know that they are incapable of feeling emotion in anything like the degree that we do, and are therefore unable to duplicate RK9.

"But to understand properly," he went on, "you have to go back to the first battle computers. R's 1, 2 and 3 were no good, we lost nearly every time with them. R4 was better, and with later models we improved until our computers were the equal of the Semran machines and we won—if you could call it that—about half the time. But you remember what it was like in those days . . ."

Henson could. Looking through the transparent dome above him, he could imagine the same things happening to the Semran forces out there.

Interstellar war was a study in contradictions. Men and machines flew ships at speeds faster than light through two continua and yet were forced to use archaic chemical warheads on their missiles. This was because atomic devices of the cruder, less balanced kind—the kind known as mass destruction weapons—became explosively unstable when the ship carrying them ducked in and out of subspace a few times. Engagements were of necessity close-range, bloody affairs, yet fought at such speed and with such a fantastically large number of variations in any given tactical situation that mere beings of flesh and blood were unable to react fast enough to them.

A favorite tactic was for a single ship—or it could be modified for the use of a fleet—to approach an enemy through hyperspace to close range, materialize to launch a missile, then flee into the hyperdimension again. It did not matter if its intended victim was in normal space or the hyperdimension, because in the latter instance any missile directed into the point of emergence of the light spillage would ultimately destroy the ship. A missile directed thus would enter the artificially created space around the target ship and remain there in stasis. But when the ship, after a long or very short time, emerged into normal space the missile would materialize inside it. Providing the problems of course and speed and timing could be solved, it was a lovely tactic.

Increasingly complex battle computers were designed to solve these problems. Each encounter became a sprawling, chaotic dogfight stretching over scores of light-years with the machines which handled the battle throwing units about like pieces in a monstrous game of chess in frantic attempts to attack and at the same time anticipate and counter an attack from an opponent. And the men inside those ships could do nothing whatever to help one way or the other. It was a battle of cold, unfeeling and inhuman machines . . .

The General was saying, ". . . It was like a game of ninepins. Or chess. There was no identification between the computers and the men taking part, they were just so many expendable chess pieces, and the carnage was frightful. The computers were so evenly matched that . . . Well, what was perhaps worse than the casualties suffered in the actual battles was those who were not sure . . ."

Ships, thought Henson sickly, whose crews thought that a missile had found its way through their tail light during the battle, a missile which hung somewhere in the artificial continuum created by their hyperdrive generators, harmless until they tried to reenter normal space. After a battle it had been a regular occurrence to see a ship come into its home system on hyperdrive only to blow itself apart on emergence. It was said that the personnel on the bigger ships stood a better chance because there was no telling where exactly in their ship the missile would materialize and if they distributed themselves about the ship some of them might survive—unless, of course, it materialized near the magazine . . .

There had been instances when whole fleets had come home, the blinding coruscation of their light proclaiming their desperation and their belief that they were under sentence of death, to disintegrate one by one a few miles above their home ground.

". . . That sort of thing had a bad effect on morale," Craig went on grimly. "Maybe our cold, unemotional friends on the other side could take that sort of thing, but we couldn't. We had to think of some way of changing the rules, and eventually we did. The R6 was the last of the old-style battle computers. There was no R7 or R8, but RK9—"

"R is for 'Robot,' I know," put in Henson. "But the K9 . . . ?"

"That will become self-evident in a moment," said Craig. "The thing we were aiming for was for our computer to have personnel identification, to *feel* for the men it was using. We could not simply tell an ordinary computer to win a battle but to go easy on the men, a computer can't be programmed that way and remain efficient—in that case doubling the objective means halving the work done. The solution to the problem lay in neurosurgery as well as in cybernetics. We decided to incorporate a living brain.

"We had lots of volunteers, naturally," the General continued quickly before Henson could say anything, "but we didn't use them. We wanted a mind and a personality which would love humanity no matter what we did to it, and all too often, I'm sorry to say, man in the singular does not love mankind in the mass. So we used a dog—"

Craig broke off suddenly to stab a button on the panel before him, and a section of the battle flashed onto the main enlarger screen. The loops and arcs and cloudy patches of light told of a sizable Earth fleet cutting out and englobing a relatively minute force of the enemy. A few long, straight shafts of light told of vessels making for home and carrying their own destruction with them. But the main force of the Semrans being englobed would surrender. They would do it not because they lacked courage but simply because they were logical about such things and knew when a situation was hopeless. They would submit to having their hyperdrive generators wrecked by Earth technicians, and, thus immobilized, would wait until the battle was over for the Humans to take them prisoner and later make use of their ships.

"Nice," said the General, and switched to another sector of the battle. He resumed, "The dog idea worked fine. It won battles for us in such sneaky, roundabout ways that the casualty figures dropped to practically nothing and morale soared. It was a perfect combination—a big, awkward, friendly mutt acting as thalamus to a super electronic brain. But in some ways she wasn't a very bright dog . . ."

The General's tone had become harsh and he was punching buttons furiously and not bothering to look at the pictures they produced. Henson felt certain that he was doing it so that he would not have to meet his aide's eyes.

". . . For instance: The Semrans resemble us so closely that it began to bother her apparently when we had to kill a lot of them, so she arranged her tactics so that more and more prisoners were taken. We didn't mind that because, among other things, we could use their ships. Then the P.O.W. problem arose and she told us how to solve that in a way easy for us and them as well. But now she has begun to do very stupid things.

"Things like collecting a fleet out by Sirius, stripping a whole sector of defenses to do it, sending it tearing half across the galaxy and then leaving it hanging there! There have been other things as well.

"Shawcross wants her destroyed."

Above them the battle was approaching its climax but neither officer looked at it. Henson thought that never had he seen such misery and desperate pleading in the eyes of any man as that being directed at him by General Craig. Instinctively he felt sympathy, an emotion he very rarely felt, but it was rapidly overwhelmed by sheer exultation as the General went on speaking. Now he *knew!*

"It is eighty-odd years since they took her brain," he said thickly. "She was little more than a pup then, and all the resources of medical science have been used to maintain her brain at full efficiency. But that could not be expected to go on forever. Her mind is becoming rapidly more senile, she has started to chase imaginary rabbits, refighting the great battles of her youth against nonexistent foes—that 'penetration in force' a while back was one instance. Shawcross says we cannot afford to maintain a battle computer which has begun to dote."

"You think she should be," said Henson in a carefully neutral voice making it sound a statement rather than a question. His eyes slid away from the anguished face of the General to the little groups of high officers dotting the floor of the dome, to the men out on the surface watching the battle through spacesuit helmets, then up to the flaring, pulsating, wide-flung banner in the sky.

Many of them, the General included, had actually taken part in this battle they were watching. It had taken place over seventeen years ago and the fact that it was being watched here and now was because it had occurred over seventeen light-years from Earth and the light had only now arrived. It was the last attempt, the Earthmen thought, which the Semrans could try at striking at the heart of the enemy culture.

Semra had been beaten to her knees, Henson knew; she was about ready to give in. But she must be capable of making one last, all-out effort, and, given the information which he now had and full data on the dispositions of Earth forces while they were unknowingly involved in refighting past battles, that one effort might very well win them the war . . .

"I do!" said the General, the words bringing back to Henson the realization that he was still in the middle of a conversation. "When you think of what we did to her—how we took her when she was only half grown, cut her off from all the sense perceptions, sound, sight, smell and all pleasure stimuli, normal in a dog. And the weeks of agony she must have gone through while we were doing all that.

"Yet she kept on loving us, the stupid pup!" Craig said, half angrily. "What's more, she learned to use and dominate the electronic senses we had given her, and many times she saved the race with them. Not only that: This war, which could have been a savage, brutal, bloody conflict bringing total extinction to both sides, she has forced us to fight clean and . . . and humane.

"The Semrans owe her a lot, too," he went on, momentarily off on a tangent, "though they don't realize it. This whole idea is impossible to them, because they don't feel friendship or love for lower life forms and it is problematical whether they will ever grow back. Not that they are cruel, or even thoughtless—they're not. But they just have not got the emotional equipment . . ."

Above them the battle which was too vast and complex for mere human brains to follow was over. It was a great, tangled mass of glowing threads now, blazing with every color in the spectrum because of their angular displacement, and already throwing out the great tentacles of light which indicated fleets going home, perhaps to die. It was a mark in the sky which would be seen all over the galaxy—a stupid scribble made by two races that had not yet grown up, but perhaps time would remedy that.

The General had accused the Semrans of being without emotion, Henson thought as he looked up with a mental struggle more violent than anything he had ever experienced before boiling within him. But Craig might be wrong. Maybe it had been the continued close contact with Humans which had done it, but this feeling in the throat, this tightness, this sense of something that was almost pain over an animal whose very existence he had been unaware of a few minutes previously . . . Yes, the General was definitely wrong, because when Henson looked upward the lights of battle were overlaid by the picture of a dog.

It was an old dog. An old, blind dog whose hair was falling out and who didn't have sense enough to come in out of the rain. A dog that shivered and twitched and whined to itself while it dreamed of its past. A dog that had given love and long, faithful service despite the kicks and beatings. And a dog, Henson thought, who more than deserved to go on dreaming for a while.

But the General had been talking, though Henson did not know what he had been saying, and was waiting for some sort of reply.

"I . . . I think you're right, sir," he said, and wondered that the General failed to notice the strain in his voice. "And I don't think you have to worry about Shawcross—RK9 has the reputation of being unbeatable, and even if she does nothing else but chase her tail from now on it will look like some devious new tactic to the Semrans. Besides, a mad dash half across the galaxy now and then is good for discipline . . ."

It was no good, Henson told himself as he talked.

Even if he sent this vital information home, and it was acted upon and Earth was overrun, it would still be no good. Semra could never win, never finally and unquestionably win, against a race that could spend countless millions on men and material movements out of kindness to a doting old dog. Nobody could win against a race which could be both so ruthless and so kind as that.

Deep within him there was a voice which cursed and reviled and called him traitor. It would continue, probably, for the rest of Henson's life, but it would never influence his actions.

He said, "Believe me, sir, I'm on your side . . ."

Nuisance Value

THE RECEPTIONIST'S VEIL was too thin to either muffle the respectful tone of her voice or hide the smile which accompanied the words as she indicated the door beside her and said, "Citizen Conlon apologizes for keeping you waiting. If you will relinquish your weapons, sir, you may go in now."

Barclay had been kept waiting for precisely two and one quarter minutes.

A fair proportion of Barclay's life had been spent waiting in outer offices like this one while he tried to find a way around or through various kinds of organic barriers. These had ranged from the weakly defended outer barricades thrown up by junior secretaries, which usually went down before a combination of persistence and an appeal for sympathy, to the rigid and impenetrable walls of silence which surrounded the highly placed people who probably knew the answer or had their own reasons for concealing their ignorance. But today, for some strange reason, the barriers were of cobwebs and he had penetrated more deeply into the Department for

Technological Reconstruction than ever before, seemingly without even trying.

He entered a small office made smaller by a large desk. On one side of the desk there was a wall TV and opposite an unmarked door. The man seated behind the desk inclined his head formally until Barclay had taken the visitor's chair—respect, of a kind, for the aged was becoming fashionable again—after which he sat down again and stared at his visitor in silence.

Citizen Conlon was in his early forties, very conservatively dressed in brown coveralls with an orange scarf knotted neatly into his hair, which he wore long over his right ear. From the other ear was suspended a gold disc signifying that it was an offense punishable by death to challenge him to a duel, but Barclay's eyesight was not good enough to distinguish whether it was the symbol of Law Enforcement or Medicine decorating the ornament.

If it was the former, Barclay could be in serious trouble.

"You are an extremely stubborn and persistent man, Citizen Barclay," said Conlon, in a tone which somehow managed to sound both friendly and critical. "You have been asking the same question since before I was born, but the answer you have been given has not satisfied you. You are without doubt the greatest single nuisance this department and those which preceded it have encountered. We deal with our fair share of crackpots, but you are a responsible, law-abiding, productive and apparently sane crackpot. I say apparently sane because monomania of this order is always suspect."

Before he could respond, Conlon went on, "The answer given you was simple and well documented with press cuttings. You were only twelve at the time, but you refused to believe it. Not only did you not believe it but you convinced your mother that it was not true. But you were young and possibly your own distress, rather than any rational process of deduction, made you disbelieve the story?"

"It *was* a story, then?"

"Please do not answer a question with another question," said the other sharply. "A story can mean a piece of newspaper reportage as well as a work of fiction. Well?"

This interview was like no other that he had experienced in the recent or distant past, Barclay thought worriedly. It was much longer than usual—as a rule, he was kept waiting two hours and dismissed in two minutes. Also, the questions were coming from the person who should have been supplying, or trying to avoid supplying, the answers. He was beginning to feel as if he were undergoing preliminary interrogation by an investigating magistrate.

At what point did a long-term nuisance become an enemy of the State?

Barclay swallowed, then said, "I did not want to believe that my father had died at all, but then I found difficulty in believing that he had died in the fashion described—"

"A moment, please," Conlon broke in. "We are discussing an incident which happened nearly fifty years ago. Before proceeding, it is necessary to identify the person concerned beyond any doubt. Is this a picture of your father?"

The wall TV screen lit with a full-color still picture of his father, spacesuited but with the helmet removed. The particular shot was not in Barclay's collection, probably because the publicity photos never showed his father looking so tired and tense—he was wearing his fussy look.

Barclay was unaware that he had been thinking aloud until Conlon said curiously, "What do you mean by 'He's wearing his fussy look'?"

"It was the way my mother described his expression when he was taking something very seriously," Barclay replied. "He . . . joked a lot and was great fun most of the time, but about some things he was very serious and meticulously careful. His job, for instance, or a do-it-yourself project at home or teaching me to swim. At times like that he was so serious my mother laughed at him. That was why I thought the story of his death so ridiculous—"

"Were these changes of mood sudden or accompanied by flashes of anger?" said Conlon suddenly. "I realize that the implications of the question are clear to you, but please be objective."

"I remember him being angry," Barclay replied, "but not violently or often. Once was when I was six and climbed a tree I'd been forbidden to climb . . . other incidents like that. But I seriously doubt that he was capable of losing his emotional control to the extent that he would fly a plane over the sea with insufficient fuel for the flight."

"The relationship between your mother and father," said Conlon. "Was it a good one? Be objective."

"How can I be objective about a family relationship?" said Barclay, unable to conceal his irritation. "They were the only parents I had. I don't *know* how they measured up on an objective basis. *I* thought we were very happy."

Conlon nodded without expression and said, "We'll leave the family relationships for the moment and return to your suspicions regarding your father's death—"

"The manner of his death," Barclay broke in. "By the time I was eighteen we were both pretty sure that he was dead. But somebody, probably Dr. Goyer and maybe a few of the others, were hiding something."

"Very well, the manner of his death," said Conlon. He cleared his throat, then went on, "Information about this period is untrustworthy, I realize, but I understand that by the time you were eighteen you had pestered everyone you could possibly reach with your questions and suspicions. In the beginning there was a lot of sympathy for your mother and yourself at the space center, but after six years of making a nuisance of yourself the sympathy began to wear thin. You lost friends. The first to go was Dr. Goyer, the technical director, who had been a friend of the family and your adopted uncle. He stopped visiting your home, found somewhere else to be when you called to see him at the center, and finally he left instructions that you weren't to be admitted at all. Is my information substantially correct?"

Barclay nodded.

"When the space center was closed to you, you started making a nuisance of yourselves with local police authorities," Conlon went on. "Each time you moved to another area to stay with relatives, or during a stopover in a large city, you reported your father as a missing person and possible accident or amnesia victim. You supplied pictures of him taken out of uniform, a very accurate physical description, but a fictitious name. It was more than four years before they realized that police authorities all over the country were looking for the same missing person under different names, and the police passed the matter to one of the Government security agencies, which investigated you. As a result, your missing person was identified, and shortly afterward you stopped being such a serious nuisance and your mother died.

"What exactly was said to you which made you lose, or appear to lose, interest?" Conlon went on, leaning forward in his chair. "Had your mother's death anything to do with it? Ah, I seem to have touched a sensitive spot."

He has no right to ask questions like this, Barclay thought angrily. Aloud, he said, "I'm simply trying to find out what really happened to my father. What possible reason can you have for wanting to know what my mother or I did or did not do fifty years ago?"

"So the constant pestering over the years may not have been exclusively your idea," said Conlon musingly. "But surely after all this time you can talk about it? However, to answer your question, the law-enforcement people have had more important things to do than waste time dealing with an apparently harmless nuisance like yourself. But the situation has changed recently, and now I must discover all there is to know about you, to help me reach a decision."

"A decision," asked Barclay, feeling his mouth go dry, "or a judgment?"

"Try not to frighten yourself unnecessarily, Citizen," Conlon said, smiling, "and answer the original question."

Barclay wondered what he had done to deserve this interrogation. He had always supposed that his offenses, even during the Mad Years, had been venial. Forcing the anxiety to the back of his mind, he began to describe his mother's initial reaction to the loss of her husband. There had been the grief and the shocked refusal to believe that it had even happened. Barclay realized later that they should both have tried to face up to what had happened and stop the stupid pretense that his father might not be dead simply because his body had not been recovered—he at least should have done so, because his mother had not been a strong-minded woman or capable of adapting to a domestic catastrophe on that scale.

She should have married again and, looking back on it, Dr. Goyer had been a strong possibility. They both liked the Doctor, and it was only his rimless spectacles which made him look old. But Barclay had practically accused him of lying about his father so often that he had stopped coming to the house—although he might still have married her if Mrs. Barclay had not discouraged him as well. But she had thought that her son would go to pieces if he was told that his father was really dead—Dr. Goyer had been a kind man, but he had not believed in allowing people to fool themselves—so she kept up the pretense that his father might still be alive for her son's sake. But she had cried a lot at night when she thought Barclay could not hear her, and it was many years later when he realized exactly what she had been going through. By then, unfortunately, she had begun to believe the pretense herself . . .

". . . I still didn't believe the story about him being lost over the sea due to a shortage of fuel," Barclay went on. "Even now I'm convinced he was not the kind of man who would make that sort of mistake. But I wanted to know what really had happened. It was curiosity, mostly, a need to tidy up loose ends so we could forget the whole thing and start over, and a feeling that it was wrong that my father should not only die but be called a fool, which he wasn't, for dying. But then I found myself carrying on the pretense that he might still be alive to help *her . . .*"

Any show of sentiment would be mistaken for the maudlin sentimentality of a silly old man, which was why Barclay made a special effort to be objective as he went on to describe the course of treatment he had devised and put into effect. He had been eighteen at the time and the therapy had been rule of a very tender thumb, because he still had not understood the reality behind the cases he had studied in the psychology textbooks. His language was coldly clinical as he described to Conlon her increasing and constant need for reassurance and the wild, seesaw swings between apparent acceptance of the situation and fits of depression so deep that for days on end she would not even acknowledge his existence.

But there had been progress, nevertheless. His academic record had been very good although he had not sought clinical experience in a psychiatric hospital or in private practice, preferring to specialize in the long-term treatment of one particular patient for whose condition he felt partly responsible. Gradually her fits of depression became rarer and less prolonged. More and more she had discussed the future, his current girl friend, his feelings about getting married and making his own way in life. She had said that she should renew old friendships from the space-center days. On one occasion she said that his father would probably not have approved of the way they both had been wasting time trying to find out what had happened to him . . .

A photograph of his mother taken from her space-center ID card appeared on the screen, but Conlon was concentrating all of his attention on Barclay.

"It wasn't that she was overpossessive or selfish where I was concerned," he resumed, looking at the fifty-year-old photograph. "She did not ask me to do the things I did for her. It was just that she was so terribly dependent on my father that . . . I mean, if it hadn't been for his death this minor flaw in her personality would never have shown up. Even by objective standards," he ended firmly, "she was a very fine person."

Conlon said, "Go on."

"Why this morbid interest in my mother?" Barclay burst out. "All I came here to find out was—"

"I know what you came to find out," the other said calmly. "But first I have to find out all about you. This includes the people and events which have made you the . . . nuisance . . . that you are today. I am especially interested in what you are today. Now, you say that your mother's mental condition showed signs of improvement, and your qualifications should make this a statement of fact rather than wishful thinking. But there was, I believe, some kind of trouble with the law which brought about a rapid deterioration?"

Barclay nodded, then explained that the police in one of the cities they had lived in became suspicious about the missing-person report he had filed on his father, and had referred the matter to an aging, irritable and overworked senior lawman belonging to an unnamed Government agency. This man had drugs, muggings, race rioting, and steadily mounting larceny and murder figures to contend with, he had told them, and they were not helping things by playing childish games with the constabulary all over the country. The file on astronaut Barclay was closed, and they should both go home and make the best of things.

They had fully intended doing just that, but Barclay had not been able to resist the opportunity to ask more questions.

The man had been simply trying to get rid of them, but Barclay had been young and emotionally involved and his mother had not progressed enough to withstand that kind of shock, and suddenly it seemed that someone had not only caused his father's death but was intent on committing character assassination on him as well.

"What, exactly, was said?" asked Conlon.

"He didn't *say* anything," Barclay replied bitterly, "but he gave the impression that my father had defected and taken valuable technical material with him to the Russians. Our people had kept quiet about it, apparently, because a lot of public opinion was building up in favor of a complete cancellation of all space projects, and a scandal like my father's defection would have given too much ammunition to the opposition . . ."

The man's words had made the desired impression on Barclay—for a few hours, at least. But then he decided that he disbelieved the latest story even more than the one about the plane crash. Because he remembered his father talking about the Russian astronauts and how closely they cooperated in space. The space agencies in both countries had been under the same kind of political and economic pressure to suspend operations; there no longer had been expensive duplication of technical effort, few if any secrets. There had been no apparent reason to defect, therefore, even if he had been the type of man who would desert his wife and son to do so—which he very definitely was not.

But his mother, while she had said that she did not believe the story either, had not reacted in a rational fashion. Once again she became desperately anxious to find out what really had happened to her husband.

Dr. Goyer had died a few weeks earlier—in an accident on the space station, a still-friendly contact at the center had told them. He also told them that the Doctor had been due to be arrested the moment he returned because of a major misappropriation of funds and equipment, so that his death might not have been an accident. His mother had wondered if her husband had become involved in some fashion with Dr. Goyer. She was sure that he was not a thief who had been found out and had suicided rather than face his family. Possibly he had discovered something very wrong going on and had been silenced. She had not even mentioned the possibility of his defecting. She became very confused and emotional and she had to find out what had hap-

pened at all costs, and it had cost them nearly all the
money they had possessed . . .

"You were an unusually dutiful son," Conlon broke
in, his tone making the words sound anything but com-
plimentary. He went on, "Was it at this point that you
started the collection of technical publications which
I've been hearing rumors about?"

Defensively, Barclay said, "I was not being forced to
learn languages and spend money on foreign journals,
at least not by her. I'd wanted to be an astronaut for as
long as I could remember and I still had the interest,
even though the Mad Years were starting and space
flight was dead. Besides, when the TV and radio stations became protest targets and dusk-to-dawn curfews
became general, there wasn't anything else to do but
read."

Conlon nodded. He said, "So you gave her plenty to
occupy her mind. At what stage did you decide to dis-
continue therapy, and why?"

Therapy!

What an offhand way to describe all those years of
careful cross-checking, of sifting and evaluating and ca-
taloging data which was very often in a foreign language. By its very nature the work had lacked excitement, and the encouragements and disappointments had
been so slow in becoming manifest that they had never
been sure at any given time whether they had been
proving or disproving his father's alleged guilt. In the
beginning the material could be had simply enough, by
subscription. But later, when their and everyone else's
society fell apart, other methods of payment than
money had had to be used or the material had had to be
"permanently borrowed without permission." But when
the owners were dead or disinterested, where was the
crime?

No doubt Conlon would be glad to tell him the answer to *that* question.

During the Mad Years the word "survivor" had very
often been synonymous with "criminal." There had
been law but no order, widespread killing for food, fuel

or simple self-gratification, and no protection other than self-protection or voluntary slavery to a local gang-leader willing to extend his protection for services rendered. The painstaking study and research his mother and he had pursued, the strict mental discipline which had been required to accomplish it, had been an escape to an unexciting but orderly world from the anarchy surrounding them. Conlon was right—it had been therapy for both of them.

"Please answer," said Conlon. He did not sound impatient or even interested. Perhaps he had lost the capacity to feel or display emotion, or was trying hard to lose it as a good lawman should.

Barclay did not reply at once, because he was remembering the aftermath of one of the early food fights between rival gangs. Nobody seemed to care how many innocent bystanders with official ration cards were killed and robbed of their week's supplies, but Barclay had cared very much about one of them. The pause was to insure that all trace of emotion was absent from his voice and expression before he went on.

"The therapy never stopped," he said, "even after my mother died. This was nearly six years later, when I was thirty-three and the collection had begun to take over the available living space. But it was growing very slowly because the material was becoming increasingly difficult to come by. The evidence I was uncovering was invariably negative, and it was becoming obvious that the exchange of technical information between the Russians and ourselves long before my father's accident made the defection idea very unlikely, in fact virtually impossible. And that is an objective evaluation based on the evidence up to that time, not the subjective reaction of a twelve-year-old boy.

"So far as I am or was aware," Barclay went on, "there was nothing irrational or fanatical about my continuing search for information about my father. It may have started like that, but at that particular time there were so many terrible things going on in the country that the idea of devoting so much time and mental effort to clearing my father's name, or some such romantic idea, was unrealistic, to say the least. I think the truth is that then, and during the intervening period up until now, the search for evidence was a habit, something to do with my mind. It happens to be an orderly mind which dislikes unexplained loose ends."

"Good," said Conlon.

Barclay stared at the other man for a moment, wondering if he was being complimented or simply encouraged to continue. The former possibility was so unlikely that he dismissed it, and went on, "I had become very well informed on the subject of space flight by then. At least, I knew enough to know what questions to ask if I could only visit the space center again . . ."

The space center had been under constant attack, both political and physical, for some time, because of the money it was costing to maintain it even in its powered-down condition and for the large quantities of fuel and other combustibles it contained. One of the reasons for the breakdown of society at the beginning of the Mad Years had been the burning of public and Governmental records by armed protest groups. Initially there had been a kind of logic behind the activity—destroying income-tax records, traffic violation or criminal records, even certain types of medical records, benefitted certain groups of people. But then the destruction became less selective and much more practical, because power and fuel supplies were diminishing rapidly and books, papers and filing cards kept one warm in winter.

His contact was still living securely and fairly comfortably within the inner perimeter of the space center, and he told Barclay that his job was more like that of a curator in a science museum than a fuel-systems engineer. He said that Barclay was welcome to call any time for a talk or a look around, but that if he was considering making the four-hundred-mile round trip to the center he would need a military escort.

As quickly as possible, Barclay set about providing himself with a military escort.

At that time Barclay was in the business of providing essential services to gangleaders and self-defended establishments in an area covering his own city and a few surrounding towns. It had been a very difficult and risky type of business to set up without losing his independence, but gradually he had been able to sell the powers that were in the area on the idea that someone like himself who owed allegiance to no particular group was a necessity. If a specialist medic or a car or TV mechanic was being bought or exchanged—technically the people concerned were not slaves, so it was referred to as a "change of protector"—a liaison man, someone neutral and therefore able to cross the heavily defended borders of the various gangleaders, was needed to arrange terms and conduct the transfer. In time he won the respect and even the friendship of some pretty terrifying characters and his people and vehicles were safe from all but a few ignorant free-lancers, and that was why he approached the local military commander with his most ambitious scheme until that time.

Unlike a few of the military establishments he had heard of, which were little more than forced-labor camps, Colonel MacIvor ran a very tight and orderly camp. He did not take people under his protection so much as offer them the chance to join his army, after which he gave them less and worked them harder than any gangleader. They became army farmers, army housewives, army schoolteachers, army children, army butchers, army bakers and, during the frequent power blackouts, army candlestick makers. Camp MacIvor covered six hundred acres at that time and was still spreading like a great khaki blot of calm and order into the surrounding anarchy. Discipline was strict and the ultimate punishment was not death but discharge, a fate reserved for persistent troublemakers. There were remarkably few of those, because although Colonel MacIvor demanded every last ounce of mental and physical effort from his people, he allowed them to keep their pride.

MacIvor's problem was that for a long time he had

badly needed certain electronics and communications specialists, vehicle mechanics and a few more decent cooks, while he had a comfortable surplus of medics and teachers. Six hundred miles away, Camp Peters had the same problem in reverse and was willing to swap. The Colonel had four transport helicopters and not enough fuel to use them for the job, and about twenty serviceable armed and armored personnel carriers with insufficient ammo to fight a six-hundred-mile running war—which he did not want to do in any case because most of the space aboard the vehicles would be taken up by spare fuel tanks for the trip, and the people being moved were noncombatants and incapable of using weapons effectively.

Besides, MacIvor was not a warlike man—a fact which he had successfully hidden from everyone except Barclay.

In the past Barclay had performed a few useful services for the Colonel, for which he had been paid in camp-grown food and maintenance on his three pickup trucks and TV set. But this was the biggest job that Barclay had ever taken on, and the negotiated terms were stiff. They included detouring sixty miles on the return journey so that he could spend a few days at the space center and using an agreed minimum of surplus space on the vehicles for his own personal purposes. In return he undertook to get the MacIvor medics to Camp Peters and the Peters specialists back to Camp MacIvor, using his reputation, influence and virtually every favor and obligation owed him to insure their safe passage.

The outward trip was not without incident, especially while they were traveling through areas close to Camp Peters where Barclay's name and reputation were not well known, but there were no casualties. One reason for this was that Barclay had advised the transfer personnel to take every possible opportunity to practice both their surgical skills and their bedside manner during stopovers. Because space was limited in their vehicles, they were therefore unable to accept the usual goods as payment for services rendered and received instead a priceless return of goodwill.

The arrival at the space center of a convoy of military personnel was welcome in an establishment whose security force was stretched to the limit. He had suggested that if his charges concealed the fact that they were noncombatants, their three-day stay would be much more pleasant all around.

Most of the center's senior technical people had left for other positions or died and only his contact, a small, graying man named Bob Saville, remembered Barclay's father. Saville did not mind answering questions or talking about the old days, reliving the past achievements while glossing over the disappointments, or retelling the rumors which had been going around after Dr. Goyer's death. But he had been a very junior member of the staff at that time. He did not know what Goyer had done to get into trouble. One rumor, later strenuously denied, was that the Doctor had falsified reports regarding the accidental loss of a shuttle, but all that Saville *knew* was that the Doc's technical material and files had been sealed in the security strongroom pending a Government investigation on his return from the space station. When he died on the station the investigation was dropped.

Saville did not know if Barclay's father had been connected with the Doctor's trouble, but the idea of his defecting was ridiculous.

Occasionally someone got the urge to look through the Doctor's papers, but there had always been someone else—an old-time friend of the Doc's, usually, with enough rank to have his way—who talked about morbid curiosity and suggested that Goyer's personal and professional effects should be left alone. Saville added that now, of course, the old-timers were dead and nobody cared anymore.

Next day Barclay wandered around the space center at will, looking through bulky flight plans in the library, examining the hardware and models in the museum and playing spaceman on one of the simulators while Bob

Saville talked excitedly about all the things they might have done if there had been more money and a little more time before their society sickened itself to death with the sight of its own warts.

At the end of one of the happiest days in his life came the most exciting night . . .

A mob breached the perimeter fence in three places shortly after midnight, forcing the outer security men to withdraw into the main complex. Unlike the earlier attacking mobs, which had acted like a beast with a thousand arms and legs and no brain, this one was being used tactically. Disciplined units within the mob were using the screamers, rioters and burners as cover to attack the center's food warehouse and fuel-storage tanks, and it was obvious that they were attacking to steal and not necessarily to destroy.

When the defenders realized what was happening and took the necessary countermeasures, the affair turned suddenly nasty. The mob was directed toward lightly defended buildings, which were quickly overrun and set alight. A few security men died at the hands of this mob and a large number of rioters perished in buildings which they themselves had set afire, but neither the food nor the fuel-storage dumps were broached.

By sunrise more than half of the center was burning and the mob had withdrawn to catch its collective breath. But it was obvious that relations between the space center and the adjoining city, never the most friendly in recent years, were ruined forever, and the most that the center's personnel and its visitors could expect was a long siege with very little hope of survival at the end of it. Barclay had therefore suggested holding peace talks with the mob's ringleaders, and before the sun had risen again he had negotiated terms.

It had been agreed that Barclay's convoy of noncombatants—who had learned to combat very well indeed during the preceding twenty-four hours—plus as many of the center's personnel as wished to accompany them could have motor transport, food and fuel for the trip back to Camp MacIvor. In return they would evacuate the center and leave the remaining food and fuel, a very considerable quantity of both, intact.

When Colonel MacIvor learned of the specialties and training of the personnel concerned he said that he would be happy to accept everyone. Barclay's convoy, grown five times larger in size, set off before the mob, which was becoming restive again, could change its mind . . .

"You seem to be an adept at talking your way out of trouble," said Conlon drily. He smiled suddenly and went on, "I suppose you were able to remove a few souvenirs, photographs, flight plans and the like, before you left?"

Barclay smiled in return, then shook his head. "I would have liked to, but items like that were in the museum block and had been burned during the first few hours of rioting," he replied. "All that was left was the contents of the security vault, so I loaded a truck with Dr. Goyer's files and filmed material and—"

"You did *what?*"

Conlon was on his feet, leaning over the desk and glaring down at him. Earlier, Barclay had wondered if the other's face was capable of showing any expression at all, but now there were so many different expressions pulling at his features that it was impossible to classify them. But one expression predominated as Conlon resumed his seat a few seconds later. It was a look of quiet exultation—the look, perhaps, of an investigator who has uncovered the key piece of evidence.

After a relatively brief but very violent dark age, Barclay thought sadly, the human race was trying to put society, technology and the legal processes back together again. But Law and Justice were not always the same thing.

The incident had occurred thirty years ago, he thought desperately, and so much had happened since then that the thought of being punished for it was ridiculous. Barclay was silent for a moment as he marshaled his defenses. Then he said, "I did not consider it an act of theft. I was simply removing valuable records which would otherwise have been destroyed."

"You removed valuable Government records," said Conlon quietly, "much of which were secret. Presumably you read this material?"

"Well, yes," said Barclay. "But you must understand that this was a chance I had of finding out about my father, studying Goyer's files. But most of the stuff was the Doctor's personal notes and photographs, a couple of the big, thick flight plans of missions my father had flown, detailed drawings of the instrument packages and experiments the shuttles had carried and things like that. But there was nothing that told me anything new about my father, and if the material was Top Secret then it still is."

"Explain," said Conlon.

"The Doctor's material," Barclay replied carefully, "was too difficult for me to understand. I tried to find textbooks which would help me understand it, and I'm still trying. But I'm a psychologist, if anything, not an experimental physicist and whatever else Dr. Goyer was. Nobody I knew could understand it, either."

"There are still a few people around who may be able to understand it," said Conlon, "and it is a strong point in your favor that you kept this material safely. But you realize that we will have to confiscate this material?"

Barclay stared at him without speaking.

Conlon frowned, then said, "Your private space collection is your life's work, perhaps? You would fall apart psychologically without it?"

As objectively as possible, Barclay considered the question. He thought of all those years of studying and cross-checking that steadily growing collection, and of the search which had been interrupted from time to time but which wealth and retirement had enabled him to resume. He had desperately wanted to be an astronaut when he was young, but now space flight was dead for lack of resources, both technical and material. Besides, if he was completely frank with himself about it, the search and the collection had been a hobby, something to do, good therapy when it was needed for his mother and himself, and really only a means to the end of finding out about his father.

His strongest feeling, Barclay realized suddenly, was not one of regret at losing the collection but of relief that Conlon might be more interested in acquiring it than in punishing him.

"You're welcome to it," said Barclay.

Smiling, Conlon said, "We should give you something in return . . ."

"No need," said Barclay. "Now that you seem to be more interested in the collection than in me, I'm so relieved that—"

"I'm still very much interested in you, Citizen Barclay," Conlon broke in, "and I am very far from being finished with you. I said that we owe you a favor, but I cannot decide whether it will be a punishment or a reward. I suppose it depends on whether or not you believe that it is better to journey hopefully than to arrive.

"Would you like to know," he went on very seriously, "what really happened to your father?"

He stared at Barclay's face for a moment, visibly coming to a decision; then he touched a button on his desk. The picture on the wall TV changed once again.

To the technically uninformed it was a boring film, simply the sound and vision record of a space shuttle mission in which a large and complex experiment package was transported from the space station to an unnamed destination. Barclay had studied similar material which he had taken from the center, and seeing it on film with a spoken commentary by Dr. Goyer did nothing to increase his understanding of what had been going on. Occasionally his father and another astronaut appeared on the film, but only because they happened to be examining the hardware of the package, which was the exclusive interest of the cameraman. Until a few minutes from the end, that is, when there was a five-second shot of the Doctor shaking hands with his father and the unfamiliar astronaut on the shuttle's flight deck, and all of them looking highly embarrassed about it.

This was followed by a sequence showing the shuttle detaching itself from the space station and shrinking from view while his father and the Doctor recited esoteric mathematical litanies to each other. For perhaps a minute the screen was black except for a few of the brighter stars; then there was an intensely brilliant flash of light in the center of the field of view and his father stopped talking suddenly.

So, eventually, did the Doctor.

Conlon cleared his throat and said, "Dr. Goyer lied to you, of course. He had no choice. That was a highly unofficial experiment, obviously, and conducted without the approval or knowledge of the authorities. Only Goyer, your father and a few top people in the center and on the station knew about the project. Only if it had been completely successful could they have announced the results and, hopefully, reversed the accelerating retreat from space and space-related sciences.

"The Doctor could not risk telling your mother or yourself about this, naturally. Your father had volunteered for the mission, which was to test the system of propulsion Goyer had devised. I am as ignorant as you are about the operating principles, except that it would make space travel, perhaps even interstellar travel, as cheap and easy as taking a trip on one of the intercontinental jets of the day. But I suspect that the Doctor felt responsible, perhaps even guilty, for what happened to your father. When you accused him of knowing more than he had told you . . . Well, he had to stop going to your house or talking to you."

For a moment Barclay stared silently at the wall TV. It showed his father asleep on a couch, his face haggard and tense despite the sedation—footage which had probably been shot at the end of a training session. In his mind's eye there was a picture of Dr. Goyer as he had been during the last few times Barclay had spoken to him—angry, somehow furtive, afraid and nothing like the smiling character with the inexhaustible supply of candy bars in his pockets who had been his only adult friend. Barclay blinked, then returned his attention to Conlon.

"Now I understand," he said. "And thank you."

Conlon nodded. Sympathetically, he said, "This film is part of material which became available only a few weeks ago. But now that your search is at an end, how do you feel? Is your father's memory still painfully fresh or have your feelings changed toward him?"

Barclay pushed back his chair and stood up. Coldly, he said, "I am grateful to you for telling me what really happened, and you have said that you are grateful to me for giving you the technical material I have collected over the past fifty years. Let's call it quits. This constant questioning about my feelings toward—"

"Be objective," said Conlon, returning to his cool and clinical tone.

"Very *well!*" said Barclay furiously. "My feelings are those of relief and satisfaction at knowing the answer at last, but I don't feel maudlin about it. Regarding my father himself, with fifty years of hindsight my feelings were bound to change. I know now that my mother and he were too emotionally dependent on each other, that if the positions had been reversed and he had lost her, the result would probably have been similar. Objectively, I would say that he was brave, dedicated, enthusiastic, considerate and, I realize now, not very tough. Subjectively, if you're interested, he was a very good father."

"I'm interested in both of you," said Conlon. "Now sit down!"

Barclay resumed his seat, then said dully, "You are grateful to me, but I have broken a very old law. I suppose the questions are an attempt by you to show your gratitude by trying to find extenuating circumstances. But now comes the sentence."

Conlon nodded and said, "From the evidence I have obtained about you I would say that it will probably be a life sentence. But before the sentence comes the judge's summing up, so please pay attention.

"Before your father's mission there were two other astronauts who suffered fictitious, Goyer-type accidents," he went on seriously, "but their families or friends accepted the Doctor's explanation of what had happened and, unlike you, did not make trouble. According to the material which came with the film I showed you, Goyer had been confident of success with your father's mission, but there was a reference to hyperdimensional travel and the danger of misplacing a decimal point when warping time and space. Just think of that. We will never be able to mount anything as expensive as Apollo again. But we still need space travel, if only as a challenge that will turn our minds outward again. We both know that, I believe. But Goyer and the others who remember his work are dead now, with the exception of one man who can't help because he is incapable of coherent—"

The other's emotional control was slipping badly. He shook his head angrily, then went on, "So we are left with one old man, yourself, whose steadfast belief that his father was a good guy, despite everything that was said or hinted about him, was directly responsible for preserving so much knowledge of the art. And we have the recently acquired film and records which are useless without—"

"Where did you get that film?" said Barclay suddenly. "I thought I'd cleaned out Goyer's files and—"

"You did," said Conlon drily. "It came back on one of the Goyer-modified shuttles, which crashed three weeks ago. It had returned safely from a very long trip in space and an incredibly short one in time, to find the spacestation deserted and deactivated . . ."

One of the two-man crew had died in the first few hours of the mission, during a period of EVA while he was trying to make adjustments to the Goyer equipment. The survivor got himself very thoroughly lost in interstellar space and had to try to find his way back by trial and error, never sure whether his next space jump would be of a million miles or twenty light-years, and even with his companion dead the ship's consumables would last for less than a week.

When he did eventually find his way back to the solar system and the space station, the station's air had leaked away. He could not perform the intricate series of tasks needed to reactivate the station while he was wearing a spacesuit, and neither could he power up the surface surveillance equipment or radio. The shuttle's radio was apparently on the blink, because he could not raise anyone with it. Dust and cobwebs do not gather in space stations so he had no way of knowing how long it had been deserted. But his air was dangerously low and he had to try for a landing without guidance from the surface . . .

"And he would have made it, too," Conlon went on, in a hushed, respectful voice, "if his old-time landing area had not been covered with homes and factory buildings. It is not an easy thing to divert in a supersonic glider on final approach, when it is close to stalling and its aerodynamic handling properties are those of a falling brick. But he managed to direct it well clear of the buildings before he dropped the message container with the film and records, then ejected himself."

Conlon canceled the picture on the wall TV and stood up. He said, "It was rough country and he was lucky to escape with a broken ankle and a few bruises, but mentally he is in very poor shape. Quite apart from any humane considerations, we, if we are to have any chance at all of rebuilding the Goyer drive, must have him sane and healthy and cooperative. That will be your job—your sentence, if you like.

"Frankly, Citizen Barclay, I have been playing games with you," he went on. "For this I apologize. You will understand, I'm sure, that when a candidate is being interviewed for a difficult and responsible job, the process is not a pleasant one for the man concerned. I am, of course, in Medicine and not Law, and I shall not be playing games with you again. Instead I shall do everything possible to assist you with treatment.

"It will not be an easy job," he continued as he moved toward the inner door of his office and opened it. "The patient came through a lot during that interstellar trip. He wasn't sure of finding his way back, and I think there are feelings of guilt regarding the death of his companion, but this may be due to a hyperdeveloped sense of responsibility. Also, he is seriously disoriented and completely out of his depth in this alien society of today, with its dueling and, by his standards, incredibly harsh laws. And despite everything we have tried to tell him, he wants to see his young wife and son, who, so far as his time sense is concerned, were alive and well a few weeks ago.

"You can see that it will need someone with patience and understanding to bring him back," Conlon said quietly. He stood to the side of the door and motioned Barclay to enter before going on. "Someone who had lived through the past fifty years and knows from experience what adaptations were and are necessary, someone with a personal as well as a scientific interest in what he is doing. In short, someone who is family . . ."

Very gently, Conlon closed the door behind him so as to leave him alone with his patient for the first few minutes. Barclay looked down at the sleeping figure on the couch with the TV camera trained on his head and shoulders, the same head and shoulders that he had seen on the screen in the outer office, while he tried to blink away the fog which was keeping him from seeing the face clearly.

Quietly, he said, "Hello, Dad . . ."

In Loving Memory

EVERY DAY ROLSTON went for a walk. Today, as he'd done daily since the beginning of Kallec's twenty-four-month summer, he left the cool silence of the Dome through one of the small ground-level seals and went outside. He walked under the swollen baleful thing that was the summer sun of Kallec, carefully picking his steps around places where the surface had become near plastic with heat, following a path that never changed. His thoughts and memories, spilling through channels etched deep by the acid of self-guilt, were also much the same every day, and his mouth had forgotten how to smile.

His feet seemed to find their own way as he walked, for Rolston's eyes were not on his surroundings, but were staring instead into a distance of time and space. The things he was seeing were reflected in them: the awful yearning, the bitter confusion, and the raging fire of impatience that burned in his soul. There were many times when Rolston's eyes shone with a light that was not quite sane.

A mile from the dome a cracked and blackened hill arose, burned free of every trace of vegetation. Awkward in the stiff confines of his heavy heat-suit, Rolston climbed it until he came to the shiny white stone at its summit. It resembled a giant, lumpy egg. He stood over it, looking down at the smooth whiteness with tormented, angry eyes.

"You fool," he whispered. "You little fool . . ."

Abruptly he flung himself on the burning ground beside where Naleen lay, and let the pain of memory wash through him again.

Why had she refused to take the shots? That was the question Rolston kept asking himself. The Medic on their team had pronounced her fit, and their Psychologist had given her a high rating in adaptability and intelligence, adding that few if any of the usual courses of reeducation would be necessary to fit her for life in any civilized society. There were neither mental nor physical barriers to stop her, yet she had refused.

It wasn't that she hadn't trusted him. The way that Naleen and he felt about each other left no doubt about that. But what made her refusal so baffling was the fact that she was the last Kallecian *not* to submit to the shots, the only one on the whole Godforsaken planet . . .

Kallec was a crazy, murderous planet. It was a small, dense world, with a shallow elliptical orbit about its primary that gave it ten years of temperate autumn-winter-spring and two years of a summer the heat of which made the planetary surface molten in places. The captain of the survey ship which had found it took one look, and named the planet "Phoenix." It was the only name that such a world *could* have, especially when he discovered that it contained intelligent, extra-human life, and found out how the natives adapted to their hellish environment.

The survey ship had established a limited form of communication. With some reluctance its captain had to erase his pet name of "Phoenix" from the ship's log and substitute the natives' name for their world, which was

"Kallec." But he made another discovery shortly afterward that overshadowed everything else. Phoenix-Kallec was under sentence of death. The ship's astronomy section reported that the planet's orbit was no longer an ellipse, but had become a diminishing spiral that would eventually plunge Kallec into its own sun. The end would not be for thirty or so years, but the planet would be rendered uninhabitable—for *any* form of life—long before then.

The captain reported the finding of an inhabited system and his astronomer's predictions at once, and told of the pitifully few natives who even then managed to survive the planet's summer. He urged that the Bureau of Extra-human Education give the planet top priority. This was done, and a team of Educators was on Kallec just two years later.

This was to be a rush job, Rolston's team had been told, to be completed before the onset of the Kallecian summer. Otherwise the native population would have shrunk still further. When they landed it was mid-spring and summer was less than two Earth-standard years away.

The survey ship had already knocked a fair-sized crack in the barrier of language. Rolston, as the team's linguist, had to widen that crack until the barrier itself collapsed and he could not only communicate, but exchange philosophical concepts without the slightest trace of ambiguity distorting his meaning. Only then could the others begin their work; the psychologist, gradually and with incredible subtlety, to change the Kallecian mind, until the natives themselves practically demanded that the team Medic change their bodies as well.

When that occurred their work of reeducation on Kallec would be complete, and not a single native would have been forced into doing anything he hadn't wanted to do. It would be smooth. Rolston knew it was for the natives' own good, but sometimes the basic ethics of it all worried him.

How could Earth humans be certain what was best

for those who were . . . different? But doubts like that troubled him seldom. He liked his work.

The Dome—a great, air-conditioned hemisphere capable of sheltering the entire native population, and feeding them, too—had been built. To impress the natives with the Earthmen's contempt for the summer heat to come, it had been placed on the planet's equator. Then the construction men, after making sure it would function properly, packed their robots and departed, leaving the team alone to do the real work.

The great Dome was thrown open to the Kallecians, and, with natural curiosity, more and more of them had come to marvel at it, and enjoy the coolness, eventually even to taste the various synthetic foods. After that the going was much easier, because the Kallecians were very human indeed.

The volumes of unwritten laws regarding Educators who formed emotional attachments for their charges would have filled a fair-sized bookshelf, and all of them began by warning against it. Rolston had taken those warnings to heart, determined that nothing like that was ever going to happen to *him*.

Then he met Naleen.

His Psychologist, Jennings, tried to make him realize the purely objective nature of the phenomenon, pointing out that what Rolston called "love" was merely a complicated but easily understood interaction on the glandular level brought about by sight, sound and tactile stimuli—a fact which he should know quite well himself. But the team psychologist's scorn was tempered more than slightly by deference—Rolston was, after all, his chief—so his warnings had no effect at all, and he was forced by honesty to admit that Naleen was, as far as he knew, a mature, mentally healthy person. The Medic, Munsen, who was over twice Rolston's age and who deferred to nobody, adopted the bluff, fatherly approach. When he saw it was getting him nowhere, he reminded Rolston sharply that one wrong move on the part of a team member could very easily turn the natives against them, thus ruining the project completely. He still wasn't getting through. The Medic lost his temper then, telling Rolston that obviously he meant to do as he liked no matter what or whose advice he asked for. Stiffly, Munsen gave his professional opinion that the native in question was physically healthy, female, and completely human except for the *grel* gland system and the skin markings associated with it. He'd added grumpily that successful interbreeding was highly probable, providing, of course, that she submitted to Standardization treatment.

But Naleen didn't submit to the shots. Rolston tried very hard to make her do so even before the realization came that he was in love with her, and when it did come, he tried much harder. During the language-instruction sessions he always guided the conversation on to the subject of the other planets and peoples in the galaxy, telling her how different most of them were, yet how basically similar, and stressing the fact to her that there could only be universal peace and happiness when there were no differences left at all.

Sometimes he didn't get his meaning across properly. He stammered, his mouth dried up, and he felt like a tightly wound spring when she was near him. He couldn't take his eyes off her.

She wore the short, white tunic that was customary on Kallec. Her perfectly formed face and limbs were tanned a deep, intense brown, and every square inch of skin was covered by the delicate gold tracery of the *grel* network—like a second capillary system laid outside the skin. This, and the mass of pure white hair that was another protection against Kallec's blazing summer heat, was the only visual difference between her and an Earth girl. But mostly it was her eyes that he watched, eyes that shone with enthusiasm and excitement when he talked of those far places and strange people. Reorientation of the natives was really the Psychologist's job, but Jennings was very busy with about a score of Kallecians who were all on the point of asking for Standardization, and doing the other's job for him was, in this case, very much a pleasure.

It was so pleasant that gradually her instruction began to make inroads into his leisure. He didn't mind that at all. The happiest time of his day was when they walked together at sunset, just before the night rains came. Spring was far advanced, and all about them the balloon seeds were almost pulling their parent plants out of the ground. Occasionally groups of them would break free with soft, tearing sounds and climb toward the surface of their atmospheric ocean like clusters of brightly-colored bubbles. He would explain or argue some point of logic or ethics with her, or sometimes just talk about nothing at all. Gradually, as the days passed and the now seedless vegetation began to shrivel and die in the fiery advance of summer, what had started as a pleasure became instead a necessity. He found suddenly that he couldn't do without seeing her, not even for a single day.

Unfortunately, the heat of their arguments kept pace with the rapidly increasing temperature, until one day they'd boiled over.

That day they stood on the hillside which overlooked the Dome and verbally tore each other to shreds. He called her stupid, narrow-minded, barbaric. She was a witless savage who could not now and who probably never would be able to understand an abstraction like altruism, or get it through her thick skull that the Earthmen were here only to help her. Only a moron, or a suicidal maniac would want to stay on this roasting-spit of a world . . .

"You want to help me selfish," Naleen cut in. Her face was tight with anger, and her *grel* lines stood out on it in sharp relief. "You not alt . . . altru . . ." She stumbled at the unfamiliar word.

"Yes. I want you for myself," Rolston admitted angrily. "But that's a different thing. That's . . ." He tried to explain, but he was hot and sticky and terribly impatient with these senseless little arguments. Suddenly he wanted away from it all—the planet, the team, everything. His explanation was delivered in a tone of such scorn that it became nothing more or less than a deadly insult.

But Naleen wasn't completely defenseless. She'd grown very close to him over the past months, far closer than he'd realized. Naleen knew his weaknesses, and she said things which hurt him as badly as he was hurting her. The quarrel raged until they were shouting at each other in their native tongues, their faces only inches apart. Then abruptly his arms were around her and her tears were hot on his neck, and he was telling her that he was rotten and contemptible and that he hadn't meant the things he'd said, and that he loved her and wanted to be with her as long as he lived.

Through her tears she told him much the same things, and it was a long time before they tore themselves apart.

They didn't argue after that for three whole days.

It should have been easy, Rolston knew. All he had to do was make Naleen realize subconsciously as well as consciously that she lived on only one world among millions, and that it was possible to live on almost any one of the others after she left Kallec. He also knew that if she would only submit to the standardization treatment, the few remaining Kallecians who hadn't taken the shots would follow her example, because they held her in very great respect. Kallec would then be evacuated on schedule and everybody would be happy.

Again and again Rolston expanded on the work of the Educators to her, and about the event in the incredibly distant past which made that work necessary.

So long ago that not even a mythology of it remained, a human race had begun an interstellar colonization program. But that expansion had been premature. Instead of first developing a fast means of interstellar travel—such as the warp drive of the Earthmen—they used ships that were nothing but giant, reaction-driven shells—relying on their tremendous knowledge of the biological sciences to see them through. By traveling for centuries in suspended animation they arrived at the planets of other suns. These planets were rarely if ever suitable for them, but because they must have lacked the technology to either look for more suitable ones or alter the existing ones to suit themselves, they were forced into the only alternative to living forever aboard their ships.

They adapted to the planets.

And on hundreds of worlds throughout the galaxy, they thrived.

On the frigid world of Wimarr Nine, the animated balls of fur that greeted the first Earthmen explorers were not at first recognizable as being human, but they were. And under the reeking, corrosive atmosphere of Toscammerlang Four there was a thriving civilization, also human. The ocean world of Resslone held a race of human amphibians, and so on.

Not all the differences were visually detectable, but they were there. The ability to breathe water, to adapt to mind-staggering variations of heat and cold, and even limited forms of physical metamorphosis in some cases. Nowhere did the Earthmen find sub- or superhuman entities; instead there were intelligent human beings who—because of the addition of certain specialized organs—were perfectly suited to their environment. *Extra*-humans.

And the extrahuman population of the galaxy meant to the Earthmen just one thing. War.

That was the part which was hard to get across to Naleen. All those planets, each with a culture and an ethical and moral code shockingly different from each other and, in most cases, mutually repugnant to each other. Luckily, none of these races had reattained interstellar flight. But when they did . . .

The Earthmen had had enough of war, and they were selfish enough not to want to become involved in some future interstellar conflict. They were altruistic enough, however, to set about trying to make such a war impossible.

Standardization, the elimination of physical and mental differences, seemed to be the answer. If every civilization held similar ethical standards, war should be impossible. At least, so they hoped. They therefore set about making—by means of weather-control installations, ecological engineering, and the specialist teams of Educators—every inhabited planet they found into another Earth.

Kallec was a different matter, just a simple shots-and-shift job—Standardize and Evacuate, in official language. The Kallecians should be glad to leave such a murderous environment. Rolston couldn't understand why Naleen seemed so fanatically attached to the place. But she was.

Even when he told her for the hundredth time that he wanted to marry her and take her with him wherever he went, she still held back. He pleaded with her. He told of the worlds she could see with him, planets where summer was no hotter than the inside of the Dome and where plants grew all the year round—and flowers, too, which were plants so beautiful that she'd have to see them for herself. And the civilizations, and cities. He told her of the gorgeous way in which the female inhabitants—both human and extrahuman—dressed. Naleen listened to all these things with wondering, wistful eyes, but she still refused to take the shots. She loved him, but . . .

Awkwardly, Rolston asked the help of the team psychologist.

"You've been trying too hard," the Psychologist told him bluntly, "overselling your product. And you've further messed things up by telling her too much—*far* too much—about the purpose of the Educators and the extrahuman problem we're trying to solve. In selling, one dwells on the quality of the goods, not on the margin of the profit, if any, that they bring.

"Naleen would have been Standardized long ago," he added angrily, "if I'd taken her. But no. You wanted to help out. You had to get emotionally involved with the girl and mess everything up so much that I can't do a thing—"

Rolston used some rugged language to the Psychologist, to which the other listened with clinical interest. Then he apologized and left to find Naleen again.

Finally he got her to agree to *talk* about the shots to Dr. Munsen.

That was a bad mistake.

The Medic was understandably impatient at the continued indecisiveness of the last Unstandardized person remaining on the planet—the person who'd already delayed the completion of the job by over two months because of the fact that none of the other natives would leave without her. The team's home office was also growing restive about the delay—the team was always needed elsewhere, urgently. And anyway, Munsen objected fiercely to spending his time just waiting for somebody to make up their mind. Perhaps that impatience hadn't been masked very well, or he too had pressed his arguments too hard.

Naleen was under intense strain, being practically split in two by the opposing forces of environmental conditioning and her emotional feeling for Rolston—both of them almost irresistible. She'd been very quiet when she'd met Rolston afterward, and thoughtful.

Rolston, believing that she was on the point of giving in, determined to finish the business for good. His pleas and arguments were forceful, undoubtedly. But a bludgeon would have had more finesse.

Naleen blew up.

She began by telling him that she was a freak, and that he only wanted to drag her around as a sort of pet animal. Dr. Munsen had told her that the skin markings would never quite disappear in her, or the *grel* gland system connected with them, though the shots would neutralize it. He was abnormal for wanting to marry a freak like her. People would laugh at her wherever she went with him, and he'd be laughing at her, too. He was a sadist, she accused, an egomaniac. She hated him, his team, and all the Earthmen there ever were—but mostly him. She didn't have enough of his words to tell him how much she hated him, but she was going to try . . .

Rolston replied harshly that she didn't know what she

was talking about, and she'd no business trying to analyze him with the few scraps of elementary psychology that the Educators had taught her. Dr. Munsen had been angry because she was the cause of his having to stay here, and this must have made him tactless and caused some misunderstanding.

But his replies didn't satisfy Naleen. Her accusations became wilder and more hysterical, and his answers to them grew angrier and more contemptuous.

The whole thing was merely a last outburst—a final release of mental pressure—before her final surrender. He should have realized that and let her blow off steam. But instead he went on making scathingly logical answers to accusations that Naleen knew herself to be silly. He should have held on, but he was every bit as impatient as Dr. Munsen to get away from Kallec, and the heat and sheer frustration made his nerves like taut wires. He needed the momentary luxury of losing his temper just a little bit; his tightly knotted nervous system demanded it.

But when he lost his temper, he lost it all.

Hazily, he knew that he had sunk his fingers into her shoulders, and shaken her until her teeth clicked together and her glorious white hair fell all over her face. He had heard his own voice shouting that he was going to shake some sense into her, but there was an unreal, dreamlike quality to it. It *couldn't* have been his voice, he couldn't bring himself to hurt Naleen in any way. Not *Naleen*. But the passion-thickened voice and the viselike fingers were his all right, and he was suddenly shocked back into reality when Naleen twisted free and ran away crying.

Desperately Rolston began running after her, for he knew what she might do.

He caught her, almost, at the exit port—the seal nearly closed on his fingers. Then she was through, and a viewer over the port showed her running madly over the burning ground away from the Dome.

With desperate haste Rolston struggled into a heatsuit, keeping his eyes on the wavering, heat-distorted image of Naleen that grew steadily smaller in the view-screen. It was early summer; unprotected, he wouldn't last two minutes in the hell outside the Dome. When he got out at last she was a hundred yards away. In an agony of guilt and sorrow he called her back. She kept on going. He tried to follow her, but the cumbersome suit held him back. She drew steadily away, and he saw her climb the hillside that they'd come to know so well, the pitiless glare of that blast-furnace sun making her hair and tunic a blob of brilliant light against the blackened ground surface. Near the summit he saw her slow, stagger, and collapse.

When he reached her ten minutes later she was lying curled up in a fetal position, and the things the heat was doing to her made him gag. He couldn't bear to lift her, or touch her even. She was slowly . . . bubbling and changing color. Great globules of sticky white stuff were forming on her skin, bursting, and spreading—faster and faster. He tried to shade her with his body, but he knew it was hopeless from the start. He forced his eyes to look at the thing that had been Naleen, and slowly, monotonously, he cursed the sun.

He was still crouching over her when the team Psychologist and two Kallecians came out to take him back. The natives were also in heatsuits—the Standardization shots having neutralized their *grel* function, they needed them now as much as the Earthmen—and were being sympathetic and philosophical about Rolston's loss in voices that were too highly amplified. Naleen, they told him solemnly, was great, highly respected and unusual . . . or words to that effect. Her parents also had been great and had lived through many summers, very many summers. The natives kept talking about how great and unusual Naleen and her parents were until Rolston felt like smashing their kindly, reassuring skulls together.

An hour after they returned to the Dome, a native spokesman informed the team that, because of what had happened to Naleen, nobody was going to leave Kallec until the end of the present summer.

All that had been twenty months ago, Rolston thought as he gave the shiny white rock on the scorched hillside a final look before he began retracing his steps to the Dome, and the pain and anxiety, the sheer frustration and the awful, maddening uncertainty were as bad today as they had been then. Worse even. The natives hadn't blamed him, he knew; they understood and left him alone. Dr. Munsen, though he still must have felt burning impatience at being forced to remain on Kallec with nothing much to do, neither talked about it nor showed it in any way; he, too, understood. But the team Psychologist, on the other hand, showed his professional concern over Rolston's condition, and had hinted several times that he'd like to do something about it. But while he had drugs and techniques at his disposal that could wipe the whole Naleen incident from Rolston's memory and make him normally well adjusted again, the same code of ethics that forbade the Medic's administering the shots to Naleen against the girl's will kept him from using his wonderfully efficient curative methods until he was requested to do so.

Rolston, therefore, continued his daily walks. Slowly as Kallec climbed toward aphelion along its eccentric, near-cometary orbit, summer merged into autumn. The night rain which converted the outside of the Dome into a world of boiling mud and superheated steam began to collect in cracks and gullies, and remain as a liquid for longer periods each morning. The naked, cruel rocks were covered and softened by layers of dried mud that increased in thickness each day, and the balloon seeds, which had been riding out the summer in the relative coolness of the upper atmosphere, fell shrunken and heavy to begin their cycle of life all over again.

Rolston discarded the heatsuit for shorts and a light cloak. Daily he walked and sat beside the shiny white rock on a hillside that was now green with new life. Sometimes he lay and talked to it, going over conversations they'd had, or saying intimate, loving things. On other days he was sullen and silent and barely looked at it. One day he lost control and beat on it with his bare fists until the white perfection was smudged red. Sanity returned to him only when he felt a hand on his shoulder, and he heard the team Psychologist's voice saying gently, "Take it easy, Prince Charming. You'll never get your Sleeping Beauty that way. Now will you . . . ?"

His daily walks continued—until the day he saw a crack in that flawless white rock.

The sight hit him like a physical blow. He felt sick and weak. All the frustration and anxiety that had been building up in his mind over the past two years of summer came boiling up, seeking release. He paced backward and forward beside it, wringing his bandaged hands together and talking to himself, and the look in his eyes was wild. As he saw the single crack, caused by the steady drop in Kallec's temperature, widen and become many, he wept a little. But not for long. When the rock began to fall apart like a cracked egg, he gave a shout of pure exultation and started tearing the loose pieces away.

Naleen rose, the last few fragments of her heat-resistant *grel* chrysalis falling to the ground. She was more than half asleep, and the golden network of lines that had exuded the chrysalis were still crusted by powderings of that rock-hard, organic insulator. Rolston brushed it gently off her face while she breathed deep, shuddering breaths—the first she'd taken since going into summer hibernation two Earth years ago. Then abruptly Rolston was trying to squeeze the recently regained breath out of her.

They held each other tightly for a very long time, until Naleen got her mouth free long enough to speak with it:

"I want to see Dr. Munsen again . . ."

The Apprentice

I

UP UNTIL ELEVEN thirty a.m. Arthur Richard Nicholson, the personnel manager of Coop's department store, had had a fairly average day.

He was savoring that warm, pleasant and positive feeling of one who both enjoys and is completely on top of a job, when the sound of feet and voices came through to him from the outer office.

The voices were low, but the quick, irregular thudding of four feet on the waiting-room carpet told him that Harnrigg was in trouble again. All his pleasure was swept away by a wave of irritation. Striding across to the connecting door, he yanked it open and snapped, "Come inside, please. And sit down. Those who can," he added sourly.

The trio which filed into his office was composed of Redmond, the ground-floor supervisor, a good-looking salesgirl whose make-up had been wrecked by tears, and Harnrigg. Harnrigg entered last, clumping softly across the carpet to stand between the chairs taken by Redmond and the girl. Watching the being, Nicholson could not decide whether it resembled a furry walrus with hooves, or an outsize skunk with arms. Harnrigg's physical aspect was centaurlike—four legs, two arms and a head which had eyes, nose and mouth in the usual positions. In addition it possessed a dark-brown furry pelt, dramatically marked by a broad white line which ran along the spine and into the tail, which was large and bushy. Chest and arms were almost manlike, and were topped by a head which might have come from a furry sea lion. The most obvious features were the eyes, which were very large and sad.

Part of the sadness might be due to the fact that Harnrigg was some thirty-seven light-years from home.

"What's the trouble this time?" Nicholson said.

Redmond cleared his throat. He said, "Horseplay at the music counter, I'm afraid. Miss Clarke and Mr. Harnrigg were, er, dancing to one of the demonstration tapes. My arrival startled them, they lost balance and a display stand was knocked over, by Mr. Harnrigg's tail. Estimated cost of damage seven pounds, three shillings and sixpence. Including tax."

Some of the other floor supervisors would have elaborated on a case like this for fifteen minutes or more, but Redmond preferred assisting misplaced shoppers and placating children who had lost their mammas to putting his staff on the carpet. That had been one of Nicholson's reasons for placing Harnrigg on Redmond's floor; only serious misdemeanors would be reported, and maybe he would get a rest from this extraterrestrial apprentice and his troubles.

But that, apparently, was not to be.

"Well?" he said sharply to Harnrigg and the girl.

"I . . . I'm sorry, Mr. Nicholson," Miss Clarke said, on the verge of tears again. "We were only tapping our feet. At . . . at first, that is . . . I mean, there were no customers about . . ."

"It was my fault entirely," Harnrigg broke in, his tremendous bass voice filling the office. "I like Earth music very much, and this piece was such that some form of rhythmic movement was forced on me. I asked Miss Clarke if she would teach me to boop-jog."

"I see," said Nicholson.

It was common knowledge that Harnrigg's race derived intense enjoyment from earthly music—their culture, although very advanced in many ways, was musically starved. Placing the being at that counter had seemed a good idea. The Clarke girl had not objected, and it was Nicholson's private conviction that the people who bought the currently popular boop-jog recordings were so far gone already that being served by a furry centaur would not even make them blink. Working so close to all that music should have made Harnrigg very happy.

Apparently it had made him delirious.

Nicholson addressed the girl. His remarks varied little from those used on similar occasions. Miss Clarke was a fully trained member of the selling staff. As well as being courteous, personally tidy and conscientious in her duties, an assistant was required to show a good example to trainees placed in her charge, especially when the trainee in question was an extraterrestrial. Miss Clarke should be ashamed of herself, Nicholson concluded.

Stopping just short of pronouncing sentence, he turned to Harnrigg. "And as for you," he went on, "I can only say that I am disappointed and very angry. You came here seeking a job which would let you meet Earth people and see the planet, and insisting that you wanted to be treated as one of the boys. Well, I can tell you that if you were being treated as one of the boys on this occasion you would have been on the street five minutes ago! Wait outside, both of you," he concluded grimly. "I have to discuss this matter with your floor supervisor."

When Miss Clarke and the centaur had gone, Nicholson said, sighing: "I know Harnrigg's record. Is there anything previous against the girl?"

Redmond shook his head.

"What do you advise doing with these . . . these boop-joggers?" Nicholson asked impatiently. "For my part, I'd run them out, Harnrigg anyway. I'm a bit sorry for the awkward so-and-so, to tell the truth, but this Harnrigg character has caused nothing but trouble . . ."

"I know," Redmond put in quietly. "But he grows on one, and the trouble wasn't always his fault. And the Clarke girl is very good at her job."

"Whose side are you on?" said Nicholson irritably.

Redmond grinned. "Theirs."

Nicholson rose and headed for the outer office, then changed his mind and sat down again. He felt angry, indecisive and discontented. These feelings seemed to have been with him more and more frequently since Harnrigg had arrived. But Nicholson told himself that he couldn't go blaming the apprentice for his moodiness and fits of bad temper.

Angrily he forced his thoughts into more constructive channels. He cleared his throat and prepared to rid himself both of the problem and this soft-hearted floor supervisor who insisted on acting like a defense counsel when it was his duty to side with the prosecution.

"Tell them they're suspended until Friday, pending my final decision," Nicholson said briskly. "That will give them a couple of days to stew in their own juice. On Friday give them a good lecture. And none of your fatherly more-in-sorrow-than-in-anger routines, d'you hear? My reason for suspending them," he ended, "is to have time to find another spot for Harnrigg."

When Redmond and the others had gone Nicholson tried to work himself into a pleasant, engaging and forceful frame of mind. He was going to try selling Harvey of the Toy department the idea of taking Harnrigg into his section again.

The Toy buyer was a "good boss." Nicholson hoped that his good nature would extend to centaurs.

"Oh, *no!*" Harvey protested when Nicholson phoned him. "I had him the first two weeks he came here. He's *awkward*. Some of the children are frightened by him,

and others want to ride him like a donkey, which fright-
ens their parents. Apparently you drummed this
customer-is-always-right stuff into him so thoroughly
that he was willing to give a kid a ride around the department if it would help him sell a doll's house. Some
of my girls thought this an unfair advantage," Harvey
added reflectively. "Harnrigg was away ahead of them
with commission. Space behind my counters is cramped
and with the Christmas stocks coming in it will be more
so. We'd trip over him and he'd break things. I'll take
him if you insist, but I'd as soon not . . ."

When Nicholson let the receiver drop he had decided
that Harvey's objections were sound. His next call was
to Furniture.

While waiting for Fielding, the Furniture buyer, to be
brought to the phone Nicholson visualized the great department, which covered nearly all the fourth floor.
There was a big central aisle along which stood lines of
tables, couches and assorted dining and bedroom suites.
The side aisles were also wide, though there were a few
awkward corners here and there. Nicholson was becoming adept at estimating Harnrigg's powers of maneuver-
ability in any given space, and he decided that there
would be a few scratched surfaces before the being got
used to the place, but then what was the polishing shop
for? He prepared to be very charming to the Furniture
buyer.

"I won't have him!" Fielding burst out. "I don't want
that hairy brute dancing about in my department. Oh,
yes, I heard all about it. You should have fired him!"
Fielding had stomach trouble and it showed in his disposition.

"Fielding, yours is one of the few departments where
he could turn around without breaking something . . ."

"I won't have him near me! Why doesn't he go
home!"

The Radio and TV department he considered and
dismissed at once, and also China, Electrical and the
other sections which dealt in valuable and easily damaged merchandise. Jewelry, Cosmetics and Lingerie

were out also; Harnrigg would have looked ridiculous in those surroundings. Men's Wear would have been ideal—their buyers raised no objections and the floor space between their stock fixtures was ample—but in those departments the assistant was often the arbiter in matters of fit, style and appearance, and what customer would believe an assistant whose dress consisted only of a watch and four hoof protectors! Pharmacy required special training and Grocery was out. The sight of meat, even tinned meat, made Harnrigg ill.

After an hour's solid telephoning, Nicholson had the possibilities narrowed down to three: Blankets, Garden Implements and Carpets. But the buyers concerned were not very cooperative. They had nothing personal against Harnrigg, but all were men close to retirement age who ran good, paying departments, and they were too set in their ways to welcome a disturbing influence.

The selling end was beginning to look hopeless, but the store employed a small army of clerical and maintenance staff. There were repair men, painters, carpenters and cleaners. Making Harnrigg a cleaner seemed the ideal solution.

But would he take a job like that?

II

AT THE INITIAL interview Harnrigg had told him that he wanted to meet people and see the sights of Earth, and that he would work hard to earn the money to do so. He further stated that it was a point of honor with him that he earn what money he received, and he wanted no special privileges. Harnrigg was a proud type despite the donkey-rides and the boop-jogging.

Contact had been made with his species ten years previously, but even now there was only a handful of his race on Earth at any given time. This meant that, despite the request that no special consideration be given him, Harnrigg was in effect a guest of the planet.

One did not set one's guests to polishing floors and mopping out washrooms.

Nicholson was still trying to find the answer, and was rapidly losing his temper in the process, when his phone rang. The abrasive quality of the voice identified the caller as Hammond, the store manager himself.

"Nicholson! I hear you suspended our extraterrestrial, and may fire him. Why?"

"Er, some disciplinary action seemed necessary . . ." Nicholson began.

"Disciplinary action my foot!" Hammond's voice blared. "You were told to find a place here where he could work happily and efficiently, and that is your *job!* The fact that Harnrigg is an e-t may entail a little more work for you, but that is all." The voice became quieter, but with a dangerous edge to it as Hammond went on: "This is the first time one of Harnrigg's race has come here to work at an ordinary job. As I've already explained to you, his presence at the store is pub-

215

licity for us of the most valuable and subtle kind. We aren't using him as part of some cheap advertising stunt, but are employing him as an ordinary member of the staff. He has trade-union protection, shares in sickness and superannuation benefits, and receives the usual apprentice's wages. This demonstrates our initiative, far-sightedness and racial tolerance. We do not want to lose him."

"I've been trying—" began Nicholson again.

"Obviously not hard enough!" Hammond snapped, and hung up.

Nicholson banged down his own receiver with a force which threatened to shatter the plastic. So he wasn't trying hard enough! What *had* he been doing for the past hour? Bouncing out of his chair, he stamped out of the office. He was fed up with this job, the store and everyone in it. He was going out to lunch before he hit somebody.

During the meal Nicholson calmed down but his feeling of angry discontent would not leave him, which was strange. He had always preferred dealing with people as people rather than as adjuncts to increasing business, and had sought promotion in the administrative rather than the selling side. Well, he had risen as far as it was possible to go. If he had not been scared of the dog-eat-dog atmosphere of the selling side, he might have been in Hammond's place today.

By the time Nicholson got back from lunch he was fed up with himself too.

There was a spaceman waiting in his office.

"Good afternoon," said Nicholson respectfully. The sight of the trim black uniform with the tight, silver-edged beret and surgeon-commander's insignia gave him a funny feeling in his chest. It was like meeting royalty. *The things this man has seen,* Nicholson thought; *the places he's been* . . . Despite the spaceport being only twenty miles away, this was the first time he had spoken to a space officer.

"My name is Telford," said the visitor, smiling and

getting to his feet. "Friends, including a mutual acquaintance called Harnrigg, shorten it to Joe."

Harnrigg again! Abruptly the aura of glamor died from around the commander.

Telford ignored Nicholson's expression and said cheerfully, "Harnrigg has to bunk at the spaceport—none of the hotel or boarding-house people will accept members of his race, I'm ashamed to say. When I saw him wandering about during working hours I asked him what was wrong. He wouldn't tell me. What *is* wrong?"

In spite of the light tone it was obvious that the commander was deeply concerned for the alien. So Nicholson gave him a quiet, objective résumé of the apprentice's record to date.

"I suppose I could tolerate having him here because of the prestige," Nicholson went on, "but none of the department heads want him, which means he isn't going to have a happy time wherever I send him. I'm beginning to think that staying here is a punishment he doesn't deserve."

"He isn't a criminal," said Telford drily.

"I know that!" Nicholson snapped. Irritably he went on, "He's a fairly normal type, not too young, unmarried and with itchy feet. The Earth team on his planet distributed a lot of illustrated literature, translated copies of the *National Geographic* and so on, and he fell in love with Niagara Falls or the Matterhorn. I've had several long interviews with him, you know, and once I had to listen to him being homesick for a solid hour. Wouldn't it be kinder," Nicholson went on seriously, "to take him out of this place? There are very few centaurs on Earth at the moment, and all except Harnrigg seem to be getting the red-carpet treatment. Why not send him on a conducted tour as a goodwill gesture, and then pack him off home? Why does he have to *work?*"

Telford leaned forward to give emphasis to his reply. He said soberly, "Because Harnrigg is the most important centaur to visit us to date, and he must earn his keep."

"But if he's such a VIP . . ."

"He isn't. On the contrary, Harnrigg is a very ordinary, not-too-intelligent and slightly maladjusted type."

I agree with you there, Nicholson said under his breath. Despite the awe he felt for the other's rank and profession, he wanted to tell the commander to talk sense.

Nicholson tried not to fidget as Telford began talking about Earth's first contacts with the centaur race. Gradually he began to realize that the commander *had* been talking sense.

During the years which followed the first contact, scientists and other great minds of both races had exchanged visits, Telford explained, and those exchanges were still going on. The beings concerned, both centaur and human, were very much aware of their responsibilities and were careful not to do or say anything which might offend the other party. And because they were sane and highly intelligent beings, these people displayed a code of ethics which was *not* representative of their respective planets . . .

"A fair analogy," Telford went on drily, "would be that of an old-time captain of a warship visiting a foreign port. The mayor and other leading citizens are impressed and delighted by the charm, politeness and friendliness of the captain and his officers and feel more than favorably inclined toward his country of origin. Then the ship's crew get twelve hours' shore leave and wreck the place!" The commander sat back and continued more quietly: "At present a millionaire couldn't afford the trip to the centaur planet, but twenty years from now a man in your own position could do so at least once in his lifetime. Thousands of people will be visiting each other's planets then, and they will be *ordinary* people. Friction will occur, misunderstanding, possibly war. We are hoping," Telford ended, "that by presenting the worst as well as the best facets of our respective cultures from the very beginning, both sides will have a fuller understanding by the time the stage of a mass exchange of tourists is reached."

"I see," said Nicholson, getting to his feet. He felt

that he had to walk around, or do some physical exercise, to relieve the excitement building up inside him. That a problem of such vast scope, affecting as it did the future well-being of two whole solar systems, was being discussed in *his* office!

He sat down again, laughed nervously, and said: "So Harnrigg is an average alien, holding down an ordinary job so that he is forced to mix with ordinary Earthpeople. I can't help feeling sorry for my centaur opposite number, with an Earthman apprentice to contend with."

"There aren't any, yet," the commander said morosely. "Oh, we've had volunteers, but they're the starryeyed idealist type—they aren't average at all! The kind we want is the person who is a good mixer, fairly adaptable and even-tempered. When I mentioned the worst and the best back there I didn't mean that we were going to use criminals or hopeless psychotics. But Harnrigg is our immediate problem. Or one of them," Telford added, with an uncomfortable glance at Nicholson. "You see, he has three friends."

"On Earth?"

The commander shook his head. "It happened during the first week he was at the store, before he began to get into trouble. He was enthusiastic about the place and wrote letters home to that effect. Three of his friends decided that they would like to work on Earth also, and asked our mission there if this could be arranged. We arranged it. They'll be arriving in ten weeks."

"Not . . . here?" said Nicholson, aghast.

Telford nodded, and began to speak rapidly. Coop's store had been chosen for Harnrigg because it was the largest on the planet and offered the widest variety of openings for an alien who would almost certainly have trouble adapting to any kind of Earth job. More important, it was a pleasant and easy firm to work for. This in turn was due to its personnel manager, who had also been investigated thoroughly and passed with flying colors. It was due to Nicholson rather than Hammond that

the e-t was here, and if Coop's was the best possible
choice for the first alien apprentice it followed that the
other three should at least serve there for a short time.
He did not have to stress the importance of the situation
which was being worked out, they were sorry that the
problem had been dumped in Nicholson's lap, but the
decision had been taken at such a very high level that
he was one of the few people qualified to handle it.

Meanwhile, what was he intending to do about Harnrigg?

Nicholson did not reply for a few minutes. He was
thinking that this surgeon-commander was a very
smooth operator. Telford had begun by dazzling him
with the scope and importance of the problem, then
stabbed him in the back with the news that three more
centaurs were coming, and had ended with a hefty shot
of flattery.

He said: "If I tell you what I intend doing with
Harnrigg we'll discuss it awhile, during which time you
will say that there is no point in waiting until Friday
before bringing him back to work. Then I will find that,
by some odd coincidence, you happen to have Harnrigg
with you, waiting downstairs! Wouldn't it save time if
you brought him up, Commander? Then I could show
you what I'm going to do."

Telford looked startled. He left the office without a
word.

Nicholson did not know which of the three possible
openings—Blankets, Garden Implements and Carpets—would best suit the extraterrestrial. Something
which Telford had said about experiencing the worst
with the best set his mind off on a tangent. Hitherto he
had been trying to fit Harnrigg into departments where
the work and people suited him. But suppose he put
him in a tough section? That way Harnrigg might appreciate the good departments more, and behave ac-
cordingly.

When the commander and Harnrigg returned, Nicholson came straight to the point. He said, "Mr. Harnrigg, I'm sending you to the Dugout. It's the section in

the basement near the TV repair workshops which services the air-conditioning system, the elevator motors, and sundry other jobs. In charge are a senior and junior maintenance engineer, the rest of the personnel being unskilled. I must warn you that some of these people are likely to feel antagonistic toward you," Nicholson went on briskly. "They are that type. Also, you will hear figures of speech which will puzzle you. Don't go asking what they mean, just forget them if you can— they will be of the kind never used in polite company."

The expression in Harnrigg's eyes, the only features not covered by a concealing mask of fur, told Nicholson that the e-t had heard all about the Dugout, and that he wasn't happy about being sent there. Nicholson decided that it was time to soft-pedal a little.

"The move is temporary," he continued, in a slightly warmer tone, "and your conduct will determine your length of stay in that department. Frankly, I want you out of my hair for a while."

"I understand, sir," Harnrigg boomed. Even when he was being submissive his voice almost rattled the windows.

"Very well," said Nicholson. "Go to Mr. Redmond, who will introduce you to your new section."

Harnrigg left and Nicholson made the phone calls necessary to arrange the transfer. The commander waited patiently until he had finished.

"What's so terrible about your Dugout?" he asked.

"The people, chiefly. When something goes wrong they have to work hard, very hard, but major breakdowns are rare. This means that they also have more leisure time during working hours than anyone else, and as they are tucked away in an inaccessible corner they do pretty much as they like."

Gambling went on, Nicholson explained, and there wasn't a thing he could do about it. The Dugout had an early-warning system, fitted by one of the electricians. It was foolproof, and the floor supervisors had long ago given up the idea of catching them gambling. Nicholson did not mind a little surreptitious card-playing during lunchtimes, providing it was for pennies and he didn't catch anyone at it, but the sums which changed hands in the Dugout were too large. Nicholson would have fired practically everybody in the section, including the two engineers, if only he could have caught them at it.

But he could not, no matter how hard or how often he tried. All that he could do was to see that the Dugout was staffed by people who would not be hurt too badly by its lawless environment: men without dependent relatives who wouldn't mind losing most of their wages in a game.

"I am hoping it will teach Harnrigg two lessons," Nicholson summed up. "The first is to make him appreciate the good spots he's been in by putting him in a rough one. The second . . . well, the Dugout men do practically every 'Don't' in the staff rulebook and get away with it. Maybe the association will teach him how to get out of trouble after he's gotten into it."

The commander rose to his feet, shook hands with Nicholson, dropped a card on to the desk and turned to go. "If you need information on his home planet, or anything at all, let me know. Good afternoon."

III

FOR A LONG time Nicholson sat staring at the door
through which the commander had passed, planning his
next moves. Several department heads would have to be
sold the idea of taking centaurs into their sections, and
starting tomorrow he would begin applying the good old
butter. Departmental buyers were always wanting something—more staff, their sections redecorated, extra
display space for slow-selling goods—and if necessary
Nicholson could wangle these things for them. For a return favor, of course. It was blackmail, a scandalous
abuse of his authority, but Nicholson did not care.
They could say what they liked about him, but gradually they would all get the idea that employing an e-t
in their departments paid.

Harnrigg was here already. Three others were expected shortly, and Nicholson felt it in his bones that
there would be more to come. He *had* to make openings
for them—the things Telford had told him made it imperative.

Perhaps it would be wiser to get Hammond's backing
before he brought pressure on his buyers. The store
manager was interested in e-t's only for their prestige
value. Providing Nicholson put it to him properly first,
Hammond would shout down any of his buyers' objections to e-t's as assistants.

Nothing happened next day, or on the one following.
The weekend came and still Harnrigg had not got himself into trouble—or any that Nicholson knew about.
On Sunday Nicholson drove out to the spaceport, partly
on impulse and partly because he had always wanted to

have a closer look at the ships and now he had a name to drop which might get him past the outer gate. He was pleasantly surprised. Telford must have been expecting him to call and had left word with the guards that Nicholson was to be admitted at any time.

The commander was a very important person, Nicholson realized, as Telford met him and suggested a tour of the port.

Telford took him through one of the larger interstellar ships, showing him the hyperdrive engines, the sleeping and recreational quarters, and ending in the control room. He indicated an acceleration chair—the captain's—and asked Nicholson to sit down. Taking the astrogator's position himself, he began to talk about some of the problems of navigation over interstellar distances. He made no attempt to talk down to Nicholson, or be offhand, or to show off. It was obvious that to Telford this ship was wonderful and the places he had been were wonderful. Nicholson's wonder was a pale thing by comparison.

When they finally left the ship, two hours later, Telford began talking about Harnrigg's home world. Nicholson had seen the pictures, of course: the strange, fleecy trees, seas that were like blue milk, and the fantastic cloud effects. But Telford's quiet, expressive voice gave the remembered pictures new depth and color. Nicholson was entranced.

"Here we are in the quarters used by Harnrigg and other visiting centaurs," the commander explained as Nicholson stared around him, trying to identify objects in that alien room. "He's paying a call on the crew of the centaur vessel on Apron Six, but I have a standing invitation here."

The dissimilarities were what Nicholson noticed first: the largeness of the rooms to accommodate a being who was much less maneuverable than a human; the low, wide doors and the fact that there were tables in the usual places but no chairs. Harnrigg's kind could relax quite comfortably on their feet, and if necessary go to sleep on them. Nicholson was very pleased with himself when after only two minutes in one of the rooms he identified a large square of brightly colored foam rubber set flush with the floor as a bed.

There were books, TV, and pictures scattered about in comfortable disorder. Most of the pictures were of people rather than places. To Nicholson, who could not tell one centaur from another, they seemed to be all of the same person. But there was one landscape, or seascape—the famous Three Islands taken just after sunrise.

As the commander was taking him back to the main gate Nicholson said suddenly, "I can't understand why anyone would want to leave a world like that."

"Oh, I don't know," said Telford, grinning. "We have a few attractions, too. Like snow, or moonlight, or boop-jog!"

Nicholson did not sleep very well that night—he was too excited by all the things he had seen and by the knowledge that he was taking part in an extremely important project. His departmental store seemed to be an unlikely place to work out centaur-human sociological problems, but that was exactly what was happening. Harnrigg's presence was an exciting challenge.

On Monday morning Nicholson began laying the groundwork for bringing in more e-t's. It was a gradual process, involving personal visits to department heads instead of the customary phone calls, carefully dropped words and half promises, and a peculiar mixture of threats, cajolery and near-blackmail. He became so absorbed in it that Wednesday came and went before he realized that Harnrigg had been almost a week in his new section without getting into trouble. He felt that this was too good to be true.

But on Friday morning Redmond phoned.

"Harnrigg wants to see you," said the floor supervisor in a strained voice. "He, ah, it looks as if he has the mange."

A horrible picture of the centaur running about like an outsize, mangy dog, of some terrible extraterrestrial disease running rife among the staff, rose up before Nicholson. Then he remembered that centaurs and humans were supposed to be immune to each other's germs. That made him feel better. He said, "What does he want?"

Nicholson heard Redmond relaying the question and the booming voice of the e-t as he replied. Apparently Harnrigg's superior had not liked having a centaur landed on him and had taken it out on the e-t by setting him to check elevator cables—a particularly messy job. Harnrigg had performed this work satisfactorily, but the detergents he had been forced to use to clean his fur had bleached his coat, causing unsightly patches of gray and yellow. He wanted to know if it would be possible for him to be supplied with protective overalls like the other maintenance staff.

"Certainly," said Nicholson, relieved. "Send him along to Tailoring. They'll have to make him a set."

"He wants to see you about a personal matter also," said Redmond.

Nicholson did some careful thinking before he replied. A point which the e-t was probably not aware of was that, in his workmates' eyes, people who visited the personnel manager's office for anything but a ticking off were suspect. Nicholson did not want them to get the idea that Harnrigg was telling tales.

"Send him to be measured," he said. "I'll be down in Tailoring shortly and will see him there."

Nicholson arrived in the Tailoring department to see Harnrigg rolling about on his back on the floor while two assistants chewed their pencils and made notes. When Nicholson appeared the centaur rolled on to his side, and struggled to his feet, displaying his bleached and scraggy coat.

"We've finished the measuring, sir, and are working out how best to fasten the garment," the senior assistant explained. "We think he should lie on his back, pull on the hind legs, then the forelegs, and finally the arms. Once upright he can fasten the garment, which will join along his back. The tail was a problem, but we've decided that it will have to be tied so as to lie flat along the spine. This, he assures us, will cause him no discomfort. There will be two pockets in the breast and two special tool pockets on each flank."

Nicholson nodded and the salesman went on enthusiastically, "It takes eleven and a half yards of material for him! Why can't we get all these centaurs interested in wearing clothes while visiting Earth?"

"It's an idea," said Nicholson, "but not my department, I'm afraid. And now I'd like to have a word alone with Mr. Harnrigg."

The salesman and interested observers moved out of earshot, and Nicholson turned to the centaur. He said, "Something is bothering you?"

Harnrigg wagged his head up and down. He made several attempts to say something, but failed to get past the second word. The expression in his eyes was of confusion and appeal. Nicholson felt himself warming to this four-legged apprentice.

Choosing his words carefully, Nicholson said: "Everything which goes on down there is known to me sooner or later—but by hearsay, so that I can't take official action. For instance, someone brought in a bottle of whisky three days ago and one of the electricians got so drunk that he was unable to clock out until eight thirty. I also know, unofficially, about the gambling. So if you are afraid of implicating someone by telling me your trouble, I can listen unofficially, too. Did they clean you out?" Nicholson ended bluntly. "Are you short of money?"

"Oh, *no!*" Harnrigg exclaimed; then, in response to Nicholson's frantic signal, he forced his voice down to a loud, discordant whisper. "Somebody started the rumor that my race is telepathic and they won't let me play."

"You were lucky," said Nicholson. "But what *is* the trouble?"

Apparently it was a problem belonging to two other people. One, a young mechanic called Sinclair who worked with him, had become emotionally involved with a girl in Hosiery. They were going steady and saving up—at least, the girl was; Sinclair found it impossible to give up his poker and betting on horses. In Harnrigg's opinion, if Sinclair could be transferred to a department where it wasn't so easy to slip out to the bookies and where there was no poker game, this would have a beneficial effect on his character and future hopes of promotion.

"I see," said Nicholson when he had finished. "Did he ask you to do this for him?"

Harnrigg shook his head. "I found out about it because Mr. Sinclair and a few others discuss this sort of problem with me. I'm supposed to have an objective viewpoint where human love is concerned. Taking the long-term view, I decided that transferring Sinclair away from Maintenance would be a good thing."

"Well, well," thought Nicholson. This was a completely unexpected development. Harnrigg had been sent to Maintenance as a punishment, and now the e-t was intent on showing his irresponsible colleagues the error of their ways—the salvageable ones, anyway.

Nicholson was about to put him in his place when he saw the hurrying figure of Redmond approaching, closely followed by Chambers, the Bedding-and-Linen buyer. Both their faces were red.

They began talking at once while they were still a dozen yards away, Chambers complaining and demanding and Redmond trying to tone down the other's demands and complaints. Nicholson suggested that they all go to his office and discuss the matter less publicly, but Chambers wouldn't have that; he wanted a showdown right now.

Gradually Nicholson began to understand what all the shouting was about. Two members of the Bedding-and-Linen sections—of opposite genders, Chambers explained delicately—had been sent into their stockroom to check off a delivery. An hour later Chambers had gone into the stock room and had been horrified to find them holding hands. Chambers had very strict views.

"Send them up to my office," Nicholson said with a sigh. "I'll deal with them there."

"Fire them!" Chambers cried. "Make an example of them!"

"I don't think such drastic action is necessary," Redmond put in.

Within seconds the two men were yelling at each other. Nicholson thought that the whole argument was highly undignified, when Harnrigg chimed in.

"If I might make an observation," he said in a conversational tone for him, but which drowned out everyone else, "a store of this size represents a system of checks and balances similar, though on a smaller scale, to the ecological balance of a continent or planet. Causing large numbers of people of opposite genders to work in close proximity and then inhibiting the attraction which they feel appears to me to be an unnatural practice, and one likely to seriously upset the ecological balance of the store . . ."

Chambers had gone plum-red with rage and Redmond's face was only a shade lighter—from suppressed laughter. But Harnrigg was warming to his subject and his tone was no longer conversational. Possibly here were a few people at the other end of the building who could not hear him now, but Nicholson doubted it.

"Take Jewelry, for instance, whose buyer keeps a special room where members of the staff can choose engagement rings—in secret, if they prefer it that way, and most do. The buyer takes care of store personnel himself, which proves that the staff trade must make up a fair proportion of his total turnover. According to a breakdown of last year's trading figures, which I read a few days ago, engagement-ring sales to store employees accounted for five and a quarter per cent of—"

Nicholson gave Harnrigg's flank a thump with his fist in an attempt to make him shut up.

"I am not advocating unrestrained lovemaking," the extraterrestrial went on in stentorian tones. "Only that certain physical contact, when people are caught at it, should not be considered an offense of such gravity as to require dismissal. If this were so the staff would not patronize the jewelry department, the trading figures would go down and the buyer would not be pleased. Neither would Mr. Hammond."

The silence which followed was broken by someone at the other end of the department clapping his hands. Nicholson glared in that direction and the applause ended abruptly. Before Chambers could get in a counterblast he said hurriedly, "Mr. Harnrigg, you are being insubordinate. Return to your section! And I suggest that you go back to your department also, Mr. Chambers. You, Mr. Redmond, bring the two offenders to my office in half an hour."

As Nicholson was leaving, Redmond caught up with him and kept pace for a few yards. "Man, that was lovely! And bringing Hammond into it at the end was a masterstroke. I'll be afraid to tick off an apprentice for bad writing now in case I upset the ecological balance—"

"That's enough, Redmond," Nicholson said sharply.

IV

BACK IN HIS office, Nicholson decided to adopt Harnrigg's suggestion and transferred Sinclair to Garden Implements.

Basically the extraterrestrial was a nice type. His attempts to gain a transfer for Sinclair proved that. Altogether, Nicholson put him down as a kindly but suggestible type—which was why his role of champion of the oppressed workers had Nicholson worried.

No store likes agitators, extraterrestrial or otherwise.

Harnrigg had settled in and been accepted by the rough characters of Maintenance—his request for overalls rather than a transfer proved that. He had made friends down there, but there must still be some who did not like him. Forbidding him to play poker suggested superstitious distrust on someone's part, and superstition and hatred were almost synonymous. That same person or persons had also learned that Harnrigg was suggestible, excitable and believed everything he was told. Somebody in Maintenance was busily feeding him with ideas which must ultimately get him fired.

According to Telford, and Nicholson agreed, the extraterrestrial apprentice was a test case. His reactions to average people, and their reactions to him, were pointers to where their respective cultures were heading when unrestricted contact became possible. The alternatives were friendship or distrust, peace or eventual war. It was crazy that a matter of such tremendous importance should depend on the workings of some malicious joker's mind. There must be *something* he could do.

On impulse, Nicholson phoned Maintenance and asked for the chief. In his best official voice he told him

231

that the apprentice Harnrigg had been down there mainly as a punishment, that the e-t must have learned his lesson by now, and that he was considering moving him out again.

"He's doing all right," the Maintenance chief replied. "Naturally he got underfoot at first, but now I think he likes being here."

"Let me speak to Harnrigg, please," said Nicholson.

He got nowhere; Harnrigg liked it in Maintenance. If it was at all possible, he did not want to be moved.

There were three ways only in which he could transfer a member of the staff: by permission or at the request of a department head, at the request of the person wanting the transfer, or if the person concerned had misbehaved and was being transferred for disciplinary reasons. Harnrigg's chief wanted him to stay. Harnrigg wanted to stay, and since going to Maintenance he had kept out of trouble. Nicholson's hands were therefore tied, and the unknown joker who was angling Harnrigg into trouble would have a free hand.

He decided to call Telford.

"I didn't know so much cloak-and-dagger stuff went on in a store," the commander said after Nicholson had given him the details of what had been happening. "I'm afraid I can't help, I'm just not qualified to cope with Borgia-type intrigues on this scale. You are."

"You're a *big* help!" said Nicholson witheringly; then he hesitated for a moment. "One thing has been bothering me, however," he went on. "I know, of course, that Harnrigg's race is not telepathic. But since he came here I've noticed a change in my feelings. I used to like this job very much and now, well, I don't know. The effect seems to increase the more I see of him. Could there be some subtle emanation given off by members of his race which—"

"*No!*" Telford snapped. It was the first time Nicholson had known him to show anger. "Start talking like that and the next thing people will be saying they eat babies."

"I didn't mean it like that," began Nicholson.

"Sorry, I know you didn't," Telford replied. "But talk like that from a person in your position can do great harm."

Two days later Harnrigg got into, of all things, a religious argument. It began in the Time Office when he was clocking out for lunch and developed so quickly that the e-t dismissed the special truck which took him to and from the spaceport so as to continue it in the staff canteen.

Over the preceding five years the staff canteen had remained the same size while the number of employees had increased, so the obstruction and disorganization Harnrigg caused was considerable. Nicholson expected the catering manageress to be banging on his door within minutes of the e-t's arrival in the canteen. But no, the catering manageress made only a faint, ritual protest by telephone, and when Harnrigg went to the canteen next day to continue the debate one of the aisles between tables had been specially widened for him.

But as the days went on the arguments which Harnrigg got into increased. He would argue about anything. At the same time he was not opinionated, and would admit that he was wrong if the other party could prove it. He argued indiscriminately, excitedly and innocently. Harnrigg ranting against income tax or giving advice—usually very good advice—to lovelorn human salesgirls was not serious, but he was just as likely to pick more explosive subjects.

For three weeks Nicholson sweated, trying desperately to put the brakes on Harnrigg's enthusiasm, and hoping that the arguments would stay confined to lower-rank personnel.

In the middle of the fourth week, it happened.

Redmond, who had tried unsuccessfully to intervene, gave Nicholson the details. Harnrigg had been talking to Harvey, the easy-going Toy-department buyer, about the ideal working conditions in Maintenance and had stated that, relatively, the staff in Toys were cowed and oppressed. Harvey, for the first time in seven years, had lost his temper. For ten minutes he matched Harnrigg decibel for decibel, and had proved to the e-t's satisfaction that if there were any oppressed minorities in this department it was himself and his charge assistant.

"Harnrigg apologized humbly then," Redmond went on. "Everything would have been all right then if Harnrigg hadn't said that if he ever came back to Toys he would be a model worker for Mr. Harvey. And when his friends arrived he would see to it, if they came to Mr. Harvey's department, that they would be the same."

"Oh, no," said Nicholson faintly.

"Harvey asked what friends," Redmond continued. "When Harnrigg told him, the ceiling was all that kept him from going into orbit. Now it's all over the store. Every buyer in the place is up in arms, there's talk of running Harnrigg out, and of calling for a strike. Did you know that we're getting fifty more centaurs?"

"Yes!" said Nicholson savagely. "But nobody else was supposed to know, yet. And it is three, not fifty. Try and spread *that* around, will you. And get that unprintable Harnrigg up here at once!"

"Why did you have to blab about your friends coming?" Nicholson yelled before Harnrigg was past the door. "You must have known I wanted that kept quiet until I had places for them. Now the staff are hostile as well as the buyers. Where the blazes am I going to put your friends when they come?"

"Two of them," said Harnrigg timidly, "are interested in TV. They are repair men—they could talk knowledgeably about the new sets that we're getting. Since Earth has begun to copy our full-color TV system the manufacturers are making a big thing out of the fact that the designs originated on our planet. I thought that it might tie in nicely with the advertising to have two centaurs selling the sets."

When Harnrigg had taken his rhetorical question literally and started answering it, Nicholson had been startled. Then he began to see the sense of what Harnrigg was saying, and his rage cooled, even though he realized that this was the effect that Harnrigg must be striving for. The four-legged so-and-so is *handling* me, he thought.

But before he could develop that thought the phone rang. It was the store manager. Hammond wanted to know what all this was about the store importing cheap labor from the stars, the trade-union district organizer was in his office threatening strike action, and what the blazes had Nicholson done *now?*

Covering the mouthpiece, Nicholson said, "Get out!" Then he began replying to the store manager's questions one by one.

V

NEXT DAY FEELINGS were still running high, though not against Harnrigg personally. There was a tension in the air that gave it an almost static charge and the staff were being too polite, keeping too busy. Some sort of diversion was needed.

Using as his reason the fact that Harnrigg no longer returned to the spaceport each midday, and in the circumstances not to build a special washroom would be needless cruelty, Nicholson requested and was granted permission to install washroom facilities for Harnrigg in the basement. The maintenance section were to handle the job and work was to begin immediately. When that got out, practically everyone in the store found an excuse to visit the basement to see what a centaur washroom consisted of.

So the staff had something to speculate on, and the humorists among them had a field day. Nicholson was able to use the time to scotch the exaggerated rumors which had been going about, and to regain some of the ground which he had lost. He was with the head of the Radio and TV department when he was told he was wanted in the store manager's office.

Commander Telford and the store manager were there when he arrived.

"I met the commander as he was coming in," Hammond said. "He was going to wait for you in your office—imagine that!" The implication in his tone was that such an important person must feel slighted at having to wait in Nicholson's small, dingy office. "This is Surgeon-Commander Telford, the director of a group studying centaur-human relations and the man responsible for Harnrigg and the others coming here. Commander Telford, this is my personnel manager, Mr. Nichol—"

"Hi, Joe," said Nicholson, for the purpose of seeing what effect such familiarity toward a space commander would have on Hammond. Hammond was stricken speechless.

"Hello, Arthur," said Telford, catching the ball neatly. "I have just been telling your chief that my group has decided that for the next four or five years Coop's store will receive all centaur immigrants. They will probably arrive at the rate of three a year. But only if we are assured that they will be reasonably happy working here. Can you absorb that number in your—"

"He'll have to!" Hammond broke in. "It's his job to do so, and if he falls down on it I can find another personnel manager."

Telford looked uncomfortable. He said, "I don't think he can be blamed too much for failing to solve a unique and extremely difficult problem." He turned to Nicholson. "How have you been making out?"

Nicholson knew that he would have exerted himself to the utmost on the problem, and Hammond's threat of the sack only angered him. If he hadn't had what he thought was the answer to the problem, now would have been the perfect time to duck out by telling Hammond what to do with his job. But Nicholson had been doing some heavy thinking over the past few days and he thought he had the problem licked. Harnrigg had to stay out of trouble until Nicholson put his plan into effect.

He was on the point of answering Telford's question when the store manager's intercom bleeped and an excited voice shouted, "Sir! I can't find Mr. Nicholson and there's a riot in the Dugout! They've locked the door but you can hear them all over the ground floor, Harnrigg anyway. Mr. Redmond says will he send for an ambulance, and the police?"

"*No!*" Nicholson yelled, before Hammond could

react. "I'm coming down!" He headed for the elevator, with Telford and Hammond close behind him.

The man who had phoned met them on the ground floor and ran with them toward the basement stairs. He said breathlessly, "Mr. Redmond is trying to get through to them. H-Harnrigg's gone mad! Listen to him, he must be murdering all around him. No lousy centaur is going to—"

"Don't do or say anything until I know what has happened!" Nicholson snapped at him.

The noise of human shouts was loud even here, and the sounds which Harnrigg was making were something which Nicholson had never heard him make before. Altogether it sounded like a bloody massacre. But still he clung to the hope that there would be an innocent explanation.

Redmond had sent to Hardware for an ax and had just about finished demolishing the door. It swung open as they came level with him.

Harnrigg was in the middle of a struggling, punching mob of maintenance staff, invisible but deafeningly audible. There were a few bodies lying about on the fringe of the mob, and one man was crawling about on his hands and knees and splattering the floor with blood from his nose. There was a lot of loose money and spilled playing cards on the floor, too. But Nicholson was relieved to see that so far nobody had been killed.

"Stop this!" he thundered. "Stop at once!"

Nobody heard him. Harnrigg was making too much noise.

"They're killing him!" Telford shouted into his ear, and dived into the struggling mass of bodies. Redmond and Nicholson followed. Nicholson did not waste time trying to separate any of the fighters; he merely shoved them out of the way or tripped them up. Telford and the floor supervisor both had split lips by the time they reached Harnrigg.

The e-t was prancing about furiously, his heavy tail protruding from the tatters of his new overalls and whipping about viciously. The furry covering made it resemble a sandbag as a weapon, Nicholson thought as it thumped him in the back and knocked him to his knees. Harnrigg was also flailing away with both hands and roaring his head off. Nicholson shouted again but still could not make himself heard. Telford caught his eye, shook his head, and dived across Harnrigg's back.

Nicholson saw his hands prodding rapidly into the fur along Harnrigg's spine. Then Telford balled one of his fists suddenly and swung it down. Harnrigg jerked convulsively, keeled over on to his side and lay gazing along the floor with a bewildered expression in his eyes.

"That's dirty fighting!" yelled a burly maintenance man, and swung at Telford. The commander ducked sideways and the blow skidded off his cheekbone.

Nicholson shouted: "Quiet! That's enough!"

This time they heard him.

"Redmond, get the medical kit," Nicholson said briskly. "And any of you men who have been injured, line up here and we'll have a look at you. Commander, will you attend to the ones on the floor?"

"I'm a psychologist," Telford growled, fingering his raw cheek. But he moved to obey. Nicholson returned to the shattered door to speak to the store manager. This was a horrible mess, and what little hope there was in it lay in his being able to handle it alone. He had to get rid of the s.m.

"I don't want you to think I'm ordering you around, sir," he said respectfully, "but I need someone at the head of the stairs to keep everybody out until I can find out what has happened. Someone with authority and a level head, who can quell any tendency toward panic among the staff up there . . ."

Hammond left and Redmond came up to Nicholson. He said: "None of the men are hospital cases. Apparently we arrived before things got out of hand."

Before he could reply, Telford came across. "Bloody noses, minor cuts and bruises is all," he said soberly. "Cold compresses, sticking-plaster and aspirin is what they need. But how will this affect the Harnrigg business?"

The extraterrestrial came wobbling over to them at that point, apparently none the worse for Telford's judo punch. He began, "I'm sorry, Mr. Nicholson—"

"Not another word!" said Nicholson sharply. He pointed to a door leading into a large storeroom and snapped, "Go in there and wait. You men with nothing wrong with you, wait there also. When we've attended to your friends I'm going to get to the bottom of this." He turned and began applying surgical tape to the face of the junior maintenance engineer. As the man was turning to go he added, "I don't want it to be said that I was unfair about this business, that I questioned any of you while you were still dazed or otherwise mentally confused. So I'm going to give you all fifteen minutes to gather your wits. You are all," he went on grimly, "guilty of two crimes which, together with dishonesty, make up the three which bring with them instant dismissal: fighting, and gambling for money. The penalty applies to humans and non-humans alike."

A few minutes later the rest of the men had been taped up and sent into the storeroom with the others. A rising hum of talk came through the thick door, frequently interspersed with Harnrigg's louder tones, reached a crescendo, died and rose again. Nicholson paced up and down nervously, kicking at the loose cards and money lying around on the floor and not daring to think beyond the next fifteen minutes.

The noise coming through the door was building up to a new high.

"It's a pity it didn't work out," Telford said sadly. "You tried hard, I know, but even I know that a store can't have this sort of thing going on. You'll fire him, of course, but don't you think you'd better keep an eye on those people in there? You said most of them will lose their jobs over this, and if they decide that Harnrigg is the cause they might turn nasty. If they injure him seriously it could mean the first interstellar incident."

Nicholson walked up and down again without speaking; then he said, "Look around, you can almost *see* what happened. I bet they let him play poker for the first time, and he had beginner's luck—otherwise there would have been no fight. Somebody, a loser, of course, remembered that rumor about him being telepathic and accused him of cheating—maybe hit him. But Harnrigg has a lot of friends down here, so the riot started. Trouble is, will I be able to prove all this? You see," he went on quickly, "this wasn't the usual sort of fracas. There were no boots, clubs or hooves used—only fists. Apparently even his enemies did not want to hurt him too much. You remember that character who slugged you because you gave him that rabbit punch in the back? If rough types like those could agree to rules for a free fight maybe they could agree—"

"*Listen* to them!" said Telford urgently. "Even if they didn't want to hurt him then, now it's different. Now they're all going to be fired. They'll kill him!"

Nicholson shook his head. "I know what I'm doing, I think," he said worriedly. "Anyway, their fifteen minutes are up."

When he entered the storeroom the maintenance staff were ranged against the opposite wall, with Harnrigg slightly front and centre. Obviously he was to be their spokesman. Considering his growing reputation for winning arguments, Nicholson thought drily, the e-t was the logical choice. If Harnrigg couldn't talk them out of this fix, nobody could.

Harnrigg made the opening move. "This trouble is entirely my fault, sir," he said miserably. "It came about through my ignorance, and also through the mistaken kindness of my friends here."

"I'm getting tired of hearing that everything is your fault," Nicholson broke in. "Maybe it pleases you to be a martyr, but the free-for-all we have just witnessed was not being fought solely by you, and the gambling required more than one participant."

"But we weren't gambling," Harnrigg boomed passionately. His eyes were large, soft and sincere. "I brought the playing cards in with me, seeking instruction, and thought that perhaps some of my friends would be able to help. My interest is purely academic, I assure you. Commander Telford knows that we have nothing resembling cards on my home planet."

Telford nodded dumbly. Redmond seemed in danger of choking at the thought of the maintenance people merely *explaining* cards to anyone. Nicholson was thinking, *What a beautiful liar he is. If only he can keep it up.*

"There was a large amount of money lying around," he said coldly. "Proof, I submit, of gambling."

"It must have been shaken out of our pockets during the fighting—"

"So there was fighting?"

Harnrigg shook his head ponderously. "Not exactly, sir. Fighting among the staff is an offense punishable by instant dismissal, I understand. But I am intensely curious about all forms of earthly activities, not only music, literature and drama. Car racing, for instance, and chess. I realize now that I should not have talked my friends into demonstrating boxing for me during working hours, but out of politeness to an extraterrestrial they agreed."

"You mean to say," said Nicholson witheringly, "that all these people were merely showing you how to *box?*"

Harnrigg remained silent, but all the battered and bloody faces behind him nodded or otherwise signaled assent.

Nicholson kept sternly to his role of Public Prosecutor, but inwardly he was jubilant. He said: "This story appears somewhat fantastic, but I haven't the time to go into obvious flaws at the moment. Mr. Hammond is upstairs trying to keep the staff from leaving in panic. They don't know what has been happening here and suspect that you are running berserk. It is more important just now that I help him calm them down. But rest assured that I'll get to the bottom of this. The day after tomorrow I'll hold a full investigation which will last, if necessary, a week!"

As Nicholson was heading toward the basement stairs again, Telford said, "I don't understand. You . . . you don't believe him?"

"Of course not," said Nicholson, grinning. "But by the day after tomorrow I'll have no choice. Maintenance people stick together, and the electricians next door are as bad. Come the investigation, there will be a dozen electrical boys ready to swear blind that a few minutes before we broke in, everyone in here was either teaching Harnrigg how to play patience or discussing the last Killer Colgan fight, or both. I'll have to transfer him again, of course."

Telford shook his head numbly. "Then he isn't being fired? There's still a chance."

Nicholson sent Redmond on ahead. Then he said: "I was about to tell you that I had the answer to the whole centaur business when the riot started. I'm going to transfer him all around the store, a couple of weeks to every department in turn. *Everyone* is going to have experience of centaurs and he's going to experience every job. If I think it necessary I'll make him do the round two or three times."

"But you can't keep moving him around," Telford objected. "That's not finding him a position."

"No," Nicholson agreed. "But it is necessary training for the job I have in mind for him. If we're going to be flooded with centaurs I need an adviser who knows all the jobs from the centaur point of view. And he's good with humans. That is why, eventually, I'll make him assistant personnel manager."

They were at the bottom of the stairs. Telford halted him with a hand on his arm and said warmly, "Neat, Arthur, very neat. I think you've got it. But . . . but don't you realize that if what you say is true about him handling humans, you've worked yourself out of a job?"

Nicholson shrugged. "I don't think I care."

Telford squeezed his arm. He said, "And I think I know why. I'll give you a job myself. You would have to take a demotion, of course."

The store manager, Redmond and assorted members of the sales staff were crowded around the head of the stairs, and Hammond was glaring down at him impatiently. That was why Nicholson did not realize the implications behind Telford's parting words until later.

"But you'll be too far away for anyone in Coop's to hear about your drop in status. And anyway, I don't suppose that you'll remain an apprentice any longer than Harnrigg did."

Answer Came There None

I

LIKE A GREEN and seemingly virginal carpet, the planetary surface unrolled five miles below the slowing ship. The grasses and small plants showed no signs of vegetable blight—the atmosphere was free of industrial pollutants and there were no cities or surface transport networks of any kind. But to the ship's sensors and the tired, experienced eyes of the crew the greenery was a beautiful lie, a cosmetic skin of apparent youth overlaying a world which for many thousands of years had been drained of all its natural resources, used up and emptied of all life above the insect level.

"We're wasting our time," said Jan, in a tone that indicated that she was looking for an argument.

Peter did not like arguing with her, especially during the last few minutes before touchdown, even though a searchship was fully capable of landing itself. He waited until the ship had recovered from a brief attack of the transonic shudders and their landing spot was centered in the forward viewscreen.

Then he said, "Probably."

She gave a short sigh of irritation and tapped for a magnified picture of the landing area on her duplicate display. He could not see the particular section she had blown up for closer examination because her head was in the way.

Lit in profile by the screen, Jan looked almost young again. In silhouette the graying hair and the fine facial wrinkles did not show. But it took more than a trick of back lighting, he knew, to cancel out the weariness and lack of hope in her body and mind—as well as his own. Like the salt used to preserve meat in ancient times, every cell and thought was soaked in it. If an old-time cannibal had taken a bite out of one of them, hopelessness and frustration would have been the strongest taste.

Eighty years, he thought, was a long time to be doing the same job.

The screen darkened as the ship's nose went up, pulling forward-facing cameras off-picture, and they began falling tail-first into the increasingly resistant softness of their antigravity landing cushion. They touched down— the cushion flicked off and the ship rocked gently as the weight forced its landing legs deep into the soft ground. The all-around viewscreens lit up and the images steadied and sharpened as the ship came finally to rest.

"We *are* wasting our time," Jan persisted. "I'm sure we have been here before."

"Unlikely," he replied, "but you could be forgiven for thinking so. One of these sites is very much like any other—the same green mounds, the same type and size of ruined buildings even, because they are probably examples of the most advanced and durable structures built by the same architect—"

He broke off because she was shaking her head. In a less conciliatory tone he went on, "Are you suggesting that I made a mistake and we've doubled back to a site already investigated? An understandable error, you are doubtless thinking, caused by my advancing years? But you are forgetting that our computer, which isn't subject to lapses caused by senile decay—"

"I could argue that point too," she broke in.

His first impulse was to tell her that the recent trouble they had had with the computer had been due to operator error and that she had been the operator, but he thought better of it. Instead he said, "Are you coming outside?"

"Yes," she replied. "I prefer talking to you to sitting here talking to myself."

"I'm glad," he said drily. "For a moment I wondered if the romance was going out of our relationship."

But they said very little while they were climbing into their protective suits, probably because he had touched on a subject to which they were both hypersensitive. He would willingly have bet that within the next hour there would be an argument about rejuvenation and that argument, he knew from bitter experience, nobody won.

Preceded by a general purpose robot which, in addition to the usual sensory and specimen gathering equipment was also programmed for medical and surgical emergencies, they moved down the ramp and onto the springy turf. The sun shone brightly out of a sky whose clouds could not have been more tastefully arranged by a landscape painter. The air was fresh and pure and eminently breathable, but their heavy protective suits were needed to protect them against the insects which crawled and flew and were incredibly vicious. Even though he knew that he would have no use for it, he wore a sidearm because the regulations required him to do so.

Jan did not wear one because, she was fond of saying, if a native life form more than two inches tall came at them she would be so pleased that she would want to hug the thing instead of shoot it.

The insects were everywhere.

Hundreds of the things died with each step the

searchers took, while the robot's balloon tires wreaked even greater havoc. But the dark and oozing tracks that stained the grass in their wake were gone before they had traveled ten yards because the insects ate each other and not, for some odd ecological reasons, the short grass that sheltered them. Any insect left defenseless by death or injury disappeared quickly, right down to the last smear of juice or edible tissue.

There had been a time when Jan and he would have examined the insects' behavior for indications of developing intelligence—some sign, perhaps, that these last inheritors of this and so many other worlds would produce an insect gestalt with which the human race might eventually communicate. Now, however, they walked between and over the all too familiar grassy mounds and ignored the senseless ferocity under their feet.

Beneath the grass and the layer of warring insects the robot's sensors reported the usual mixture of indestructible plastic debris and metallic oxides. Toward the end this particular civilization had used a lot of plastic because no metal had been available. Nevertheless the beings had built well and the plastic ruins still stood impressively tall in a few places, even though the builders had long since gone down before the insect enemy.

"That one looks interesting," Peter said, pointing toward a squat, five-story building that seemed to be structurally complete except for its missing roof. Many of the plastic windows were still in place, but rendered virtually opaque by weathering and the mosslike growth that also covered the walls. The ground-level entrance was large and clear of rubble. He added: "Do you still think that we've been here before?"

"The familiar can look strange," she said stubbornly, "if you approach it from a different angle."

"And the wrong angle of view," he replied, "can make the strange look familiar. But let's stop arguing and start looking inside. We are supposed to examine at least one building on every site and more if we should turn up something interesting . . ."

His voice trailed into silence. He was thinking that

one indication of approaching senility was the habit of explaining things to someone who already knew the explanation.

A few minutes later the robot placed sensors against a wall and emitted high-pitched squeaks as it sonically analyzed the building for structural defects. Satisfied that the place was safe for human searchers, it preceded them inside.

With the robot's main beam trained at full intensity on the ceiling there was more than enough light for them to see around the big entrance hall. The remains of what might have been desks and possibly some clear-walled display cases were spaced at intervals about the floor, while the walls were covered with large pictures. A heavy dusting of living and long-dead insects over everything made it difficult to pick out details.

The contents of the display cases, if they once had been display cases, were no longer recognizable. Most of the pictures, for some reason, were less obscured by insects and showed machinery with natives busy around it—Peter deduced a large factory complex and what looked like a supersonic atmospheric flyer of conventional design. A bank of elevators was framed against the wall facing the entrance, the doors collapsed outward under the pressure of the rubble that had collected in the elevator shafts.

A broad ramp curved upward to the level above. The searchers began to climb.

From their studies of sites visited earlier they had formed a vague idea of what the natives of this world had looked like and of the way they moved when they were not riding in cars or flyers. Physically they had resembled short, wide-based cones with a number of specialized appendages—manipulators, visual equipment and possibly eating and breathing orifices—sprouting from the top. Presumably their brains were housed somewhere inside the stubby, legless bodies, which had moved snaillike—but not necessarily slowly—on a wide apron of muscle. Stairs or ladders inside the dwellings had been conspicuous by their absence.

As he mounted the ramp Peter's eyes were fixed on the robot, which was capable of climbing anything, when Jan gripped his arm tightly and pointed ahead.

"Look at those sculptures," she said excitedly. "And undraped, too. This will answer a lot of the physiological questions."

Two enormous figures, five or six times larger than life, dominated the floor space at the top of the ramp. They had been cut from hard rock and the insects had left them alone—Peter saw that every muscle and joint and wrinkle was rendered in perfect detail. No wonder Jan was pleased.

"I suppose," he said, "the smaller of the two is the female of the species?"

"It's easy to tell who is the medic in this family," Jan said, shaking her head. "No. I'd say that the small one with its eye glaring aggressively at us is their equivalent of Neanderthal Man, while the tall one with the more specialized appendages, whose eyestalk is pointed skyward, represents the builders of this once-mighty civilization."

. . . *Which rose to its greatest heights,* he added silently, *and signaled its presence to the rest of the galaxy and then died, two thousand years ago* . . .

"We're lucky," Jan went on. "We've found a cultural center designed for posterity—maybe even us. Look around you. Some of those display cases are still complete and their contents are undamaged—which isn't surprising since most of them contain oddly shaped pieces of rock—"

She broke off and turned away from him. The robot was busily photographing the alien tableau and concentrating its main beam on the subject it had chosen. Jan switched on her suit light and picked her way along a cluttered aisle to the next ascending ramp. She went up it at a near run. Peter followed more slowly. By the time he and the robot found her crouched over a collapsed display case, she was still trying to catch her breath.

"You shouldn't run like that," he said. "Overexertion is dangerous at our age."

She waved his words aside and went on excitedly, "I was pretty sure below, but now there is no doubt in my mind. We've found a museum. The ground floor level is devoted to the race's prehistory—crude stone implements, knives, early attempts at working clay or mud. On this level they have progressed to agriculture and weaving. Most of the specimens were of perishable vegetable matter, so time and the insects have done for them. But the wall pictures are well preserved and clearly show the level of culture of that period. Succeeding levels should bring us to the time when this civilization began to fall apart. We may even find the reasons for its collapse."

"We know the reason why it, and all the others, collapsed," he said tiredly. "They had too many, smug, self-satisfied, selfish beings eating up too few natural resources. We've pieced together that particular picture too many times—what's begun to impress me is that nearly every culture we've found has left us a lesson of its past; not one a lesson for survival."

"I know," she replied, some of the enthusiasm fading from her tone. "But finding this building was a piece of rare good luck and there might be another piece just waiting for us. We're due some good luck and I have a feeling—"

"You always have a feeling," he broke in. "It's called wishful thinking."

"Are you trying to be nasty or can't you help it?" she said angrily, then went on: "Right here we may be able to piece together a complete picture, instead of searching all over the planet for pieces of the jigsaw—and probably missing most of them. I'm glad you made that mistake and doubled back here because—"

II

"DAMN IT," HE said furiously. "You keep insisting that we landed here before, but we can't have done so. The computer isn't your specialty, so I can't completely convince you that when I program the ship for a search it cannot possibly make that kind of error."

"It couldn't—but maybe you could," she snapped back. Then, more quietly, she went on, "You are sure that you didn't make a mistake and I am sure you did. So we are having this stupid argument and letting it blunt our powers of observation and reasoning. We've found something I think we missed before and you don't. That doesn't alter the fact that we could be on the point of learning the workings of an extraterrestrial culture that—in all respects save one—might make ours look medieval by comparison.

"This is all wrong," she went on seriously. "We're losing our sense of proportion. I think we've let ourselves grow too old. We seem to do nothing these days but argue and snap at each other and we could be missing important data simply because we are squabbling instead of looking."

"I know we're growing old," he said. "But the last time this subject came up we agreed that there would be no more rejuvenation programs unless we found—"

"You agreed. I had reservations."

He took a deep breath and tried to hide his anger at having to say something he had already said too many times before.

"We've already undergone three rejuvenations. There is no problem about getting another. Even though the treatments are restricted because there are too many people, our work insures our being made young again with no quibbling. At the same time—if we go through the process once again we'll be morally obliged to continue our work as searchers. And I, for one, do not think that I could stand another twenty years doing—this. Even as a youthful, vigorous, clear-eyed graverobber instead of an elderly specimen with hardening of the intellect. We've already known lifetimes of disappointment. To extend it by another twenty years is more than I could take. I'm sorry. But if *you* want to apply—"

He could see her head shaking inside her helmet.

She said, "No. I do as you do."

"But—" he said drily.

"But," she said softly, "I miss the fringe benefits."

For a few seconds they stared silently at each other. Then he grinned and suddenly they both laughed. The problems were still there—nothing had changed so far as their personal difficulties were concerned but, for a short time at least, the senseless arguing was over.

"Is there anything special I should look for?" he asked when the therapeutic laughter had ceased. "Something to indicate species survival?"

"I don't know," she replied. "Look for something different, some new idea or facet in the culture that would make it unlike any of the others we've investigated. It could be a scheme for population control or feeding—maybe an idea that came too late to do these creatures any good, but one we might use on Earth before we go the same way. But I would especially like to find some indication that—before their culture fell apart—some of them were able to get away and plant a colony. In the two thousand years since this world stopped signaling a flourishing colony could have come into being in another system. A colonization project like that is important enough to have a place in a museum," she added, "and its position in space would almost certainly be included in the exhibit."

In short, he thought wearily as they moved toward another ascending ramp, *we are still looking for our own image . . .*

They had been looking for "people" on the first search mission, Peter remembered, but on that occasion it had not seemed to matter too much when they had not found them. The prospects had been too new, strange and exciting—setting out in one of the first searchships with everyone wishing them well. In many respects it had been like a honeymoon—for Jan and himself it had been their honeymoon—and those tend to be perfect in every way, especially in retrospect.

Using the newly developed stardrive, they had jumped ten light-years into interstellar space, deployed their vast antennae and listened. More accurately, the ship's sensors had listened while the personnel carried out explorations of a more personal nature. The weeks of waiting had passed pleasantly enough while the antennae scooped up mush from stellar objects that radiated on the bands above and below the visible spectrum. Then, suddenly, a signal had come that could only have had an intelligent source.

It was simple, repetitious and as individually unique as a signature. As expected, it faded out within a few minutes and returned, again for only a few minutes, just over a day later.

During their training on Pluto Station they had listened to recordings of many such signals. The theory had been that the "messages" emanated from antennae on worlds that could well lie halfway across the galaxy and that the periods of silence corresponded to the rotational period of the transmitting planet. It was also thought that the transmitting antennae were steerable, so that they painted virtually all of the surrounding space in measured, vertical sweeps. This theory proved true in the majority of cases, the searchers discovered later, but there had been a few worlds where the signals had been sent from a transmitter in orbit.

Peter had taken a fix on that first signal and he and his bride had jumped one hundred light-years closer. Then they had taken another fix and jumped again. There was no need to make sense of the signal, although they had often tried—it was simply an alien voice saying over and over again that it was there.

Then, abruptly, it was no longer there.

They had back-tracked until the signal was coming in again, then made a long jump at right angles to fix the system's position by triangulation. Within a few weeks they had found it—and arrived on a world wiped clean of intelligent life.

The system had been something like four thousand light-years from Earth and in all probability its signals had been coming long before human technology had reached the level of being able to detect them. Radio-frequency emissions traveled at the speed of light, and their ship had continued to encounter those signals for more than half of its four-thousand-light-year journey, so that the civilization which produced them had lasted for at least two thousand years.

But even long-lived, stable and technologically advanced cultures come to an end and, when such a civilization fell—it fell hard.

Peter's and Jan's feelings on finding that first dead world had been of mild disappointment rather than sorrow. They had been unlucky first time out, they told themselves, and next time there would be *people*—new, alien and perhaps dangerous *people*—to contact.

The risks involved were not great because a race that advertised its presence all over space would probably welcome contact. But on that first world there had been only insects and the remains of a great civilization in a remarkably good state of preservation. Jan and Peter had taken back specimens and records that had advanced Earth technology by a half-century. Their debriefing had lasted for nearly three years, during which they had been heaped with academic and other honors, as had, to a lesser extent, the other searchship crews which had brought home smaller pieces of the alien bacon.

Finally they had been allowed to try again.

The second world they found had also died long before its radio signals had finished their slow journey to Earth. There were interesting artifacts and useful processes on that world, too, and on the many others they visited. At home everyone benefited from the steady feedback of alien know-how. But the searchship crews grew tired of robbing technological tombs.

They wanted to find people . . .

"Next time we'll ask for a trip into the Galactic Center—" Peter began, then stopped. He had made the same suggestion at this stage of the investigation of nearly every planet they had visited.

"We tried that once and were nearly killed," Jan replied. "If you remember—stars there have young planets and it is easy to have the ship wrecked by an extraterrestrial mammoth or an outbreak of volcanic activity. But you know all this," she went on irritably. "Why bring it up again when you'll end by arguing that it's better to follow a signal—because then we are sure of something having been there—than to launch ourselves into a forest of stars where life as we know it has not had a chance to evolve.

"We've never delayed our rejuvenation treatments as long as this before," she added, "and I think that we're becoming forgetful as well as bad-tempered, myself included. Or have you a fresh idea about a Center search?"

He shook his head. "Not really. My idea is that we take rejuvenation again and, young and healthy and with our reflexes speeded up, we make a three-year random search of the Center. The planets we find may be composed of primeval magma, but there is still a chance that we will find intelligent life. Maybe young life—but intelligent. A fresh start. We can't go on forever trying to talk to alien ghosts."

"Neither can we talk to alien children or mindless alien embryos," she replied. "We must find someone our own age to play with."

"Yes," he said.

They had climbed from the third floor of the building

and were beginning to explore the fourth. The equivalent of the industrial revolution had been left behind and nuclear energy had been released, although not in time of war. In common with all of the other dead cultures they had studied, this one had had very few major wars in its recorded history. Progress in all of the arts and sciences had been slow and at every stage the culture had remained stable. The beings appeared to have been cooperative, easy-going and seemingly happy. Their world had been a nice place to live.

The display cases on the fourth floor were relatively undamaged, but their metal contents were irregular masses of corrosion. Plastic components and models, although discolored and encrusted with dead insects, were in good condition. And the searchers were encountering more and more specimens of plastic books—great, thick-paged tomes whose text seemed to float above the pages and whose illustrations gave an illusion of perfect three-D on a flat surface.

"They'll be interested in that particular effect at home," he said. *At least I hope they will,* he added silently. The people at home were becoming disinterested in everything—including themselves.

"Yes," she replied, "and the contents of this building will enable me to finish this mission in two or three months instead of a year. We were lucky finding a museum—"

"Landing here wasn't a waste of time, then?"

He did not know what was driving him to restart the argument which, only a few minutes earlier, he had been so glad to end, but he felt angry, frustrated and depressed and suddenly he wanted someone besides himself to suffer.

"No, it wasn't a waste of time—" she began testily, then stopped. For a few seconds she stared at him as if he were her patient and she a doctor or nurse, her expression sympathetic rather than angry. Then she went on: "Look at that mural over there. One of their interstellar radio transmitters, wouldn't you say?"

Feeling even more annoyed by her sympathy, he

looked in the direction she was pointing and nodded. The murals were large and in a very good state of preservation and, like those in the lower levels, they were displayed in chronological order, beginning at the right of the entrance ramp and running around three walls to end on the left of the ascending ramp to the next level. Two sets of transmitting antennae were pictured on adjacent murals, one built on a snow-streaked headland overlooking an angry sea and another set in desert land.

The next few murals in line showed advanced agricultural processes on land, sea and under the sea—a lot of wall space had been devoted to the solutions, however temporary, of the problem of feeding a rapidly increasing population. The desert transmitter was shown again, its bright metal dulled by the passage of centuries and the surrounding desert converted to a green and yellow patchwork of field tended by agricultural robots.

His eyes moved to the next picture and he laughed sardonically.

"Well, now," he said. "It seems they built their interstellar signaling devices several centuries before they attempted their first space flight. They were a smug, self-opinionated bunch of—"

"Maybe they had their priorities right," Jan broke in. "After all, they must have realized that there was a strong possibility of life in other star systems as soon as they outgrew the idea that their particular world was unique and the center of the universe. They probably decided that an interstellar drive was beyond their technical capabilities."

"The stardrive was beyond our technical capabilities, too," he said drily, "until we began looking for unlikely solutions instead of obvious ones. The whole concept is so obviously impossible that it was sheer—"

"So they chose instead," she continued firmly, "to signal their presence to the rest of the galaxy in the hope that someone with a stardrive would come to them, and they could then do a spot of high class technological horse-trading. They were an intelligent and patient race who obviously believed that everything comes to those who wait."

"We came," he replied grimly, "two thousand years too late."

III

THEY DID NOT speak again until they had completed their circuit of the murals and were moving toward the top of the last ramp. The robot's lighting was no longer necessary because the roof of the topmost level had fallen in, wrecking most displays and covering the floor with rubble, which was in turn covered by patches of grass. But here, too, the murals showed clearly through their thin coating of living and dead insects.

"They must have had a pretty potent insect repellent," he said, "to be able to keep the surface of those pictures clear after all this time."

"But they weren't able to kill them all," she said softly. "Nobody ever succeeds in killing them all."

The murals showed space missions to the nearer planets and bases being set up. But there were no indications of the colonization of the worlds concerned, much less the building of generation ships for a sublightspeed attempt at planting an interstellar colony. The transmitters were shown again, still patiently sending their signals to the stars, which this race would never reach. There were pictorial examples of high-density living structures and high intensity agriculture which was being troubled by some kind of blight. One of the pictures showed enlarged images of various types of insects with what could have been the chemical symbols representing the insecticide that would kill them.

There was no sense of urgency or fear in the pictures—the museum had been built by a long-established and stable race which did not frighten easily. But to a searchship's crew which had seen it all before the signs were plain. Another flourishing culture, severely weakened by diminishing food and energy resources, was about to go down before an enemy too small and mindless even to know or care that it had won.

"Let's go back to the ship," Peter said dully.

Jan nodded, still looking at him as if he were ill, and said, "Then what?"

"Then we'll talk about something other than graverobbing for the rest of the evening. Tomorrow I'll help you begin to evaluate this material until it is time to go home."

"And then?"

He had taken her hand to help her over a pile of rubble, and now that they were retracing their steps along a clear section of ramp he continued to hold it, for reasons he could not define. He was still angry. He knew that she had always been argumentative and strong-willed. But there had been times when even the serious arguments had been of no real importance and had been quickly forgotten, instead of dragging on interminably and poisoning their conversation and their work for days on end.

"Then we'll go home and rejuvenate for one last trip," he said. "You're right about our condition, of course—we spend too much time arguing and not enough searching. And we really should make our last trip in top physical condition. We just might find something."

"And if we don't?"

"We resign," he said firmly. "I'm pretty sure there will be no opposition. The number of searchship missions has been reducing steadily over the last ten years and even our top people are beginning to lose hope. There are also signs that our culture, too, is becoming self-satisfied and self-centered and beginning to die on its feet. One of these decades we'll lose our sense of adventure, our insatiable curiosity about the universe and the beings who inhabit it. We'll begin to set up interstellar radio transmitters and settle back to let the Others find us.

"By that time," he added, "we two will have used up our fourth period of youth and our final old age in sampling the delights of our smug little culture, while trying not to notice the news flashes about insects—or other rivals—adapting to our latest pesticides."

"That might not be much fun."

"Of course it won't be fun," he told her. "So maybe we'll make two last trips or even three—the more last trips we make, the greater will be our chances of finding something."

"This is hopeless," she burst out suddenly. "It always has been hopeless. We're wasting our time."

"I know," he said.

But the searchship crews had been chosen very carefully from that large, but rapidly diminishing, number of people who could not give up hope. An unbiased observer, while considering this particular psychological type, might have said that steadfastly refusing to face inevitable failure was utter stupidity. But it had been stupidity of this order that had taken the race so rapidly, if at times violently, to its present cultural and technological eminence. And certainly momentum powered by persistent stupidity had produced both the stardrive and gravity control and—now that humanity had finally renounced war—an even higher order of stubborn, self-aware stupidity was driving them to find a partner before their culture became too ingrown. And before the stupidity that had made them great became lost in a rising tide of intelligence and philosophical acceptance of static realities.

As they followed the robot to the ground-level entrance Peter remembered the other planet-sized graveyards they had visited. The inhabitants of those worlds had been humanoid in the majority of cases, but some of the others had been visually unpleasant. But in each instance they had built civilizations for themselves that were rich, stable, peaceful and, by Earth standards, extremely long-lived. They had matured early and given up such childish and destructive pursuits as war and racial or religious/sociological discrimination while they were still young. Their cultures had been nice places in which to live—and perhaps a pleasant life was all that any life form could reasonably expect.

"Sometimes," Peter said suddenly, "I think we'll never grow up."

"That could be a better way to live," she argued, "than growing up too soon and having nothing to live for but the contemplation of the racial navel."

Jan's first instinct was to argue, he thought tiredly, and it always had been for as long as he had known her. But nowadays the arguments were lifeless, hopeless and petty instead of being the intellectual challenge they once had been. He relaxed his grip on her hand, but she tightened hers and would not let go.

She said, "Species with a long period of gestation and preadolescence have a much greater potential for development than—well—alien butterflies. Maybe we aren't really stupid, just too young to know any better. And now we may have passed the post-puberty stage and have left home to look for a mate. An intellectual mate," she added. "I was speaking figuratively."

"I realize that," he said and laughed in spite of himself.

"I'm sorry," she continued, in a tone that was both apologetic and defensive. "From the very beginning I warned you that I would always speak my mind and tell you whenever I thought you were wrong. You used to say that my candor was stimulating and — Well, it really doesn't matter. I don't want to win every battle. And we certainly did not waste our time landing here."

He waited until they were outside the building before speaking. The sun was close to the horizon and the bright green mounds of rubble and the few intact structures were bathed in a dramatic orange light—the area had the sharp clarity of a stage set. From all around came the buzzing of the insect audience.

"On the very few occasions when you were wrong," Peter said carefully, "you used to apologize and admit it. This time you apologized without actually admitting that you were wrong, which means that you still think that you are right and that we came down here through my error."

"Oh, let's forget the whole thing and stop fighting. Please."

He shook his head. "I'm not fighting. But if I made a mistake I want to know about it. Show me proof."

"You'll also be annoyed about it for weeks—" She broke off and began looking around carefully, obviously taking her bearings; then she pointed.

"It should be about four hundred yards in that direction," she said. "It could be a patch of diseased vegetation or a trick of the light, but only a searchship makes a mark like that and I caught a glimpse of it as we were landing."

He saw the saucer-shaped depression as they breasted the next high mound. It was about thirty feet across and carpeted with vegetation whose color was a shade lighter than normal because the grass in the area had been flattened both by the landing and takeoff of a searchship and the new growth had had to struggle through the crushed remains of the old. Many such depressions had been left on this and other worlds in their eighty years of searching.

"Judging by the age of the new growth," he said, "this must have been our first planetfall. But the robot can check it against the known growth rate and give a close approximation of the time of landing. Then I'll know exactly when the mistake was made in the search pattern—if in fact a mistake was made."

She pulled her hand away from his and said angrily, "Don't be so childish! Rather than admit you made a mistake, you are suggesting that some other searchship wandered into the galactic sector assigned to us and landed here. That is ten times more impossible than the impossibility of your making an error. Maybe I should instruct the robot to run an ID check on the depression to make sure that it was our ship that landed here."

He had been staring at the ground while she had been speaking, studying the deeper and more well-defined hollows around the circumference of the depression that were the marks left by the stabilizers and landing legs. His pulse was thumping so loudly that subjectively it seemed much louder than his voice.

"Yes. Do that."

"No. *You* do it!"

"My mental state at the moment," he said quietly, "makes it unlikely that I would be able to frame the instructions in a sufficiently coherent manner for the robot to understand."

"You framed that sentence well enough—" she began, then stopped to stare at him. He could see the concern returning and replacing the anger in her face, and he knew that the sunlight reflected on his visor made it difficult for her to see his expression. She gave the necessary instructions to the robot and they stood back to enable it to work freely.

"You're taking this very badly," she said worriedly. "I'm sorry. You don't make mistakes as a rule and this was such a small one that—"

"Promise me one thing," he said very seriously, gripping her arm and squeezing it to accentuate his words. "If at any time in the future you feel like expressing an opinion likely to displease me, or you feel the need to criticize something I have said or done, or failed to say or do, or you want to make an observation about anything important or even trivial, go right ahead."

She opened her mouth to speak, looking completely baffled, but he waved for silence. The robot had completed its investigation of the depression and the markings around it and was making its report.

SOIL COMPRESSION AND CONTOUR OF DEPRESSION INDICATE LANDING AND SUBSEQUENT TAKEOFF OF A VESSEL OF SEARCHSHIP MASS USING FOCUSED ANTI-GRAVITY THRUSTER OF CONVENTIONAL TYPE, said the precise, mechanical and toneless voice in their suit phones. CONDITION OF VEGETATION SUGGESTS ELAPSED TIME OF TEN WEEKS. RESIDUAL RADIATION AND DEPTH OF MARKINGS LEFT BY STABILIZERS AND LANDING SUPPORT STRUTS CONFIRMS MASS FIGURE FOR SEARCHSHIP. CONFIGURATION OF STABILIZERS AND LANDING-SUP-

PORT STRUTS DOES NOT CONFORM TO ANY EARTH VES-
SEL TYPE ON PAST OR CURRENT RECORDS. IDENTIFICA-
TION OF THE VESSEL IS THEREFORE IMPOSSIBLE.

She turned toward him and said warmly, "I'm glad
you didn't make a mistake——" Then she stopped as the
implications began to sink in.

"It also means," he said, "that somebody else is
searching for people and finding graveyards. It means
that somebody else has discovered the stardrive and is
using a conventional antigravity thruster for takeoffs
and landings—probably because there is only one way to
build the thing.

"It means," he went on, "that we will have to go on
searching for long-dead civilizations, because they were
the only kind that signaled their presence over a period
long enough to attract the attention of ourselves and the
other searchers. It also means that instead of robbing
graves we carve our initials and a message on them—
more accurately, we will devise weather- and insect-proof
radio beacons containing data on Earth and its position in space. We will scatter them over the new worlds
we find, as well as the ones we have already covered,
because we have no idea how many of them have yet to
be visited by the Others.

"Most of all," he ended jubilantly, "it means that one
day a beacon will be discovered and opened by people
who, like us, were not content to sit and wait."

Suddenly they were hugging each other, a ridiculous
and senseless thing to do considering the thickness of
their protective suits. But it did not matter. Her face
was younger than he could remember for a great many
years—more animated and vital. She was looking, he
realized suddenly, the way he felt—as if he had just undergone rejuvenation.

Gently he pushed her away from him and said, "Let's
go back to the ship, dear. We're wasting time."